"We will not speak of Belinda."

Heavy lids narrowed Luq's eyes, giving him a predatory look. "I have warned you before not to pry into my affairs."

"And I've told *you*," Dene snapped, "that it's unnatural not to speak of your wife, and forbid other people to mention her. Even the girl's own mother— You accuse Englishmen of being cold, but you...you're solid ice!"

The words died on a strangled gasp as he came around the desk and seized her. His kiss was pitiless: demanding and punishing. Finally he thrust her away. His lean face was twisted with hatred.

"Let that be a lesson to you, *señorita*. Perhaps in future you will not seek to meddle in things that do not concern you, or pass judgment on me without fully understanding what it is you censure!"

Villa of Vengeance

Annabel Murray

Harlequin Books

TORONTO • NEW YORK • LONDON
AMSTERDAM • PARIS • SYDNEY • HAMBURG
STOCKHOLM • ATHENS • TOKYO • MILAN

Original hardcover edition published in 1983
by Mills & Boon Limited

ISBN 0-373-02612-9

Harlequin Romance first edition April 1984

CHAPTER ONE

So this was Spain! Mentally, Dene Mason crossed another item off her list of ambitions, the list of places she had always wanted to visit. In obedience to the stewardess's instructions, she fastened her safety belt and held fast to the lucky black cat she always wore on a chain about her neck. Her sapphire blue eyes were alight with anticipation, as the aeroplane banked steeply in preparation for the approach to Malaga airport.

There, spread out below her, was the coastline, with its beaches, casinos, hotels and swimming pools; and once again she congratulated herself on having insisted on a week's holiday before taking up her new post . . . a post which promised to be somewhat out of the ordinary, a challenge which Dene, with her insatiable appetite for new experiences, rather relished.

Tyres screeched on the tarmac and the aeroplane rolled to a halt. Minutes later, Dene was standing on Spanish soil for the first time, every sense, every faculty alert, receptive as always to the unknown.

It was rather deflating to find that the experience produced no immediate reaction in her. Somehow she had expected to be instantly aware of a difference in atmosphere, to be at once enfolded in the exotic Spain of her imaginings . . . the Spain of Don Juan, Don Quixote, Carmen . . .

True, it was considerably warmer here than in London, which she had left experiencing April showers, but the runways, the airport buildings were prosaically unromantic and there were Customs and passport formalities to be endured, luggage to be collected. But Dene, despite her mere twenty-three years, was a seasoned traveller and in a very short space of time she was on an airport bus, spinning along the dual carriageway en route for Torremolinos, whose sandy beaches, she had heard, extended for miles along the Mediterranean coast and where she intended to spend the intervening days between arriving in Spain and reporting to her new employer.

Eagerly she scanned the passing scenery, reflecting meanwhile on the combination of circumstances which had so unexpectedly brought her here . . . not least her own determination, which she had pitted against the advice and wishes of her family and her boy-friend.

'I can't think why you want to leave England to work. You have a nice steady job here. How can you leave *me*?' Barry had declared pettishly. 'Especially now, with the spring and summer ahead of us. I was hoping you'd go on holiday with *me* this year, to the Lake District, instead of gadding off abroad somewhere. I really don't understand you, Dene.'

No, Barry didn't understand her, Dene agreed inwardly, and until she *did* meet a man who was on her wavelength . . .

Dene's generous nature inclined her to give everyone the benefit of the doubt during the early stages of a new friendship. She was slow to condemn, to find fault in others. But even she could no longer make excuses for Barry.

To all external appearances he was boyishly ingenuous, good-humoured and entertaining company, and she knew that many of her friends envied her his assiduous attentions. But this outer façade covered a shallower nature than she had at first supposed. Barry was boring. He was narrow, conservative, unimaginative in outlook, pooh-poohing her more extravagant flights of fancy. To a girl of Dene's independence, he seemed more than usually possessive. She knew that if she were ever unwise enough to give in to his importunities, agree to marry him, her life would become one of stultifying, claustrophobic boredom. But she was not fool enough to tie herself down.

Despite her trusting nature, Dene could be extremely stubborn where her own interests were at stake and though she was practicality itself so far as her career was concerned, she had a streak of romanticism, a longing for new experiences. Born in a small village, where she had lived until her schooling was complete, she had an irresistible urge to travel, to widen her horizons, before settling down to the ties of domesticity. Indeed, happy with her chosen career of nursing, she wasn't sure that she wanted to get married at all, with all the restrictions that implied. Besides, not one of the men she had met so far came anywhere near the secret dream in her heart.

Since she had been earning enough to do so, she had taken all her holidays abroad . . . would have liked to work abroad. But Barry scorned foreign travel, declaring that there were places enough to be seen in his own country; and from this view Dene had been unable to move him.

Her elderly, similarly staid parents were even less understanding about her need for constant new stimuli. They had lived in the same Hampshire village all their married life, had always taken their one annual holiday at the same seaside resort. They had no social life, but worked on their house or garden by day and watched television in the evenings. They were visibly uneasy when confronted by the unknown or unexperienced.

The Masons thoroughly approved of Barry and could not understand their only daughter's reluctance to become engaged and in due course married to this stable young man, with his steady career as an accountant and his excellent prospects of promotion.

'I don't know what more you could possibly want, Nadine,' her mother had said on more than one occasion, exasperated by what she considered to be her daughter's perversity and ingratitude.

'I want colour and excitement in my life . . . adventure . . . romance,' Dene had answered, and though she loved her parents, she was irritated by their complete failure to understand her nebulous dreams . . . perhaps unfairly so, she often admitted to herself, for she scarcely understood her own restless urges towards the unknown, did not really know for what she was seeking.

Even so, despite all her vague, unformulated longings, she had not expected quite such a drastic upheaval in her way of life, even though her stars in that morning's paper had indicated that a surprise was in store; and for a while even *her* adventurous spirit had been daunted by the proposal laid before her.

'It's tailor-made for you, Dene,' Mr Harvey had said, as he outlined the post for which he was urging her to apply. 'I wouldn't have suggested you for the position if I hadn't felt you have uniquely suitable qualities.'

Gerald Harvey, specialist in rheumatology at St Philomena's and whose patients she had nursed for the last two years, looked at her earnestly over his horn-rimmed spectacles.

'You're always saying you want a chance to travel, to work

abroad for a while. Here's your opportunity. For many reasons I'm reluctant to lose you. But I know you, Dene. With or without my help you'll take off into the blue some day. This job would serve two purposes. You will at least be employed by someone I know and trust, which is a big consideration . . . and then . . .'

He paused, and Dene looked at him enquiringly.

'And your other reason?'

Gerald Harvey spoke slowly, choosing his words carefully.

'It won't be easy . . . the position for which I'm recommending you is an unusual one, to say the least. You'll have to tread carefully . . . very carefully. But I have tremendous faith in you, Dene. As I said, I feel that you have a special quality, something which I believe is very much needed there, which will be of help to my friend, in more ways than one.'

Dene couldn't help but be flattered by this testimony from a man whose opinion she valued very highly, and her curiosity, as he had judged it might be, was piqued by the circumstances at which he hinted but refused to enlarge upon.

'I leave it to your instincts . . . and common sense,' he told her firmly.

But still she hesitated, which was unusual for her, she realised. She did not usually step back from the brink of adventure. Why did she have this strange foreboding?

'It *would* be an opportunity to get away *now* from that odiously stuffy boy-friend of yours,' he urged, a twinkle in his eyes.

'Yes,' Dene admitted. 'But Spain? It's true I've always wanted to go there, but I only know about a dozen words of Spanish. How could I possibly . . . ?'

'No problem!' Gerald Harvey waved an airy hand. 'Your patient would be a Mrs Travers, an Englishwoman living in Spain, which is why I've been asked to find a suitable, English-speaking nurse-companion. If you want to talk it over with your parents . . . ?'

'No!' Dene said decidedly. She had discovered long ago that this was an unrewarding, negative experience. Her parents just wouldn't want her to go. They had hated her going away to work in London. Goodness knows what objections they would raise to her going abroad. 'I'll go,' she told him.

*

Dene swiftly became bored with Torremolinos. True, it was a sophisticated resort, with many fine hotels, elegant shops in attractive, traffic-free alleyways, packed with bars, restaurants, boutiques, bookshops, art galleries and high-fashion clothes shops . . . every amenity in fact for the tourist. But *this* was not the romantic Spain she had come to see.

In fact, she might just as well be working. She was anxious to meet her patient, to come to grips with a new challenge, to discover for herself the unique problems at which Gerald Harvey had hinted. She was going to make a tremendous success of this, she vowed, to show him his faith in her had been justified.

So it was with a feeling of relief that she made her way back to Malaga, for her rendezvous with a certain Señor de Léon who, she understood, was to conduct her to her patient. The meeting had been arranged to take place in the foyer of one of the larger hotels. She dressed carefully for the occasion in a yellow linen-look suit. Yellow, she had been told, was her lucky colour.

He entered the foyer of the hotel Sancho Panza, the cynosure of all female eyes and, Dene thought, very much aware of the fact. Elegantly slender, with a gipsy-like grace, his clothes flamboyantly coloured, he swaggered over to the reception desk, shoulders square, head arrogantly erect, his breezy blue eyes and infectious smile winning an instant, adulatory response from the female clerk. His deeply tanned face was haloed by a square-cut mane of blond hair, which had an unruly tendency to curl.

From observation of the clerk's irrepressible giggles and simpering looks, he was also of a flirtatious manner. Dene judged him to be in his late twenties, and though not as a rule impressed by brashness in men, she could not help wondering, with a curiosity prompted by his good looks, who he was.

Then the desk clerk was pointing in her direction and she felt a tremor of nervousness . . . a premonition as to his identity, as the bronzed, daredevil face was turned towards her, before, pivoting on his heel with the supple movement of a dancer, he crossed the thickly carpeted floor.

'Señorita Nadine Mason?'

There was a note of surprise, almost of shock, in his voice, a surprise reflected in the expression of the blue eyes. This reaction, however, was swiftly mingled with appreciation of her appearance and something else . . . a kind of pleasurable anticipation? almost . . . deep satisfaction?

Dene stood up, noting automatically that, for all his air of presence, he was not very tall, perhaps about five feet seven. His English was fluent, but accented.

'*You're* Señor de Léon?' She had expected somebody older, more responsible.

He bowed slightly from a slender waist, taking her outstretched hand, holding it just a little longer than was strictly necessary.

'José Mañara de Léon, very much at your service, *señorita*. But you should address me as "Mañara" not "de Léon", which is the name of my mother's family.'

He looked at her, his fair head slightly on one side, his expression quizzical.

'And *you* are truly an experienced nurse? So young . . . and so beautiful?'

Dene flushed. She found José Mañara's behaviour rather disconcerting, after the graver manners of her countrymen. She gave him her assurance, however, that she was indeed a trained nurse of several years' standing.

'And you like this work? Caring for the sick?'

'Most certainly!' Her vivid little face lit up with enthusiasm. 'I love meeting new people, and it's marvellous to see people recovering and know that you've had a part in it.'

José Mañara shuddered and crossed himself.

'Me, I detest any sickness. I would rather,' he said dramatically, 'be dead than crippled.' He gestured towards the door. 'But my car is outside, *señorita*. Shall we go? We have a long journey.'

As he held open the passenger door of the long, rakish sports car, he asked:

'You have eaten, Nadine? I shall call you Nadine, I think.' And, as she nodded, '*Bueno!* For we will not arrive in Seville until late afternoon.'

'Seville?' she repeated in astonishment. 'But surely that's north of here? I thought . . .'

'That we would be travelling south?' José Mañara eyed her askance, as the powerful car shot away from the kerb, gathering speed in a manner which made her catch her breath. 'Eventually, perhaps, but first we go to Seville.'

Though a little worried at this apparent change of plan, Dene was more concerned about the excessive speed of their passage, and the lucky black cat around her neck came in for more fingering, but eventually she managed to relax in her seat, admiring the luxurious comfort, as they drove first in a westerly direction over the Sierras, finally turning north, to where the *autopista* ran towards Seville. The country on either side was level and rich, with great herds of fighting bulls peacefully grazing, at the sight of which José slowed his car almost to a crawl, the only occasion on which he did so for the whole duration of the journey. He was a good driver, Dene thought, but although she was not as a rule a nervous passenger, she did wish he would slow down just a little.

But on the whole, she was enjoying the drive; could not help but be enchanted by the unfamiliar luminosity of the air, the breadth of the horizons stretched before her. Everywhere was so much *larger* abroad, she thought.

Despite the excitement of this totally new experience, she was still a little concerned over the change of destination, having understood from Gerald Harvey that her patient resided in a remote, almost inaccessible village south of Granada, in the Alpujarras, an area she had not even heard of two weeks ago. She had expected, since there was apparently such great need of her services, that her escort would drive her straight there.

If it had not been for José Mañara's confident approach, his enquiry for her by name, she would have been even more apprehensive. After all, she was a complete stranger, in a totally unfamiliar country. But she judged that José, despite his flamboyant, flirtatious manner, his bland assumption that he might use her first name, was harmless enough.

'Will Mrs Travers be in Seville, then?' she asked, after some moments spent in considering how to broach the subject uppermost in her mind.

'No.' Her companion shook his blond locks. 'She lives in Pajaro, a village in the Alpujarras. Her disability keeps her housebound.'

'Then why . . . ?'

'*Por favor*, Nadine, save your questions for my cousin.'

The request was pleasantly put, with a flashing smile, but his reluctance to give her the information she desired made her still more uneasy.

'Your cousin? But I thought you . . .'

'I am not your employer,' José informed her. 'A fact I much regret, now that we have met. I am merely your chauffeur, deputed to collect you on my way from Pajaro to Seville.'

He gave her again his wide, engaging smile, a smile that in some way reminded her of Barry's facile charm that she had once found so beguiling.

'Tomorrow, if all goes well, it will be my pleasure also to drive you to Pajaro . . . entirely my pleasure,' he emphasised.

Dene wondered just what he meant by 'if all goes well'. What could go wrong? This was just a formality, surely . . . a meeting with someone employed by Mrs Travers to engage her. She looked around the car seeking wood upon which to knock. It was obvious, however, that José either could not or would not enlighten her further, and for the remainder of their journey she thought he seemed preoccupied; though, from time to time, she was conscious of sidelong glances from his bright blue eyes, glances which, she was aware, were not unappreciative.

He smiled to himself once or twice too, a smile which seemed indicative of some deeply felt pleasure.

As José Mañara had forecast, it was late afternoon when they reached the outskirts of Seville, passing the Torre del Oro and the Plaza de Toros. Wistfully, Dene wished there were time for sightseeing, but her visit to this city would be all too brief, if it was planned that she should proceed to Pajaro next day. As they entered the side streets, passing the Cathedral and its campanile, the Giralda, Dene craned her neck to look up at this great minaret, with its trellis-like diaper of pink brickwork, dominating the city.

In the Avenida de los Santos, José braked sharply by an iron gate set in a high wall, which hid from public gaze the ground floor and garden of the house within.

'La Casa del Léon,' José announced, 'the House of the Lion, you would say? It is a typical Sevillaño house. You like?'

Indeed she did. Inside the gate, Dene studied the building with interest. The front of the house had made a plain, continuous façade with the rest of the street, the minimum of windows overlooking the Avenida de los Santos. Instead the house looked inwards, towards a square patio, reached via an archway and overlooked by four rooms at ground level. Wicker chairs and palms in tubs gave the patio a pleasant appearance and the surrounding garden gave off the intoxicating scent of jasmine and orange blossom.

A staircase led up to the first and only other storey. Both inside and out the walls were of dazzling white; all the floors were tiled.

Dene was attacked by a feeling of wonder, of unreality. Could this really be her . . . Nurse Dene Mason . . . in a real Spanish house, accompanied by a real, honest-to-goodness Spaniard; and heaven only knew what other novel experiences awaited her! The thought brought an added sparkle to her blue eyes and flushed the small pointed face with excited expectancy.

The room to which José led her appeared to be a living room, but it was difficult at first to adjust her eyes to the dim light, for the interior was darkened by shadows, cast by large ilex trees, just discernible beyond the elaborate *rejas* which barred the windows; but, as her vision improved, Dene was able to assess her surroundings.

It was not an attractive room, she thought with some disappointment. She was not sure what she had expected, but this apartment was large and square, with lofty ceilings, furnished with a spartan regard as to the necessities of life. It *could* be a beautiful room, she thought consideringly, given a woman's touch. The dwelling of a crusty old bachelor, this, if she was any judge. No woman would tolerate such barrenness, such lack of ornamentation. One or two religious paintings were all that relieved the bareness of the white walls.

Dene thought that José Mañara seemed tense, moving continually around the room, his tread reminiscent of a caged beast. But it was a tension, she felt, that savoured of anticipation rather than fear, as if, for some obscure reason, he look forward with an almost malicious glee to his cousin's appearance. He had not even suggested that Dene should sit down. His restless mood was infectious, and despite her normal self-composure, Dene found herself becoming more and more apprehensive about this coming interview.

'Señor Mañara!'
'Nadine!'

They both began to speak at once. He bowed.

'*Por favor?*'

'No . . . no, it doesn't matter. What were *you* going to say?'

'That you must not be dismayed . . . discouraged, if my cousin's manner seems a little strange.' Again that delightful smile flashed out. 'You are not exactly what we were led to suppose and I fear . . .' He paused, as if selecting his words with care. 'I think it is only fair to warn you that . . . regrettably in my opinion . . . it is quite possible my cousin will refuse to employ you, that you will be sent back to England.'

Dene stared at him in disbelief. He couldn't be serious! He struck her as being essentially a frivolous person. Perhaps he was teasing her? She was about to protest, to question him further, when the sound of an uneven tread upon the tiled floor of the outer passageway informed her that the encounter she had suddenly begun to dread was close at hand.

She had always prided herself on being totally unflappable at times of crisis, and had proved this many times in her nursing career, but it was not reassuring to find that José had moved closer to her side, since she felt that it was a protective gesture. Glancing swiftly up at him, she felt sure she detected again that odd glitter of excitement in his blue eyes. But his manner was formal, his tone equally so.

'Señorita Mason . . .' He *was* being formal! 'May I present my cousin, Señor Luqillo de Léon Rivera. Luq, this is Señorita Nadine Mason . . . from England,' he added somewhat unnecessarily.

Dene felt that his air was that of one who throws a lighted squib and then steps back to observe the effect of his action. For her own part, she had been forced to stifle a gasp; but she could not prevent her sapphire blue eyes widening and darkening, a fact not lost on the man who had entered.

She was suddenly glad of the confidence engendered by her most becoming outfit, the linen-look suit in glowing yellow emphasising the pale, ashen-blonde of her thick, straight hair. Her hand went to its heavy tresses, in a selfconscious, instinctive gesture, that was as old as time, as she stared up at the man who confronted her, his own expression one of uncompromisingly surprised displeasure.

Never in her life had she encountered a man quite like this, and the cool poise earned in many a tricky hospital situation almost deserted her, as she experienced an unaccountable thudding sensation against her ribs, which bore no resemblance to her clinical observation of the heart's normal behaviour.

Tall and lean, with broad shoulders fanning out from a narrow waist, he was perhaps a little too spectacular-looking for her taste. He would be supremely aware of his own attractions, she felt. His swart-skinned face, below thick, blue-black hair, was narrow and dangerous, terminating in a square-cut, decisive chin. A dominant, jutting nose separated long-lashed, brooding black eyes and the firmly outlined, full lips were drawn into an angry line.

At his first sight of her he appeared to have been rendered temporarily speechless, but when he finally spoke, his voice was deep, but cold and clipped, the underlying fury barely restrained. It was to José Mañara that he addressed his words, patently ignoring Dene's slim, outstretched hand, her tentative smile.

'Why, *por el amor de Diós*, have you brought *her* here? This is intolerable! She should have been put on the next aeroplane to England. You must have realised straight away . . .'

'Realised *what*, Señor Rivera?' Dene asked, small fists clenched at her side, in an angry reaction to his discourtesy.

She wasn't vain, but she *did* know that she was not unattractive and she wasn't used to being ignored and overlooked in this fashion. Both on duty and in her private capacity, she was accustomed to attention, to being consulted, her opinion being respected; and if this man had the normal, common courtesy . . .

'If you have any questions about my suitability for this position, will you please address them to *me*?'

José Mañara laid a restraining hand on her arm.

'Nadine,' he said, 'it is my cousin whom you should address as Señor de Léon. Rivera is his mother's name. You see, in Spain . . .'

'Enough, José!'

The dark eyes had narrowed at the familiar use of her name and now the deep voice was edged with asperity, as Luquillo de Léon interrupted his cousin's explanations.

'Since Señorita Mason will not be in Spain long enough for the information to be of use to her . . .'

'Will you kindly stop talking as if I'm not here!' Dene stamped one neatly shod foot, the creamy pink of her pointed face flushed with annoyance.

This man was stunningly good-looking, but he was an out-and-out pig! How dared he talk over her head, speak of sending her back to England, when he hadn't even spoken to her . . . given her a chance? Despite her slightness of stature, Dene was always more than ready to fight for her rights.

'I insist on knowing what you've got against me . . . or *think* you have.' The small, determined chin, with its delightful dimple, tilted defiantly at him. 'My references from Mr Harvey . . .'

'I have seen your references.' Luquillo de Léon's bass voice was still icily controlled, as at last he deigned to look at her. 'Your professional qualifications are above reproach. I have no fault to find with them as such. However, there was one point on which my friend Gerald Harvey saw fit to deceive me . . .'

Dene bristled at the implied slur on a former superior and a good friend.

'Mr Harvey never told a lie in his life.'

'*Señorita*, your loyalty does you credit!' The sarcastic tone destroyed all possibility that he was sincere. 'But there are other ways in which one may perpetrate a deception. There are sins of commission and there are sins of *omission*. Gerald Harvey omitted to mention your age, when he knew very well . . .'

'My age?' Dene had often been told that her diminutive height and gamine looks made her seem younger than her actual twenty-three years, but surely he didn't think Gerald Harvey would be irresponsible enough to send an inexperienced teen-ager for this position? 'My age?' she repeated, lifting delicately arched eyebrows at him. 'What has age to do with it, as long as I'm capable . . . ?'

'I made it quite clear that I required a mature, responsible person, someone on whom I could rely to . . .'

'Señor de Léon!' Her husky voice interrupted him with some of the asperity she would use to a junior nurse who dared to question her authority. 'May I remind you that maturity is an attitude of mind, not necessarily something acquired with age. I would also inform you that I *do* consider myself to be a respons-ible and reliable person.'

The more she considered his unreasonable attitude, the more furious she became. On occasions, she had been in sole charge . . . save for emergencies requiring a doctor . . . over a whole ward of patients; and here was this arrogant foreigner . . . a *layman* . . . daring to doubt her ability to care for one woman!

The heavy black bar of his eyebrows was drawn together, his finely carved features unrelenting.

'I will *not* employ anyone of such extreme youth for a post which demands dedication, discretion and considerable tact. It has not been my experience that girls such as you . . .'

'How dare you!'

Dene glared at him. What right had he to imply . . . no, it was stronger than that . . . how dared he *assert* that she did not possess those qualities? Why, they were the very things for which Gerald Harvey had constantly commended her, the reasons why he had urged her to come to Spain, because she was so admirably suited for the post. This man was just determined to find fault with her; and if one pretext failed him, then he would surely find another. Why? Why *should* he be so prejudiced against someone he had just met for the first time?

She turned with an imploring look at José Mañara, forgetting in her need for support the brash manner which had jarred on her. Although he had not uttered another word, she sensed in him a sympathetic ally against his cousin's high-handed behaviour.

But José was avoiding her gaze, the toe of his highly polished boot tracing the diamond pattern of the tiles. There was something . . . she could not quite analyse it . . . in his manner, that told of a quiet enjoyment of his cousin's annoyance. So she must fight this battle alone?

Dene was usually in complete control of her emotions, despising weakness of any kind, or its use in defence. When things went wrong on a busy ward, it was of no earthly use weeping; you just coped. But suddenly the excitement, the tension, the fatigue of her journey, and now the anti-climatic effect of disappointment, were all too much for her. Despite her determination not to give ground before this implacably hostile man, to her horror and annoyance she felt an ominous pricking behind her eyelids and her curvy, generous mouth drooped, the lower lip developing a decided tendency to tremble.

Luquillo de Léon gauged her reaction with irritating accuracy.

'And I am unmoved by tears, or any other such feminine wiles,' he warned her.

Yes. *He* would be! Of all the men in the world with whom she might have had to deal, why did it have to be this one with his arrogance and his preconceived ideas? Dene asked the Fates indignantly. Her horoscope hadn't mentioned anything like this. Was *this* what Gerald Harvey had meant, when he'd said special qualities would be required? That she would have to overcome the prejudices of this man? And why . . . what had *he* to do with Mrs Travers?

A sense of blazing injustice dried the unshed tears, as Dene drew her slim form erect, unconscious dignity in the set of her head, straight, ashen blonde hair framing her determined little face.

'You're the most unfeeling, arrogant, rude and prejudiced man I've ever met!' She could almost feel José's silent applause and it gave her added courage. 'Just *who* do you think you are? What gives you the right to condemn me, without a fair trial?'

'She has a point, Luq,' José interposed at this point.

Luq de Léon turned upon his cousin.

'You of all people should understand and respect my reasons. I can only guess at the spirit of . . . of mischief . . . I am reluctant to call it "evil" . . . which prompted you to bring Señorita Mason here, when you could quite easily see for yourself . . .' He spoke to Dene. 'Listen to me, *señorita* . . .'

'No!' she interjected, '*you* listen to *me* for a change. I'll have you know I gave up a very good job to come out here. I went against the wishes of my parents . . .'

'You should have listened to your parents.'

He was becoming impatient, darting frequent glances at his wristwatch, his voice increasingly censorious.

'Against the wishes of my parents,' she continued, as if there had been no interruption. Dene in a temper was unstoppable . . . 'and . . . and against the wishes of my . . . my fiancé,' she invented for good measure, determined to paint her feeling of ill-usage, his injustice to her, as black as possible, 'because Mr Harvey impressed upon me that there was a worthwhile job to be done here . . . a real *need* for my help.'

Firmly, she subdued the brief pang of conscience at the lie about Barry. Though she had most decidedly given that young man his congé before she left England, she was doing him no harm by this expedient falsehood.

Somehow she had to persuade Luq de Léon to let her stay. Obscurely, she felt she would be letting Gerald Harvey down if she failed in this assignment he had given her, and Dene hated to fail anyone, if it was in her power to meet their demands on her.

As she spoke, Luq de Léon's expression had altered, almost imperceptibly it was true, but the change *was* there.

'You have a *novio* . . . a fiancé . . . in England?'

Uncomfortable, because she was not normally a liar, Dene gave a defiant toss of satin-smooth hair, crossed fingers concealed in the folds of her skirt.

'Yes! Is there anything wrong with *that?*'

'On the contrary,' he said slowly, with less edge to his voice, 'it may make a considerable difference.'

'Anyway,' Dene continued, intent on pressing home her advantage, 'I don't really see what any of this has to do with *you*. I understood I was being employed by a Mrs Travers.'

'I am acting for the Señora Travers,' Luq informed her. 'The Señora is *mia suegra* . . . my mother-in-law.'

She could imagine him with a mistress . . . several mistresses . . . but though she tried, she failed utterly to imagine the kind of woman who would have the courage to marry Luquillo de Léon. Such a woman would need to be possessed of an independent, uncrushable spirit, or alternatively, to have the temperament of a doormat. Any woman falling between those two extremes would be utterly destroyed by his ruthless, domineering nature.

It was vaguely disappointing, somehow, to learn that Luq de Léon was married . . . not that *she* was attracted to him in the least, she assured herself. In fact, she couldn't remember ever feeling so antagonistic towards a man on so short an acquaintance. She supposed it was just the normal reaction of any woman, on finding that yet another attractive man was spoken for.

Luq was moving restlessly about the room now and Dene recognised the reason for the earlier unevenness she had detected in the forceful sounds of his arrival. He walked with a pronounced limp, and she found herself thinking what a pity it was that, a perfect physical specimen in every other way, he should be marred by this one defect.

He was consulting his watch again ... gold, expensive, banding a sinewy wrist, roughened by short dark hairs. He gave a sharp exclamation of irritation.

'I have an appointment. Already I am late. Reluctantly, I must postpone this discussion until the morning. In any case, it is far too late to do anything tonight ... about returning you to England.'

He was *still* going on about sending her home.

'*Señor*—!' she began her protest, but he raised one hand in an impatient gesture.

'*Mañana!* It seems I am forced to offer you overnight accommodation. I trust *you* will need no such consideration, José?'

The younger man made a swift disclaimer.

'*Muchas gracias*, Luq.' His tone was ironic. 'But I too have an engagement for tonight. My ... accommodation is arranged.'

Luq's response was a mirthless grimace.

'I see!' He managed to imbue the two words with distaste, a disapproval which baffled Dene.

Why should he be annoyed that his cousin had his own plans, when he obviously did not wish José to spend the night at the Casa del Léon? In all probability, he also resented *her* presence.

'I can go to a hotel too,' she put in hastily.

She had no wish to be beholden to an unwilling host, one who had not even the courtesy to accommodate a relative. But even this did not please him.

'Certainly not,' he said sharply. 'All accommodation prices are doubled just now, for the period of the festival ... and in any case it is unlikely you would find a room at such short notice, and at this time of year. Seville is swarming with tourists. Besides, the city is no place for a woman alone, one, moreover, who does not speak Spanish.' He made it sound like a criticism.

'I was told it wasn't necessary,' she said, immediately on the defensive. 'Besides, I do know a few words, enough to ...'

But he ignored her, moving unevenly towards the door, where his voice, raised in clipped command, produced a comely but elderly woman, dressed in severest black, whom he introduced as his housekeeper.

'Maria will attend to all your needs. *Buenas noches, señorita.*

José, you are leaving now?' It was framed as a question, but Dene knew instinctively that it was an order.

José Mañara lingered only a moment or two after his cousin had left and the housekeeper hovered, probably, Dene thought, to see that her employer's injunction to his cousin was observed.

'I will see you in the morning, Nadine,' he said, his bright blue gaze intent upon her strained face.

The relaxation of tension produced by Luq de Léon's departure had not improved her state of mind, but by removing the need for strict self-control, made her feel more strongly her utter aloneness, her powerlessness to sway Luq, if he should refuse to employ her. Her always expressive face revealed her depression.

'Do not despair, Nadine,' said José, taking both her hands in his. 'All is not lost. My cousin, despite certain . . . *prejuicios* . . . is not without justice. He is also human, believe it or not. I think you have made an impression upon him.' For a moment, his smile was wide, wickedly complimentary, 'as indeed you have impressed *me*.' He bent and kissed her fingers. *'Estupenda!'*

A disapproving sniff from Maria reminded José that his departure was awaited.

His admiration, though exaggerated, was soothing to Dene's bruised feelings, but his statement was about the unlikeliest thing she had heard today. To believe that she'd had an effect of any kind other than irritation upon Luq de Léon was patently ridiculous, she thought, as the sound of José's footsteps on the tiled corridor faded away and the housekeeper indicated by signs that Dene should follow her. The only lessening of Luq de Léon's hostility had been at the news . . . an entire fabrication on her part . . . that she was engaged, and she didn't see why that particular fact should impress him, unless it was with surprise that she was capable of attracting a man; and surely she wasn't *that* unprepossessing? Never before had any man proved so coldly resistant to her infectious smile, her vivid loveliness. Nor had anyone ever complained about her being too young. Most of her patients were agreed that her energy, her youthful enthusiasm brightened their lives . . . no mean contribution to their recovery.

After a luxurious bath and a meal served in her room, another severely unattractive apartment, Dene sought consolation from the heavy, old-fashioned mirror, which, even at her own modest assessment, gave back very favourable confirmation that she was far from unsightly. Even with her shining fair hair swept up into the severe style which she affected when on duty, there was no detriment to the sweet serenity of her gamine features, which did not, however, disguise the strength of character revealed in her steady gaze, the firm set of a dimpled chin. In fact, the neat hairstyle enhanced the delicate bone structure of her face, drawing attention to the candid honesty of the sapphire blue eyes, the gently humorous curves of her soft mouth, which could, when necessary, firm into stubborn lines.

'Not bad, my girl,' she told herself aloud, 'though obviously not up to Spanish standards!'

Her fatigue relaxed by the bath and her hunger pangs appeased, Dene felt capable of more rational thought. She was not beaten yet. Somehow she would find a way of persuading Luq de Léon that she should stay. In the meantime, she shelved the problem of her future. Worrying all night would do nothing to further her cause. She must take pains to appear next morning her most calm, resolute self.

Consequently she slept soundly, and when she woke to the sound of the bells of the Giralda, she felt refreshed and cautiously optimistic.

CHAPTER TWO

THOUGHTFULLY, Dene surveyed the contents of her large suit-case. The balance of her wardrobe was already on its way to Pajaro. Let *him* sort *that* one out! she thought triumphantly. If *he* sent her back to England, *he* could just bear the expense of returning all that luggage!

Perhaps, she decided, the sparkling yellow of yesterday's suit, her lucky colour or not, had been a little too frivolous, too informal, giving him a totally incorrect impression of her. Today she would aim for sobriety and efficiency. She settled for a demure, cap-sleeved dress in midnight blue, relieved only by a large white collar and a broad belt, which emphasised the neatness of her tiny waist.

She breakfasted alone and was made to understand, by the housekeeper's combination of sign language and broken English, that the Señor had risen even earlier, had gone out, but would be back in due course.

As time passed, Dene found herself becoming increasingly restive and wondering wistfully when José Mañara would arrive. She felt that his ebullient, slightly disrespectful presence would do much to relieve the tension of her next encounter with his cousin.

The telephone began to ring and Dene waited expectantly for Maria to appear. But there was no sign of the housekeeper, and Dene regarded the instrument doubtfully. It could be important . . . could even be Luq de Léon, ringing to tell her that he had been delayed. On the other hand, if it were not he, she doubted that her Spanish was equal to taking a coherent message.

The telephone was still ringing; there was still no sign of Maria and all Dene's instincts revolted against leaving the instrument unanswered. Hesitantly she lifted the receiver, still diffident about doing so in someone else's home. Immediately, a female voice began to speak, in rapid Spanish, and Dene could understand only the opening words.

'Luq? *Caro mio* . . .'

'Ex . . . excuse me,' Dene faltered. 'I . . . I don't suppose you speak English?'

There was a tangible silence. Then the voice began again. It was a melodious, seductive voice, but suspicious now and hostile.

'Who *is* that?'

'This is Dene Mason. I'm . . .'

'Oh, the nurse . . . the Englishwoman.' There was a perceptible note of relief in the voice. 'Is Señor de Léon there?'

'No. But I think he'll be back soon.'

'Then you can tell him to call me, as soon as he returns.' The voice was peremptory now, the tone of one accustomed to giving orders to inferiors. His wife?

'Who . . . who shall I say called?'

'Tell him Elena . . . and tell him it is urgent.'

The line went dead and Dene replaced the receiver.

Ten minutes later she heard the sound of a car, the clang of the heavy iron gate and the unmistakable sound of Luq de Léon's uneven stride. She tensed herself. Would this morning prove to be a repetition of last night's battle, or would he have relented? Somehow she didn't see the formidable Señor as a man likely to change his mind lightly.

'*Buenos días!*'

He was dressed formally, in a dark suit of impeccable cut; his greeting was curt, with no sign of friendliness in the austere, handsome features.

'I am late,' he continued. 'I apologise. My car was held up by a military parade and the streets are swarming with tourists . . . here for the Semana Santa.'

Of course, Dene thought, doing a rapid translation . . . Holy Week. In all the hustle of the past fortnight she had lost track of the days. The next day would be Palm Sunday and the beginning of the traditional Easter celebrations, more spectacular, she believed, here than in England.

Abruptly he motioned to her to be seated, but he himself remained standing.

Dene's heart sank. Undoubtedly she was about to receive her

marching orders. But at least there was one way of postponing the evil moment.

'Señor de Léon! I . . . I think your wife wants you to get in touch with her.'

'*Madre de Dios!*' His dark eyes were riveted on her face, a white line of sudden tension around the firm lips. '*What* did you say?'

'There . . . there was a telephone call,' Dene faltered, one slim hand indicating the instrument.

He relaxed visibly, but his voice was still harsh.

'Did the caller leave no name?'

'J . . . just . . . Elena . . .'

He gave her a withering look and she wondered what she had done now to displease him, as he turned his back on her, lifted the receiver and dialled. There followed a rapid, totally incomprehensible conversation, during which Dene, with nothing else to do, found herself studying the back of the dark head, its proud contours, the dark springing hair, badly in need of a trim, so that one or two unruly curls lay upon the muscular nape of his neck; and she felt her fingers itching with a sudden crazy desire to touch them. She was severely shaken by this quite irrational impulse and flushed hotly as he replaced the receiver and turned towards her, the thick black line of his eyebrows quirking derisively.

'That, for your information, was a colleague of mine, Elena Pareja. *Not* a very impressive beginning, *Señorita*. It is as well, when taking messages, to contrive to get one's facts correct.'

Dene opened her mouth to protest, then changed her mind. She had determined not to antagonise this man any further . . . at least, not until she had heard his decision regarding her future. If, as she feared, he continued in his insistence that she was unsuitable, ordered her back to England . . . *that* would be the time to indulge herself in the luxury of telling Señor de Léon just what she thought of him. Besides, he had mentioned a 'beginning'. Was there any significance in that word? Automatically, her fingers went to the lucky black cat at her neck.

He proceeded to study her, so intently that Dene felt her cheeks grow hotter still. It seemed important, however, to endure the close scrutiny of those enigmatic dark eyes, and she continued to meet his regard unwaveringly, though it cost her an effort to do so.

'Tell me more about yourself, *señorita*.'

It was so completely unexpected, his tone so mild, that Dene felt she must be gaping like an idiot; and he was waiting. This was her opportunity to show herself in a good light. She mustn't muff it.

'I . . . there isn't much to tell. What do you want to know?'

'About you,' he said firmly. 'Whatever you wish to tell me.'

Stumbling at first, then with growing assurance, she told him about her background, her family, the desire she had cherished during her schooldays to become a nurse, to travel the world . . . and if possible to combine the two ambitions.

A slight frown appeared between the dark bars of his brows.

'A career woman, an ardent traveller . . . yet you are engaged to be married?'

'Oh yes,' Dene confirmed hastily, 'but I don't want to get married yet . . . not for ages and ages.'

His expression was quizzical.

'And your fiancé . . . he accepts this?'

Dene's expression became mulish.

'Yes, of course. He *has* to.'

'Hmm, curious! What is he like, this fiancé? Is he also of an adventurous nature?'

'N . . . no,' Dene admitted. 'He never goes abroad. He . . . he can't see any point in it.'

'But you insist on *your* right to do so . . . a *very* determined young woman,' Luq said musingly, and then, with a brisk return to business, 'and you have had experience in caring for patients handicapped by arthritis.'

It was a statement, not a question, for he had been given full details of her career to date. Nevertheless, she nodded. There was an air of authority about him today, a businesslike briskness, totally different from yesterday's indifferent arrogance.

'You are aware of the importance of maintaining mobility, by regular exercise, of avoiding excessive weight increase?'

Again she nodded.

There was a brooding silence, during which Dene was well aware that her fate hung in the balance. She would not plead with him, she resolved, unaware of the eager question in her lovely blue eyes, intent upon his face.

Suddenly he swooped.

'What *is* that thing that you wear, that you constantly touch?'

In examining the charm about her neck, his warm fingers accidentally brushed against her flesh, and Dene was startled by her own electrified reaction to the brief contact. She looked down, almost expecting to see a burn mark where he had touched her.

'It . . . it's a lucky charm . . . you know, for good luck,' she chattered inanely.

'You believe in such things? You are *supersticiosa*?'

'I suppose I am a bit. Isn't everyone, in some way?'

'I am not,' he said curtly. 'Superstition makes one suggestible, dangerously so sometimes.

She wished he would stop this fencing . . . come to the point of the interview. He shifted restlessly under her regard.

'I will not pretend, *señorita*, that I am reconciled to your extreme youth.'

'I'm not *that* young,' she interrupted indignantly. 'I'm twenty-three.'

For the first time she saw his long, sensual mouth yield into a smile, and though it was threaded with cynicism, the effect upon his already spectacular good looks was quite devastating. If he were to smile more often, she thought, dazed by the transformation, he would be a far more likeable and approachable person.

'When you reach my age, *señorita*, twenty-three seems as distant and desirable as childhood itself.' His dark eyes clouded over. 'Infinitely desirable,' he mused. 'If I could have my time again, I would not . . . When I was twenty-three . . .' He broke off, the nostalgic, bitter-sweet relaxation of his mouth vanishing, as it assumed its former hardness. 'But we digress. As I said . . . for many reasons, I do not really consider you suitable for a task, which, *Diós sabe*, will be no sinecure. There are . . .'

'I'm not expecting a holiday, *señor*, just because I'm in Spain.' Dene leant forward eagerly as she spoke, her piquant face gravely lovely in its earnestness. 'I *am* accustomed to working hard, and . . .'

'If you would refrain from constant interruption,' he said, his bass voice irritable, 'I could arrive at the point of this conversation.'

Dene subsided, making an effort to subdue her indignation.

She felt like asking him, 'what conversation?' So far it seemed to be a monologue on his part, consisting mainly of his doubts as to her capabilities.

'I will be frank with you, *señorita*. The position I am offering you . . .' The dark warning in his eyes caused her to close her mouth hastily upon the delighted exclamation. 'The position is not one which I have found easy to fill. It requires strength of character and has certain drawbacks and disadvantages . . . not least the situation of the village. All this I freely admit. It is not everyone who could . . . But enough! With some reluctance, I propose to give you two months' trial.'

'Oh, thank you!' Dene was not one to bear a grudge and her words were heartfelt.

After all, it *would* have been wrong of him, for the sake of all concerned, to employ someone unsuitable. Obviously he was just extremely cautious and conscientious.

Her smile irradiated the whole of her vivid little face, bringing to prominence a second, hitherto unrevealed dimple in her cheek.

'I promise you, you won't regret it. I . . .'

'It is to be hoped that *you* will not regret it,' he returned gravely, repressively. 'And if you have any doubts at all, *señorita, now* is the time to withdraw.'

'I've no doubts . . . none at all,' she said firmly.

Again, weary cynicism twisted his lips into a travesty of a smile.

'The sublime confidence of youth!'

How he harped on age . . . and he couldn't be *so* old himself, Dene thought. Mentally, she had categorised him as being in his mid-thirties . . . a lot older than her, of course, but not *old*.

Now that her employment was assured, she felt that the time had come to learn more about her patient.

'Can you tell me anything about Mrs Travers . . . as a person, I mean, apart from her illness. Is she . . . ?' She hesitated, as his face assumed once more its closed in expression.

'I would prefer you to make your own assessment of Señora Travers, unbiased by anything that I or anyone else could tell you. There are case notes on her medical history at Pajaro, which will be available to you, when we go down, in about ten days' time.'

'Ten days!' Dene squeaked. 'But . . . but I understood I'd be going there now . . . today.'

'It is quite impossible for me to leave Seville until after the Semana Santa.'

'But I thought . . . José . . . he said . . .'

'Quite unsuitable,' he said firmly. 'I should prefer to take you down myself, to introduce you properly to my patient.'

'*Your* patient? *You* are a doctor?' Dene was mortified. Why hadn't he told her before?

He nodded brusquely.

'I am Cirujano Mayor . . . Senior Surgeon . . . at the Rivera hospital here in Seville. I did my training in England . . . which is how I am acquainted with Gerald Harvey. We were medical students together . . . the best of friends too, and we have kept in touch.'

So it was Luq de Léon to whom Mr Harvey had been referring, when he spoke of his friend . . . and not Mrs Travers. Dene wished Gerald Harvey had been more explicit. It might have saved a lot of embarrassment. Still, she supposed it was reassuring that Señor de Léon and Mr Harvey were friends. She was sure her former employer would not have sent her to work for anyone he could not personally vouch for.

'The Semana Santa can be a busy time for the hospitals,' Luq was explaining. 'It is a time of great religious fervour . . . passions sometimes run high . . . there are accidents, or an over-zealous penitent may find himself in need of medical aid.'

'I'm not familiar with your customs,' Dene said shyly. 'Since I have to remain in Seville, would it be possible for me to see something of the ceremonies?'

He inclined his head.

'But the streets will be crowded,' he warned, 'the mood of the crowd excitable. It would be best if you were escorted. When I am not on duty at the hospital, I will accompany you myself. When I *am* otherwise engaged, it would be more prudent for you to remain indoors. My house is, of course, yours, for the duration of your stay. You are satisfied that Maria provides adequate chaperonage?'

'Oh . . . Oh yes . . . yes, of course,' Dene said hastily, her cheeks a little pink. 'Besides,' she said indignantly, 'I'm well aware that you're a married man, and as such to be entirely trusted.'

The look that crossed his face was a strange mixture of pain, irony and displeasure.

'You are very naïve, *señorita*. However ... You will find our observance of Eastertide very different from that of your country. You are Catholic?'

'No,' she admitted. 'I don't think I'm anything really, though I suppose my parents are C of E. But I *am* interested in religious festivals, simply as a spectacle.'

He smiled wryly.

'Do not let my aunt hear you speak so. She is *muy religiosa*. She will immediately seek to convert you.'

'Your aunt?'

'*Si* . . . José's mother.'

'And you,' Dene said diffidently, 'are you very religious? I mean, it *is* only another form of superstition, isn't it?'

'No, *señorita*, to us it is of great meaning, great importance. I should not like to think you were serious in likening religion to superstition. Superstitions were instigated by man, religion by God.'

She felt chastened by his manner, but then he smiled, a perfectly genuine expression, unspoiled by weary cynicism, and Dene found the effect somewhat overwhelming. For the first time she found herself debating the wisdom of spending a whole week under the roof of this intriguing man, with his potent masculinity, with no one else present but a practically invisible house-keeper.

'Let us not grow too serious, *señorita* . . . for the moment we concentrate on the spectacle of the Semana Santa, no?'

Palm Sunday was a day of perfect sunshine, and Dene came down to breakfast to find Luq just returned from early Mass. Maria had produced what she described triumphantly, in her imperfect English, as 'the breakfast British' . . . a doubtful concoction of bacon, eggs and beans, running with olive oil.

'You don't *have* to eat it,' Luq told Dene, seeing her doubtful expression. 'I can ask Maria to make something else.'

But Dene shook her head.

'No, I wouldn't hurt her feelings for the world. She's obviously gone to a lot of trouble to make me feel at home. I knew the food would be different, and the sooner I get used to it the better.'

He did not express it, but she sensed that she had pleased him and her spirits lifted a little. Perhaps these next few days would not be such an ordeal after all; now that he had decided to employ her, perhaps he was also prepared to be friendly.

About mid-morning, they made their way through the crowded streets to the Cathedral, where, Luq told her, they would witness the convergence of many processions.

He had timed their arrival well. As they neared the Cathedral, the sound of music could be heard in the distance, the tattoo of drums, the sombre tones of brass bands. There was sudden activity on the part of the police, who began clearing a way through the milling sightseers.

Then the procession came into view, long lines of white-robed, hooded figures, carrying silver crosses, candles in magnificent gilt candlesticks, lanterns, embroidered banners . . . and life-size statues. These were of two kinds . . . porcelain Virgins of Sorrow, under heavy jewel-encrusted canopies, depicting scenes from the Passion, and persecuted Christs of almost frightening realism. The Virgins, without exception, wore robes of velvet, lace and brocade, jewellery, rings and diadems of pearls.

Dene found the ceremony haunting in its strangeness, dignity and reverence, and she could not forbear a swift glance up at the man beside her, wondering what effect a lifetime of such observances must have had upon his character.

'This goes on for hours,' Luq warned Dene. 'You will scarcely wish to stand here all day?'

'Could we just see what goes on *inside* the Cathedral?' she begged.

'*Cierto que sí!*'

Again he seemed pleased and, superstitiously, Dene crossed her fingers behind her back. Could she possibly keep him in this amiable frame of mind until she was safely conveyed to Pajaro, with no risk of him changing his mind?

On the Monday, there were more processions to watch, more pomp and circumstance to wonder over, more Virgins, more Crucifixions, more accompanying bands. But on the Tuesday, Luq was on duty at the hospital and Dene, relaxing in the spring

sunshine warming the patio of the Casa de Leon, was quite glad
of the respite, feeling that she had exhausted the possibilities of
the Semana Santa. Wednesday, however, when Luq stated that
once again he would not be available, she felt slightly piqued,
even though he had warned her that, on some days, this would
be the case.

The sun was not so warm, and besides, Dene was not in a
mood to sit still. Unexplored Seville called to her. She fidgeted
about the house. There was nothing to do . . . no books to read.
The hands of her watch scarcely seemed to move. By afternoon
she could bear it no longer. Surely there could be no harm in her
going out alone? Luq was being ridiculously old-fashioned. She
had lived and worked in London for two years, had explored
cities in other countries on her own. She simply could not bear to
waste this opportunity. Last evening, Luq had not returned until
the meal was on the table. If she made sure she was back long
before then, he would be none the wiser.

She was going out!

She had no definite destination in mind, but wandered where
the will took her . . . along narrow streets, down wide boule-
vards, through plazas, discovering unexpected, small, quiet
squares, filled with the scents of jasmine and orange blossom.
She passed cafés, public buildings, and shops . . . their windows
dressed for the following week's *fiesta*, with high tortoiseshell
combs and mantillas, fans painted with bullfight scenes, posters
and coloured postcards of matadors. How she longed to go to a
bullfight, she thought wistfully. Would she ever have the opportunity? She wrote and despatched postcards to her parents and
to Gerald Harvey, but after hesitation decided not to include
Barry on her mailing list.

At last it was time to turn back in the direction of the Avenida
de los Santos, and Dene was thankful for the landmark provided
by the Giralda, visible from all parts of the city. She had
deliberately avoided the more crowded areas, with their inevitable crowds and still more processions, preferring to explore
more unfrequented places.

Luq met her with a thunderous face. Dinner had been held
back for her. She had committed the ultimate discourtesy. She
was late for a meal.

'I . . . I'm sorry,' she stammered, as the dishes were brought to the table, Maria's countenance taut with affronted susceptibilities.

At least Luq had restrained himself before the housekeeper, she thought thankfully, but once Maria left them to their meal, he made sure that Dene was in no doubt of his displeasure.

'Where have you been, *señorita*? I returned home early this afternoon, only to find you missing. It is almost dusk. *Por Dios*, I have been imagining . . .'

'Oh, but you don't need to worry about *me*,' Dene assured him earnestly. 'I'm really quite capable of looking after myself, and . . .'

'*Señorita*,' he said grimly, 'at the hospital today, we have dealt with countless numbers of tourists, suffering from exhaustion . . . broken limbs, whose owners have climbed to risky vantage points . . . and two young girls, of about your own age, who have been set upon in alleyways, beaten and robbed. You *knew* my feelings . . . that you should not go out unescorted. While you are here in Spain, your safety is my responsibility. If you wish to *remain* in my employ, you will not repeat today's escapade, *if* you please.'

For the rest of the meal, conversation was non-existent, and afterwards Luq retired to his study on the plea of urgent paperwork to be dealt with; and Dene did not see him again that day.

Though still simmering at the peremptoriness of Luq's manner, Dene was not willing to risk being dismissed before her employment had even begun. She came down to breakfast on Thursday, determined to be placatory, to assure Luq that she would abide by his commands. But her resolution was wasted. He had already left the house—an emergency at the hospital, Dene managed to ascertain from Maria. Bother, she thought. Luq was supposed to have been free today and she had been hoping that he would suggest more sightseeing. Now she would be stuck in this dull house all day.

She was feeling decidedly sulky, when she heard the iron gate clang shut. Luq must be back, the emergency dealt with. Her face transformed, she turned towards the door, unaware how drastically her expression changed, her smile faltering as she saw José Mañara.

'*Buenos días*, Nadine!' He took her hand, pressing a kiss upon it. 'I was desolated to find that I should not have the pleasure of driving you to Pajaro. However, I called, in the hope that I would find you alone. It seems today is my lucky day. You have no previous engagement?'

'None at all,' Dene admitted. 'Your cousin forbade me to go out unescorted.'

José's brilliant smile flashed out.

'Then your problems are solved.' He bowed formally. 'You *have* an escort, *con su permiso*? At your service, *señorita*.'

His manner was so absurdly old-fashioned that Dene's delighted laughter rang out, but she answered him in kind, dropping a graceful curtsey.

'*Gracias, señor!*' Then, with a return to normal, 'Oh, José, will *you* take me sightseeing?' She wrinkled her nose. 'But no more processions, please.'

'*¡Como nó!* Come, we shall . . . what is that so expressive English saying . . . paint Seville crimson?'

'Red,' she corrected. 'Oh yes, let's!'

José led her on an even more rambling tour of the city than she had followed the previous day. But it was much more enjoyable with a lighthearted companion to point out, to comment, to explain. They visited a street market, watched a butcher skin sheep as easily as peeling an apple; at his feet bundles of live chickens, tied together, waited to be sold; mendicant traders sold assortments of dried herbs. They sipped Manzanilla and ate seafood at José's favourite street café, visited gardens and parks, had their fortunes told by an itinerant gipsy, who shook her grizzled head over Dene's palm.

'What did she say?' Dene asked.

José's face was unwontedly serious.

'She said, "At the villa, you must beware".'

'Villa? But I don't know any villas.' Dene laughed nervously. 'Besides, can they *really* tell fortunes . . . it *is* all rubbish, isn't it?' But the unease persisted as she said: 'Come on, where to now?' And she couldn't resist a surreptitious rub of the lucky black cat as they went on their way.

She would have been happy now to return to the Casa. Luq would soon be home and the bleak rooms would not seem so empty. But José was insisting that there was more to be seen, that he wished to take her for a meal.

'Oh no, I can't!' She looked up at him in dismay. 'They'll be expecting me for dinner. Maria will be put out again, and your cousin annoyed with me. Some other time, perhaps?'

But José would not accept her refusal.

'Leave it to me, *querida*. I will telephone the Casa, make your apologies . . . assure them that you are quite safe. You want to make the most of your stay in Seville, *si*?'

'Yes . . . yes, of course, and yet . . .'

She was still doubtful, but José returned from the telephone kiosk, smiling broadly.

'*Bueno!* That is arranged. Come, Nadine. You shall see Seville, not only by day, but by evening . . . and by night.'

The warm day had cooled to a balmy evening, full of sweet smells, as they strolled along the embankment of the Guadal-quivir, arriving eventually at the café where José planned to eat.

Dene noticed that the patron and his wife greeted José with pleasure and a certain deference, sending their daughters to wait at his table, before serving others who had certainly been there before them. But the other diners seemed to bear no grudge, saluting him, the men with wide grins, the girls with simpering smiles, fluttering eyelashes.

'*Olé*, José!'

A bottle of Manzanilla was placed on their table.

'With the compliments of Don Felipe, *señor*!'

And José waved his acknowledgement to an elderly man at a corner table.

Dene was a little embarrassed by the attention they were attracting and was glad when their food was placed before them and a guitarist struck up a tune.

'Shall I order?' José had asked, and as Dene nodded, he had settled for *gazpacho*, an Andalucian soup, followed by trout Navarrese, a large, firm fish, sautéed with bits of salty ham.

After the guitarist's performance, quite a cabaret developed, as singers and dancers held the central area of the dining room. Later, a single dancer took the floor, a snake-hipped girl with dark, glowing eyes under a tangle of hair. Knees slightly bent beneath her fluttering dress, she began to dance in a wild rhythm, torso erect, neck supple. With a swaying of hips and pelvis, she contrived that the eddies of her skirt should brush against José's thigh. Her provocative gestures were suggestive of the spasms of love, as she offered him her pouting lips, before leaping away, her heels hammering the floor in a staccato beat, echoed by the handclaps of the spectators.

José seemed to take all this as his due, but Dene, unused to such public exhibitionism, felt her cheeks growing hotter by the moment. Everyone seemed to be drinking freely, glasses of wine going round from hand to hand, from mouth to mouth and outside, almost without warning, night had fallen.

Now that the entertainment, apparently, was over, couples were beginning to move on to the floor and José held out his hand to Dene.

'You will dance with me?'

She nodded and slipped into the waiting circle of his arms, disconcerted to find herself immediately pulled close, held tightly against the hard muscles of his lithe body. He was more than a little drunk, she thought somewhat apprehensively, as they circled the tiny floor space, scarcely moving. It seemed less like dancing than an excuse to be locked together in what was becoming embarrassingly like an intimate embrace.

She was just wondering how she should suggest that José take her home and whether he would accede to her request, when she saw a familiar figure silhouetted in the doorway and felt her heart leap into her throat with fear, as she saw that Luq de Léon was very, very angry.

With surprising rapidity, considering his limping gait, he crossed the floor and plucked José away, as if he were no more than a featherweight.

'How dare you bring Señorita Mason here?' he snapped, his features cruelly distorted. 'This may be a suitable place for the *putas* you consort with, but not for a young English lady in my care!'

He did not give José time to reply, but cast him aside with such violence that the younger man staggered and would have fallen, but for the supporting arm of another customer.

Dene found hard fingers clamped in a vicious hold around her elbow, as Luq marched her out of the riverside café and practically flung her into a waiting taxi.

The journey back to the Casa del Léon was made in total silence. Dene had too much dignity to protest at his cavalier behaviour in the hearing of the driver, and she knew that similar

motives ruled Luq's tongue. But once back at the Casa, he did
not spare her, and though she was no coward, she flinched before
his invective. The door of his study had barely closed behind
them before he began.

'Are you totally lost to all sense of propriety? *Madre de Diós!*
When I heard from Maria that José had taken you to that . . .
that haunt of *putas*, I . . .'

'If you have some complaint, *señor*,' Dene interrupted coldly,
'some justification for breaking in on my date with your cousin,
kindly be more explicit. I've no idea what you're talking about
. . . or what this *puta* means.'

Interrupted in mid-tirade, he glared at her, his face a cold,
angry mask.

'You do not understand what I complain of? When once again
you have disobeyed me?'

'You said I couldn't go out *alone*,' she defended herself. 'I
wasn't alone. I was with José, your own cousin . . .'

'*Si, my own cousin*,' he agreed grimly, 'would that it were any
recommendation! My cousin, *señorita*, frequents low places,
keeps low company. For your information, the word *puta* means
"whore".'

She gasped, outraged, but he swept on.

'Oh yes, *señorita*, my cousin is not particular about the women
he befriends. Do you really wish *your* name to be associated with
such a one?'

'But I had no idea,' she faltered. 'José telephoned the Casa . . .
he said it was all arranged . . .'

'José spoke to Maria. He told her where he was taking you,
gave her no chance to protest. There was nothing she could do,
until I returned from the hospital, tired and ready for my bed.'

He *did* look tired, Dene thought, with sudden compunction.

'I'm sorry . . . truly sorry,' she whispered, tears not far away.

His austerely carved features relented somewhat and he
reached out and brushed the long fall of hair aside from her
downcast face. The touch of his fingers on her cheek was
strangely disconcerting and she looked up at him, a startled
awareness in her blue eyes.

'Perhaps after all no harm has been done,' he said softly. 'Do
not look so sad, *chica*. I am partly to blame. I should have warned
you about my graceless cousin.'

His black eyes held her wide gaze for a second, but he was the first to look away.

'I think perhaps,' he said, his low-pitched voice suddenly husky, 'that the chaperonage I have provided is inadequate. Maria is no longer young enough to . . .' He paused, then seemed to reach a decision. 'The hospital must do without me for a few days. Tomorrow we go to Pajaro.'

CHAPTER THREE

DENE could not sleep that night. At first she told herself that it was fatigue. Many times, when overtired after a busy day on the wards, she had passed similarly restless nights. But then, as she grew more desperate for sleep, depression gripped her.

She did not want to go to Pajaro. She wanted to stay here, in Seville, near Luq; and that was ridiculous, because it was neither possible nor permissible. It was not possible, because she had come here to do a job, and that task still awaited her; it was not permissible, because Luq was a married man, and tonight something had sparked between them . . . something which was now endangering her peace of mind. Had he recognised it too? Was that the reason for his sudden decision to cut short her stay, to bring forward her journey to Pajaro? Was he anxious to be rid of her?

It was a warm, sultry night and she tossed and turned on the narrow, old-fashioned bed, more miserable than she had ever been in her life.

Luq was briskly matter-of-fact at breakfast, though not exactly meeting her eyes, as he spoke.

'I had thought it might prove salutary if José returned to Pajaro for a time.' His lips tightened. 'But on telephoning his . . . his accommodation, I find he is . . . indisposed. It seems we must depart without him.'

That the prospect of a journey alone with her gave Luq no pleasure was all too evident, and Dene wished that it was not necessary for him to accompany her. But even had she been able to drive, with a car at her disposal, she knew she would not dare to tackle the unfamiliar journey alone, or the mountainous route which must be traversed before reaching the valley of the Alpujarras.

Because of the arrangements Luq must make for his unscheduled absence, their departure from the Casa del Léon was delayed until mid-afternoon. The oppressively hot night had been succeeded by an equally warm day, the sun blazing down, as if in a determined effort to roast the whole countryside. Great thunderclouds hung uneasily overhead, as they retraced the route over the Sierras, which she had made in the other direction with José . . . was it only five days ago?

Luq's car, though more conservative than his cousin's, was equally powerful and luxurious, but Luq was a more considerate driver, travelling at a less breathtaking speed, paying more heed to the rights of other road users.

'Do you get many storms?' Dene asked a trifle nervously.

Storms were the one thing she really feared. Superstition was a nebulous, intangible enemy. The portents that troubled you might never happen; but storms had many times fulfilled their potential menace . . . people had been killed by storms. She felt less anxious indoors, but out on the open road, climbing ever nearer to the lowering sky, she felt particularly vulnerable.

'A few,' Luq replied laconically, unconcernedly.

It looked as if they might be in for one of the few, Dene thought. But it wouldn't do to reveal her fears to Luq. She was in a position where she must continually prove her stability, reliability. She felt he would have no patience with feminine vapours. She tried to distract her mind from the weather by reflecting on the many questions she still longed to ask.

'Señor . . .' she began diffidently.

He shot her a perceptive glance, a faint smile curling the edge of his mouth.

'I have been anticipating this moment, señorita. You have decided once again to ask me the things you wish to know, sí?'

'The things I *need* to know, señor,' she corrected him. 'You implied that there would be certain . . . difficulties. Surely it's only fair that I should be prepared for whatever eventuality I may have to cope with?'

'Ciertamente!'

'Then my patient . . . her circumstances . . . the house, the village, its amenities . . . oh, so much!'

For a while Luq concentrated on his driving, his lean, capable hands steady on the wheel. Surgeon's hands! Dene, looking at them, was almost irresistibly fascinated by their shapely strength. A man's hands were very important, she thought, remembering the faint distaste she had always felt for Barry's short, stubby . . . almost fat . . . hands.

Despite his expressed willingness to answer her queries, Dene had the distinct impression that he was choosing his words with care.

'As to the village, *señorita*,' he said at last, 'its amenities are few . . . one might say, non-existent. It is small, isolated . . .'

'Not the ideal place for a sick, disabled woman to live,' Dene observed. 'Why doesn't she move to a more convenient place?'

'She was not disabled when she first arrived,' Luq told her, 'And Señora Travers lives there as *my guest*. The Villa Venganza is *my* house . . . the original home of the Léons.'

So it was a 'villa' towards which they were heading . . . where she would be staying . . . Dene thought uneasily, and her hand crept up towards the lucky charm, as she recalled the gipsy's warning about 'a villa'.

'The Casa in Seville is also Léon property,' Luq continued. 'You would say . . . town house? It is convenient for my work at the hospital.'

'And Señora del Léon,' Dene ventured to ask the question which for some while had been uppermost in her mind. 'Is *she* at the family home, with her mother?'

A loud crash of thunder made her start uneasily.

'No,' said Luq, as the reverberations died away, his voice curt with an added note of . . . could it be bitterness? 'At Pajaro, you will find only my dependents . . . the Señora Travers, Tia Teresa . . . José's mother . . . José himself from time to time, and a few servants.'

'But . . .'

Dene thought better of what she had been about to say. She had been going to press for further information concerning Luq's wife. But she decided, in view of his abrupt reply, that it might be tactless to persist. If the Señora was not to be found in either of the Léon homes, perhaps the couple were separated . . . even divorced? Though surely that was unlikely, in a Catholic country?

She was curious, too, over Luq's claim that José also was dependent upon him. Had José no occupation of his own? He certainly gave the impression of irresponsibility . . . yet seemed to have plenty of money to throw about. Nor did it fit in with what she had learned of Luq's character. She could not see him bearing patiently with a relative who led a drone-like existence.

There were so many unknown quantities in her present situation, so many unsatisfactory gaps in her knowledge. Dene hated to feel inadequate, and it was important to her to have all the salient facts regarding her work at her fingertips. The exhilaration she had felt, when Luq de Léon had relented . . . agreeing to employ her for a trial period . . . had faded slightly, shadowed by a distinct sensation of apprehension, increased by the menace of the storm, and . . . she admitted it . . . by his mention of a 'villa'.

Lightning flashed whitely and she cowered in her seat. She could not help the feeling that even the elements were not in favour of her arrival at Pajaro.

Steadily, it was growing darker, and it was difficult to see the road ahead, except when the lightning flickered violently over the countryside. Pajaro, seen by this evil yellow light, was a small village of grey, box-shaped houses, with flat roofs, lying in a deep hollow, half huddled among orange trees and olives; though without Luq's commentary, Dene would never have recognised them from their twisted black silhouettes. Owing to the storm and the lateness of the hour, there were no signs of life, no lighted windows to lessen the illusion of gloom. It was like a ghost town, Dene thought, with a fanciful shudder.

Luq turned the car into a crudely constructed shelter . . . three walls and a canted roof.

'We cannot take the car any further, señorita,' he announced. 'The track up to the villa was constructed in the days when mules were man's sole form of transport.'

'You . . . you mean, we have to walk . . . in this?'

Dene was horrified, looking down at her light cream suit and pastel-coloured court shoes.

The storm had burst, the threat becoming actuality, and the rain was coming down now with torrential force, filling ruts, turning the road into a river; a fierce wind had blown up as if from nowhere, trees bending to its sudden squall, and lightning flashed incessantly; and still it seemed as though the storm had not reached its full fury.

Luq shrugged at her words.

'*Claro!* Unless you wish to wait out the storm in the car? This *could* continue for most of the night.'

The prospect was not one which appealed to Dene. Despite the size and luxury of Luq's car, the idea of being so closely confined with him for an indefinite period was deeply disturbing. Besides, she was travel-weary and hungry, with another pressing need that she knew would not wait much longer.

'All right, we'll walk,' she shrugged.

'Just take whatever you need for tonight,' Luq advised. 'I'll send someone down for the rest in the morning.'

'Will my things be all right in the car all night?'

'No one here would dare to tamper with the property of Léon,' Luq said, and for a moment, in the lurid light of the storm, his profile was fiercely arrogant. 'Why do you think our family home is so named . . . the Villa of Vengeance?'

'I . . . I didn't know it meant that,' said Dene, dismayed by the forbidding title.

'It was not always called that. It was renamed by an ancestor of mine, who killed the man who stole his wife, then possessed his enemy's lands and house.'

'How . . . how barbaric,' Dene said faintly.

With what kind of family had she become involved? In Seville, once his early hostility had abated, Luq had seemed a perfectly normal, if unusually attractive man. But the nearer they approached to his roots, the more mysterious she found him; and now, this revelation . . . of violence in his ancestry . . .

'Our family motto,' Luq added, apparently unmoved by her distaste, 'is, "I avenge".'

Her first impression of the Villa Venganza was of an irregularly shaped muddle of rambling buildings, crouched like a giant, menacing figure on the side of the hill. The lightning had held off for a moment, but, just as they reached the enclosed grounds, it flashed forth once more, lighting the house, and Dene could see that, like the Casa in Seville, the villa was two-storeyed, running around an inner courtyard.

But this house was not painted white; its walls were as dismal and unrelieved a grey as those of the village below. Here too, no lights showed, and recalling not only the words of the gipsy fortune-teller, but also Luq's own vague hints, his unnatural reticence about the occupants of his home, Dene had the panicky sensation that she did not want to enter the villa.

She hung back, staring up fearfully at the dark façade of the old house, as it loomed against the lowering night sky. But she hadn't much choice; the torrential rain and an impatient Luq at her elbow made entering the house the lesser of two evils.

He hustled her up the sweeping, iron-railed outer staircase, which led to a gallery. Unlit iron lanterns hung on either side of a stout main door. But despite the lateness of the hour, it seemed that someone had observed their arrival. Before Luq could open the heavy door it swung open and in the interior darkness a woman's face was just visible, eerie, disembodied, illuminated only by the candle she held.

The woman had piercing dark eyes and a haughty, arrogant nose, which clearly proclaimed her relationship to Luq. She stepped forward, lifting the candle, the better to see their faces, then recoiled, dismay, annoyance . . . or was it fear? . . . mingling in her aristocratic features.

'*Por el amor de Diós!*'

It was not a greeting to inspire confidence in someone already apprehensive and dispirited, and Dene shrank back, turning instinctively to Luq for protection, as her only source of reassurance.

'What's wrong? Why is she annoyed?'

'*Más tarde!*' he said irritably. 'Let us get in out of this benighted weather.'

He marched her into the thick, waiting blackness of the house.

'Light the lamps in the parlour, Tia Teresa, *por favor.*'

Though he added the polite phrase which etiquette demanded, it was, nevertheless, a command. Luq de Léon, Dene thought, was evidently very much the master here.

The interior of the house was no more reassuring than its exterior . . . than the greeting they had received. The room into which the woman addressed as Tia Teresa led them was spacious but murky, even after all the oil lamps had been lit, casting isolated pools of light amongst the heavy furniture, leaving dark, unfathomable corners. Gloomy, heavily framed pictures adorned the walls, the subjects austere, religious, their oil paint blackened by years of smoking lamps. The centre of the room was occupied by a large round table, covered with a hand-made lace cloth. Around it stood upright, uncomfortable-looking chairs. Against one wall was a massive, carved, heavily ornamented sideboard, and the room was crowded with other superfluous cabinets and tables. It was totally featureless, more like a furniture repository than a room in which people presumably lived. The whole atmosphere was one of stagnant respectability. Could this be Luq's taste . . . his aunt's? Surely not his wife's . . . an English girl?

Now that she could see Tia Teresa more clearly, Dene beheld a tall woman of rather formidable aspect, dressed in dark clothes of good quality, but unrelieved severity. Her yellowish complexion was not flattered by straight, thin hair, pulled tightly back over her head. Could this really be the mother of the golden-haired José?

'Tia Teresa, this is Señorita Mason, the new nurse. *Señorita*, my aunt . . . Señora Mañara de Léon. You will address her as Señora Mañara.'

As he spoke, Doña Teresa pulled out the chairs, which proved to be as comfortless as they looked, and they all sat around the table, their attitudes formal . . . like some bizarre tea party, Dene thought with a touch of hysteria.

Doña Teresa had acknowledged the introduction with a slight inclination of her severe head. Now she spoke to Luq de Léon, in a voluble stream of words, causing him to frown in displeasure.

'All this we will discuss later. For now, speak English, Tia Teresa. Señorita Mason has little Spanish.' He hesitated, then continued, 'How has our patient been since my last visit?'

Teresa Mañara shrugged black-clad shoulders, her expression indifferent.

'*La Inglesa?* As usual.' Then, with a sideways, almost sly glance at Dene, 'How much longer does this go on?'

Luq sighed.

'*Diós sabe!* Not much longer, I hope. I have consulted Elena. She has promised to pay us a visit, when she can find the time. In the meantime, I will see the Señora in the morning. You have prepared a room for Señorita Mason?'

'*Sí.* And what will *la Inglesa* have to say about *this one?*'

'Later . . . later . . .'

Luq turned to Dene, a silent witness to their enigmatic conversation.

'Tia Teresa will see you to your room.'

Dene rose, slowly, reluctant to accompany the grim, forbidding woman, who had not seemed pleased by her arrival, or her appearance . . . any more than her nephew had been a few days ago, she reflected.

'How . . . how long are *you* staying here, *señor*?' she asked, feeling that Luq was her one link with the normal outside world.

In response to the unconscious wistfulness in her voice, he shrugged.

'*Eso se depende!*'

Which told her precisely nothing, Dene thought despairingly, as she followed Teresa Mañara's uncompromisingly upright figure along seemingly endless corridors. Their dark shadows, intensified by the poor light of Teresa's flickering candle, were not reassuring, and it was a relief when they stopped and Teresa opened a door.

'This will be your room, *señorita* . . . for the duration of your stay.'

It was said cynically, as if, Dene thought, Teresa Mañara did not expect this period to be a long one. Was that what the older woman hoped, she wondered miserably . . . what they were all hoping, or were circumstances really so difficult here that staff was hard to keep?

'It is only a few doors away from that of your patient. I will light the lamps for you . . . this once. If you intend to remain here, you must learn to do them for yourself. We have few servants.'

As she spoke, her gnarled, work-worn hands were busy about the task. Whatever José's position in this house, Dene reflected, his mother did not spend her time in idleness. Right at this moment, Dene wasn't sure that she *wanted* to stay, that she *would* be here long enough to learn any of the ways of this formidable household. What on earth would her patient be like? Her only comfort at the moment was that at least Mrs Travers was English, like herself, and should, therefore, be less incomprehensible than the enigmatic Señor and his equally bewildering aunt. It was, she thought again, difficult to believe that this was the mother of the insouciant José.

'You're José's mother, aren't you?' she ventured, as Teresa

moved around the room, demonstrating its sparse, but adequate facilities.

Teresa Mañara looked at her sharply, suspiciously.

'Sí . . . but what is that to *you*? What is José to you?'

'N-nothing. Nothing at all,' stammered Dene, taken aback at the ferocity of the unexpected inquisition. 'I was just curious, that's all. I . . .'

'Curiosity is something which does not pay dividends in this house,' Doña Teresa informed her brusquely. 'I suggest that you do the job you have come to do . . . if you can do it,' she added obscurely, 'and seek to know nothing more.' She gave Dene a sharp jerk of the head, which seemed to underline her words, then left the room. Dene heard her firm, brisk steps fading away down the corridor.

With the door closed behind Teresa, Dene looked around the bedroom. Like the parlour, it was large, square, high-ceilinged . . . functional, but with few concessions to charm or comfort. There was very little furniture, only the bare necessities, and over the head of the high, old-fashioned bed was the inevitable religious painting.

Spain had not turned out to be *exactly* as she had expected, Dene thought ruefully. For a few days, it was true, she had experienced the colour, the spectacle of the Semana Santa, had encountered colourful, exotic characters. But the only two houses she had entered were bleak, with no stimuli at all to her romantic imagination. Was *this* the real Spain, the Spain the tourists did not see? Were all houses, all the people, as dour and unwelcoming as these?

It was late morning before she awoke and sunlight filtering through the grille of the tall window made bright bars across the wooden floor, with its sparse scattering of rugs.

Someone had brought in a ewer and basin while she slept. Possibly it was the sound of their departure which had awoken her. With a nostalgic sigh for the modern plumbing at the Casa, she washed in the lukewarm water and donned one of the dresses she wore when on duty . . . crisp, white and efficient-looking. Her thick hair she brushed until it shone, then whisked it up in a neat coil around her head, pinning it firmly in place.

If she was going to be living in such primitive conditions, Dene thought ruefully, she might have to sacrifice her long hair for greater ease of management. Washing and drying it was a long enough task, even when all modern conveniences were available.

A girl of about her own age was hovering in the corridor . . . dark-complexioned, sloe-eyed, she was beautiful, even in the dark, shapeless servant's dress. She seemed to scrutinise Dene's face with a curious intentness.

'*Buenos días!*' Dene smiled at the girl.

Slowly, hesitantly the smile was returned.

'*Buenos días, señorita*. I am Lucia. You slept well?'

'Very well,' Dene admitted, realising with a certain amount of surprise that she *had* slept extremely well, far better than she had expected in her uneasy state of mind.

The maid's dark eyes seemed to reflect Dene's own surprise.

'People do not usually sleep well in this house,' she observed as, hips swaying, she led the way along the interconnecting corridors, their gloomy secretiveness contributed to by shadowy doorways.

Her manner caused a responsive shiver to run along Dene's spine.

'Oh! Why not?'

Lucia shrugged, her face suddenly expressionless, as though she had suddenly remembered an injunction against gossiping.

'Maybe the *señorita* will discover for herself. Me, I am glad that I go down to the village each night.'

'Do any of the servants sleep in?' Dene asked.

The girl shook her head.

'Not since . . . no, *señorita*. We prefer to return to our families at night. By day . . .' she shrugged. 'By day, the house is light, less . . . *mala* . . . and we are busy.'

So it had not been her imagination . . . the atmosphere in this house, if even the family servants had a superstitious fear of it.

'You speak English very well,' Dene observed.

The compliment was a genuine one, but she had a motive behind expressing it. Not only was she anxious to cement at least one alliance in this house, but also she sensed that Lucia would not be able to forgo chattering for long. From her she might learn something more about the things which perplexed her. Dene did not look upon this as gossiping with servants. She was not accustomed to a household where such distinctions existed. To her the other girl was a possible friend of her own age.

'*Sí*,' Lucia nodded complacently. 'Don Luquillo insist on English-speaking servants ... because of *la Inglesa* ... the Señora Travers. It is necessary that we understand.'

She gave Dene a shy, diffident glance.

'You are very young, *señorita*. This is not usual at the villa. You must be very special exception?'

Since Dene herself did not understand the emphasis on age in this house, she could not answer the implied question; nor could she, in her turn, question Lucia further, since they had reached a room which was evidently the kitchen and nerve-centre of the house.

A massive room, its windows catching the best of the morning sun, it was the most cheerful apartment Dene had seen yet in the villa. There was an enormous open fireplace, empty for the moment, but which Dene could imagine as a focus of warmth and comfort in the colder months of the year. Great built-in cupboards of dark walnut wood lined the walls and a large, scrubbed table was set with one place.

'Your breakfast, *señorita* ... the breakfast English!' Lucia added proudly, placing a plate of bacon and eggs before her.

For a brief moment Dene felt insulted at being expected to eat in what appeared to be servants' quarters, but then she thought of the gloomy parlour and decided that she preferred the bright, homely kitchen. Remembering that Maria at the Casa de Léon had also proudly claimed to have produced the 'British breakfast', Dene was a little wary, but discovered to her delight that the food was undetectable from that served at her mother's table.

As she ate, she looked around her, glimpsing through an open door another area, which seemed to be a storeroom, for preserved hams and dried vegetables hung within her range of vision and she could see shelves bearing rows of bottled preserves.

At a smaller table in the kitchen another woman, stout, doughty, thick of arm and body, was busily making pastry. She gave Dene a cheerful smile, but said nothing.

'Asunción is the only servant who does not speak English,'

Lucia said with conscious superiority. 'For her it is not necessary. She does not see *la Inglesa*. Besides, she has been here many years, since the Señor was *bebé*.'

Asunción seemed greatly interested in Dene's appearance, as did Lucia . . . openly regarding her, as her hands plunged in and out of the enormous mixing bowl, giving little nods of her head and strange clicking of lips and teeth as she did so; but whether this was indicative of approval or otherwise, Dene could not determine.

A rapid stream of words from the elderly cook obviously constituted questions about the new nurse, since the dark eyes, made smaller and brighter by the crinkling of the surrounding flesh, never left Dene's face; and in both Asunción's questions and Lucia's reply she caught several times the words '*guitarra*' and '*música*'.

'What is she saying?' Dene asked, thinking perhaps that the cook was interested to know if she played an instrument.

Lucia seemed reluctant to reply, then, after a swift glance about her, as though to make sure only Asunción was within earshot, she muttered;

'She asks if you heard guitar music in the night.'

'No.' Dene was puzzled. 'Should I have? Does someone here play the guitar? Did Asunción hear it . . . I thought none of the servants slept in?'

The sound of horses' hoofs, somewhere below, put an abrupt end to Lucia's chatter.

'No, no one plays. Asunción just wondered . . . but the Señor returns. He will require the breakfaut also.'

And leaving Dene to muse on the strange question, she rattled off a stream of incomprehensible instructions to the placid Asunción, who nodded goodnaturedly, removed her floury arms from the bowl and turned her attention to the stove, which Dene had already noticed was powered by butane gas cylinders.

It seemed that she had jumped to conclusions in assuming that her status in the household was the cause of her relegation to the kitchen for meals. For, shortly after the sounds of his arrival, Luq de Léon entered the kitchen by an exterior door from the gallery and seated himself at the table, with a brief greeting for Dene and a flow of what appeared to be goodhumoured badinage for Asunción; for the old woman laughed and preened and set his breakfast before him herself, receiving a caressing slap upon her ample buttocks as she did so.

Dene could not believe that this was the same man, the severe disapproving autocrat. Even though his manner towards her had gradually relaxed, she had never imagined that he could behave so boyishly, and the realisation gave a betraying warmth to her sapphire blue eyes.

He caught her look of glowing, wide-eyed incredulity and his smile included her, making her catch her breath sharply, that unfamiliar sensation fluttering once again beneath her ribs.

'Asunción has been here since I was a small boy. I am told I took my first steps holding on to her hand. I believe she was young and pretty then, but alas, I cannot remember. She has always been just Asunción, always ready with a caress or a titbit for a small boy . . . To her, I believe I shall always be that child.'

It was the most self-revealing speech he had ever made in her hearing, and his words told of emotions she had not believed the severe Spaniard capable of expressing. The thought of him as a small, hungry boy, coaxing food from the cook, was curiously endearing.

'What are you thinking, *señorita*?' he asked curiously.

'I was trying to imagine you as a child.' She smiled at him, warmly, unreservedly, unaware just how lovely her creamy English-rose complexion seemed to the swarthy Spaniard, and caught a flicker of awareness in the dark eyes, before his face assumed once more its habitually rigid mask.

'No doubt you are anxious to meet your patient at long last, *señorita*?' It was a sudden and complete change of subject, his voice grave, formal once more. 'If you will join me in her room, when you have finished your breakfast, I will introduce you.'

'I'm ready now,' Dene assured him, and with a word of thanks for Lucia and Asunción, left the kitchen in his wake.

In spite of his uneven stride, he moved so quickly that she had to run almost, to keep up with him. Yet, as thay neared the patient's bedroom, his pace slackened and at the door he turned to look down at Dene, his lean, dark features sombre, yet with something inscrutable in his look, which puzzled and slightly disturbed her. There was a tone in his voice, moreover, which she found impossible to fathom.

'*Señorita*, you pride yourself, I believe, on being sensible,

level-headed. Are you also discreet, capable of forming unpre-
judiced judgments?'

She met his eyes, her own level, honest . . . if slightly puzzled.
'I hope so, señor.'

'I too hope so.' He sighed. 'For in the next few weeks, you will
have need of all those qualities.' There was a tautness behind his
words. Dene was aware of a rekindling of her apprehension.

'Is Mrs Travers so formidable, then?' she enquired, her voice
low, aware that her patient was inside the room they were about
to enter.

But he had shaken off his mood, whatever it had been, and was
businesslike, practical once more.

'I should prefer you to form your own opinion, señorita. After
all, it is you who will be spending most of your hours with my
mother-in-law.'

It gave her a little start, this reminder of his relationship to
Mrs Travers. It was so easy . . . so dangerously easy to forget
that he was married; and she wondered again as to the whereabouts of his wife. But she would find out very shortly, she told
herself. She had found that, amongst all the elderly ladies she
had nursed, not one could resist speaking of her family, relating
even most intimate histories, sometimes in embarrassing detail.

She put out her hand to open the door, at the same time that
Luq attempted to do so, and for a fleeting moment their fingers
brushed.

Dene could not repress a gasp, as she snatched her hand away,
startled at the rush of sensation their brief contact had engendered. It was as potent, if not more so, as on the previous
occasion, when he had touched her cheek. She glanced at him
hastily, to see if he had noticed her instinctive reaction, but his
expression was remote, grim, as he gestured to her to precede
him into the room.

Still shocked by her growing awareness of him, a feeling
which, despite all her efforts, she seemed unable to curb, she
entered the room, all trepidation at the thought of meeting her
patient temporarily forgotten in the greater fear of her own
troublesome susceptibilities.

Then, as she saw Mrs Travers, she couldn't imagine why she
had ever experienced any anxiety at all; for her patient was
entirely different from her expectations.

The woman awaiting her could not, by Dene's estimation, be more than forty. She was daintily, if somewhat frivolously, dressed in a flounced nightdress and matching negligee; and even though she was seated, it was immediately apparent that she was tall and though with a tendency to overweight had once been of graceful and fluid proportions; and there was no trace of grey in the carefully coiffured jet black hair.

Dene wondered, with a stabbing sense of envy which she could not repress, if Señora de Léon, Luq's wife, had inherited her mother's good looks. Still, at least this was no elderly dragon; this was a comparatively young, chic and intelligent-looking woman, with whom she felt immediately she could be friends.

At first glance, Dene thought she perceived a widening of the older woman's eyes, as though something had startled her. But it was a fleeting expression, soon replaced by one of friendly welcome.

'Miss Mason?' Mrs Travers' mobile lips parted in a welcoming smile. Her voice was light, fluting, with a slight trace of what Dene termed a 'posh' accent. 'I've been so looking forward to meeting you. I can't tell you how wonderful it will be to hear a real English voice about the place . . . even though dear Luq *has* done his best for me.'

From Dene, her large, luminous bronze eyes moved in Luq's direction, and though there was no visible change in the expression of either, Dene had the strangest feeling that the atmosphere in the room had become highly charged with an undefinable emotion.

'As you surmised, Isobel, this is your new nurse, Señorita Nadine Mason. We are very fortunate to have her, since she is engaged to be married . . . is that not so, *señorita*? We hope to keep her for as long as her fiancé can spare her. I will leave you to become acquainted. *Señorita*, as to the case notes . . . we can discuss them later, perhaps in about an hour, *por favor?*'

He had barely entered the room and now, already, he was anxious to leave. But Dene no longer felt any need for his presence. Mrs Travers was not at all alarming and she felt sure she would easily establish a rapport with her patient. She drew up a seat, swiftly, but with a discreet professional eye assessing the progress of Mrs Travers' arthritis. The only really visible signs were in the swollen and misshapen hands, but another clue lay in the need for the two walking sticks close at hand.

'So Luq de Léon brought you here himself?' Mrs Travers said, and Dene had the impression that she was not just making conversation. 'Just the two of you?'

'Yes . . . Señor Mañara was really supposed to drive down with us, but apparently he's indisposed.'

'Oh, I see!' Mrs Travers leant forward, laying one distorted hand upon Dene's knee. 'My dear, I'm afraid that was probably a discreet fiction on Luq's part.' She shook her dark head deprecatingly. 'Young José has quite a reputation.' The fluting voice became hushed, insinuative. 'A case of wine and women, to put it politely. From experience I would diagnose José's indisposition as a severe hangover.'

Remembering the evening at the riverside café, Dene thought Mrs Travers was probably correct.

'If no one else has seen fit to warn you,' Isobel Travers continued, 'I feel it's only my duty to do so. Don't allow yourself to be deluded by that young man's apparent charm. You don't mind me speaking frankly?'

'Oh . . . no of course not.'

But Dene felt a little uncomfortable. She knew only too well that the blond, handsome Spaniard was popular with women . . . of all kinds . . . but she still had a sneaking liking for him, believed that he was not as black as people would have her believe; and how he spent his time was none of her concern, nor of Isobel Travers, and she didn't feel she should encourage the turn the conversation had taken.

'Well,' she said, with the brisk good humour that had stood her in good stead with her patients, 'we've been left to get acquainted. Suppose you tell me something about yourself . . . your illness. How long have you suffered from arthritis?'

Mrs Travers laughed. It was an attractive, tinkling sound, as light as her voice.

'Miss Mason . . . may I call you Nadine . . . such a pretty name? I'm too accustomed to nurses not to be aware of your disapproval. You think me a scandalmonger and a gossip. Very well, I won't say another word. But as you're a young, lovely girl, with a fiancé to consider, I felt it was only fair that you should be warned of young José's philandering ways . . . especially since he lives here from the end of one season to the beginning of the next.'

Despite her reluctance to gossip, Dene's rarely dormant curiosity was roused and she looked at Isobel enquiringly.

'I don't understand. Season . . . what season?'

'You mean you don't know who José is? No, I see you don't. My dear, what a blow to his pride! How did he actually restrain himself from bragging of it?'

Dene had decided that, for the moment, it was virtually impossible to check the other woman's slightly indiscreet conversation. She was well acquainted with the type . . . talkative, slightly malicious, but harmless enough. Probably, once the novelty of being able to speak freely had worn off, the flow of information would stop; and after all, there couldn't be much here to occupy the mind of a woman who, though handicapped, was still young . . . apart from the activities of the people with whom she lived.

'That young man is an anachronism . . . one of the last representatives of a cult that's fast dying out. José Mañara de Léon is known nationally as the Golden Spaniard.' Then, as Dene still looked blank, 'He's a bullfighter . . . typical of his kind . . . drinking, frittering his money, womanising . . . a swaggering, arrogant young man, though not too arrogant to sponge off his cousin, when things aren't going well for him.

In spite of her own recognition of José's faults, his wild thoughtless nature, Dene could not help being thrilled by the knowledge that she had actually met and spoken with a real live bullfighter. The idea appealed to all that was romantic in her. Despite this remote, inconveniently situated village, the gloomy house with its ill-assorted occupants, Spain, the real Spain, *had* for a few days touched her life; and José would be coming home again, she reminded herself, with a tinge of pleasure at the thought, and he would bring a much-needed warmth to the Villa Venganza; she would ask him about bullfighting, encourage him to describe one of his own engagements . . . But she was not here to dream of such things.

'What about your rheumatism, Mrs Travers?' she reminded her patient gently.

A slight frown marred the other's smooth brow, as she lifted her hands and regarded them with obvious displeasure.

'Ah, yes . . . such a bore . . . very restricting, and very painful
. . . and I used to have such pretty hands. They were much
admired, you know. Luq once said . . .' She stopped, then
continued, 'I find it very frustrating. I don't get out and I can
scarcely move about the house. Luq is all in favour of this
new-fangled surgery . . . steel plates in the hips, plastic pins in
my knuckles. He did once suggest that I go to his hospital in
Seville, but he hasn't mentioned it since.'

'It's a technique which has proved very successful at my
hospital in London,' Dene assured her. 'Have you never thought
of going back to England for the operation?'

Mrs Travers sighed and looked embarrassed.

'I'm afraid it's a question of finance, my dear. I have very little
money of my own. I'm totally dependent upon Luq.'

'He must be quite wealthy,' Dene said diffidently. 'If you'd
rather go to England, perhaps your daughter could persuade
him to . . .'

'No!' Mrs Travers face twisted into an expression of distress.
'Did no one tell you? Goodness, how strange! Belinda died,
nearly two years ago.'

CHAPTER FOUR

'BELINDA was only nineteen,' Isobel continued.

'Oh!' Dene gasped with dismay. 'I'm so sorry, I had no idea.'

Why couldn't someone have told her, she thought furiously, so that she need not have made such an awful gaffe, distressing this nice woman unnecessarily. She shrank with embarrassment too, as she recalled the incident at the Casa de Léon, when she had told Luq that his wife was trying to get in touch with him. No wonder he had looked at her as if she were insane! A bubble of hysteria welled inside her. Perhaps, for one moment, he had even suspected her of mediumistic tendencies.

But if his wife was dead . . . in natural progression, Dene's thoughts moved irresistibly in another direction . . . this meant that Luq was free . . . free to marry again. She felt herself begin to shake at the thought. Stop it! she adjured herself sharply. Just because he has no wife, it doesn't mean he's the slightest bit interested in you, or ever likely to be. *He* knew he was free and he hadn't said or done anything to indicate . . . Because he thinks you're already engaged, self answered.

But she must pay attention. Mrs Travers was still speaking.

'It's not your fault, dear, that you didn't know about Belinda.' She dabbed at her strangely beautiful eyes with a wisp of handkerchief. 'I'm not a bit surprised that nobody took the trouble to tell you. No one here ever speaks of Belinda. They're very hard, unfeeling people, these Spaniards . . . and as for Señora Mañara . . . but there, I'm gossiping again!'

'You can talk to *me* about Belinda as much as you like,' Dene said warmly. 'But perhaps we should discuss *you* first. Señor de Léon will expect . . . Just how long *have* you had your rheumatism?'

'Two years. It came on very suddenly, almost overnight, after . . . after I lost Belinda. They told me it was the shock.'

'And what treatment have you had to date?'

57

'Oh, my goodness! All sorts. I'm quite sick of it. You'll have to talk to Luq about that.'

'I'd much rather you told me about yourself, Nadine. Whereabouts in England do you come from? What's your fiancé like? Whatever made you want to work in Spain? How did you meet Luq? You've no idea how boring it is here. No one seems to have time to talk to me, though they gossip enough amongst themselves.'

'Now that I'm here you won't lack for someone to talk to,' Dene promised. 'Let's see ... to answer your questions in order ...'

As Dene satisfied Mrs Travers' curiosity, regretting the necessity for enlarging on her fiction about Barry ... she couldn't think why Luq had seen fit to even mention it ... only half her attention was on the replies she gave. A separate compartment of her mind seemed capable of dwelling upon other matters. She felt sorry for Mrs Travers.

At least one thing had been cleared up, during her conversation with her patient. There was no mystery after all as to the whereabouts of Luq's wife. He was neither separated nor divorced. No wonder he hadn't the appearance of a happily married man!

She became aware that she was woolgathering and had not heard Mrs Travers' last question.

'I suspect I'm boring you,' Mrs Travers said sadly. 'It's very hard to expect a young girl like you to keep an older woman company. I'm sure you'd rather be at home in England, with your fiancé?'

'Not at all,' Dene denied vehemently. 'I'm nowhere near ready to settle down yet. There are far too many things I want to do, places I want to see. But I do feel that I've told you enough about myself.'

'You think I'm being nosey?' Isobel asked diffidently. 'Is that it?'

'No,' Dene reassured her, 'of course not. I've no secrets, but I *would* like to know more about you, if I'm to be of help to you. Perhaps it would be a good idea to tell me about your daughter?'

'Poor little Belinda! That's very sweet of you, Nadine. I'm afraid I've rather got out of the way of talking about her ... though of course I'm always thinking about her. Nobody here even mentions her name. Teresa Mañara for one had no time for my little girl . . . and I've a good idea why. If Luq had remained unmarried, there was a good chance that her son would inherit the Léon money some day. He has that chance again now,' she added bitterly, 'unless . . .'

'But surely you could talk to Señor de Léon about Belinda,' Dene began hastily, before they could descend to the realms of gossip once more.

'Luq!' Mrs Travers sighed. 'Poor Luq can't bear to hear her name mentioned either.'

'Perhaps the memory is too painful,' Dene agreed. 'Men aren't as good at talking about their feelings as women, don't you think?'

Mrs Travers nodded her head.

'Such a perceptive girl, but . . .' She hesitated. 'I can't help wondering if it isn't guilt that makes him . . . but there, I keep forgetting, you don't approve of gossip.'

It was infuriating to have one's curiosity aroused in this way, Dene thought, wondering why Mrs Travers should imagine Luq had feelings of guilt about his late wife. But though she hadn't exactly stated her views on gossip, neither had she denied Isobel's supposition that she disliked it, so she could not very well encourage the woman to enlarge upon her provocative statement.

'How did your daughter and Señor de Léon meet?' she ventured.

'Actually, I met him first,' Isobel explained. 'After my husband died . . . I've lost two husbands, you know . . . I felt I had to get away from England for a while. Belinda was in her last year at college, so I came to Seville alone. I was befriended by some Americans, staying in the same hotel . . . and it was at one of their parties that I met Luq and his cousin. The Americans,' she added scornfully, 'were lionising José, of course. I liked Spain so much that I decided to come back the following year and Belinda accompanied me. It was natural that I should renew my acquaintance with Luq.'

'She must have been very beautiful to attract a man like Señor de Léon,' Dene suggested. 'Have you any photographs of her?'

Like her clothes, Isobel's room was ornate, frilled and flounced in pastel colours, an oasis of frivolity in the dour villa, but among all the personal knick-knacks there were no photographs.

Isobel shook her head.

'No. You know how it is, I'm sure . . . when children are small, you photograph every stage of their development. Then, as they get older, the intervals between photographs increase . . .'

'What about wedding photos?' Dene persisted.

'No!'

Isobel's voice was almost sharp, and Dene decided that she had probed the wound sufficiently for the moment. Adroitly, she changed the subject and even succeeded in making the other woman laugh at past incidents in her nursing career.

The hour Luq had allotted her had long since passed, and as she knew to her cost, he was a stickler for punctuality. Suddenly she was eager to see him again . . . in order to discuss her patient, of course, she assured herself. But deep down, she knew that she was anxious to regard him in his new light, as an unattached man, to see if it made any difference to her reactions to him.

'Must you go?' Mrs Travers said wistfully, as Dene rose to leave. 'I *have* enjoyed out little talk. You can't imagine.'

'Well, you'll be seeing a great deal more of me in the next few weeks,' Dene reassured her. 'The Señor had engaged me for a two months' trial period.'

'Nadine!' Dene paused in the doorway. 'I should like it so much if you would call me Isobel?'

'Of course,' Dene agreed willingly, 'and you must call me Dene. No one ever uses my full name, except my parents. *They* like it, of course, but I think it sounds terribly old-fashioned.'

Outside Isobel's door, Dene drew a small breath of satisfaction. It was going to be all right after all. She *liked* Mrs Travers, knew they would get on well together. So much for Luq and his aunt and their doleful prognostications, she thought. She was longing to see their faces, to hear them admit they had been wrong . . . and after a few days they would be forced to make that admission.

Enquiry of Teresa Mañara informed Dene as to Luq's whereabouts.

'You will find him on the patio, *señorita*.' Her hard black eyes surveyed Dene curiously. 'So you have met your patient . . . *la Inglesa?*'

'Yes, *señora*,' Dene said warmly, pleased by Teresa's unexpected interest. Perhaps Doña Teresa was human after all.

'And how did the Señora react to you?'

'She was very friendly. She seems a sweet person. Such a shame that she's had so much to suffer.'

Teresa Mañara made an unintelligible noise, which to Dene sounded remarkably like a scornful comment on her words.

'Others have suffered more and complained less,' was Teresa's audible reply, as her sturdy, black-clad form moved away in the direction of the kitchen. 'This way, *por favor, señorita*.'

Oh dear. It certainly seemed that there was no love lost between Doña Teresa and Isobel Travers. Each had spoken disparagingly to her of the other. Still, Dene reminded herself, it was hardly to be expected that two women, with such a wide difference in their ages and from two such different cultures, would be compatible, and this remote, isolated house, with its lack of distractions was hardly the ideal breeding ground for harmony.

As Teresa Mañara had said, Dene discovered Luq seated on the patio, a book upon his knee . . . a book which she doubted his eyes saw, for he seemed to be deep in reverie . . . the thoughts, apparently, far from pleasant, judging by the twin creases between his dark eyes, the sombre cast of his lean features.

It was not a particularly cheerful place to sit, Dene thought, as she crossed the cobbles, disturbing the multi-coloured pigeons that scavenged between the stones of the patio. With his obviously affluent circumstances, it was a wonder to her that Luq had not made more pleasant places of his two homes . . . the Casa in Seville and his villa. Perhaps with the death of his wife, he had just lost interest in home-making.

A sudden pang of longing smote her soft heart; how wonderful it would be, if by *her* presence she could bring some light and happiness to this house, make Isobel Travers' lot easier, reconcile her with Doña Teresa; and Luq . . . if only she could bring a much-needed warmth to his expression. She was filled with a sudden crusading spirit . . . after all, there was no harm in trying.

But these romantic urges were hard to sustain in the face of Luq's prosaic manner. He looked up at her approach, rose courteously and indicated that she should share the stone seat at the side of a fountain, which looked as if it had not played for years.

They sat in silence for a while, Dene waiting for Luq to question her, or to make some comment about their patient.

'Now that I've met Mrs Travers, perhaps you'd like to discuss her case with me,' she suggested at last.

'I am still not sure that I did the right thing in bringing you here,' he said, as if he had not even heard her words.

Dene stiffened.

'If you still have doubts about my capabilities . . .'

He shook his head in negation. It was a weary gesture.

'Strangely enough, it is your *welfare* that I am considering at present. This is no place for a young, attractive girl. *I* should know that better than anyone.'

'Wasn't Belinda happy here, then?'

The words came out unthinkingly and she gasped with dismay at the anger that leapt immediately into the dark eyes. His hand shot out to take her arm in a punishing grip.

'Who has been speaking to you of Belinda?'

'Why, M-Mrs Travers, of course. Surely it's quite natural that she should speak of her daughter?'

'Natural, yes . . . but unusual.' It was said sneeringly.

'Perhaps,' Dene snapped, completely unnerved by the strength and warmth of his hand, 'Perhaps because no one else seems willing to talk about Belinda.'

'*She* told you that?'

Dene nodded.

'Yes . . . and it seems very bad psychology to me, not to let someone talk about their bereavement. Perhaps if she didn't have to bottle up her grief . . .'

'*Señorita*, you are a nurse, not a psychologist,' Luq interrupted impatiently, at the same time releasing her arm. 'Kindly keep to things which you understand.'

Surreptitiously, Dene rubbed her bruised flesh.

'I should have thought that *you* at least would sympathise,' she said rashly. 'Considering that Belinda was *your* wife.'

'But then you know nothing about me, or my feelings, *señorita*. I warned you that, for this job, you would require maturity, discretion and tact. Prying into things which do not concern you hardly demonstrates such qualities.'

He rose abruptly, handing her a thick buff folder bearing the name Isobel Travers, the word 'Confidential' stamped across it.

'Perhaps instead of unfruitful speculation upon the *psychological* condition of others, you could employ your time more usefully in reading and digesting these notes. Please return them to me in my study, when you are *completely familiar* with the content.'

Dene was seething with a multitude of conflicting feelings for some time after Luq left her, so much so that she was unable at first to concentrate upon the notes which swam before her unseeing eyes. Luq was devastatingly attractive, and she was drawn to him as she had never been to any other man . . . even to the point where she was dangerously close to imagining herself in love with him. But it *could* only be imagination, aroused by his exotic masculinity.

Wasn't it always the case that girls found foreign men irresistible, because of the sheer unfamiliarity of surroundings, the allure of a foreign accent? But such men did not necessarily make ideal husbands. She could not deny her recognition of the fact that Luq was hard and unfeeling, the existence of evidence that he must have been a swine to his late wife, for it was obvious that, whatever Isobel Travers thought to the contrary, he entertained no sentimental memories of her Belinda. Why on earth had he married the girl in the first place? and how dared he accuse *her* of prying, when her sole concern was for her patient's welfare?

But hadn't there been a *little* self-interest in her remarks . . . *hadn't* she been testing his reactions to Belinda's name?

At last she forced herself to concentrate upon the content of the file. Not to do so, not to be completely versed in Isobel's case, would only bring down more wrath upon her head. Briefly summarised, it told her that Isobel Travers, forty last birthday . . . as Dene had surmised . . . had lived in Spain for three years and that two years ago had suddenly contracted rheumatoid arthritis. It was not an unlikely contingency, since there was a family history of the disease, both her mother and grandmother having suffered. Her next of kin was named as an older sister, still living in Hertfordshire in England. There followed a list of treatments, those already tried . . . and current treatment and medication, with the senior surgeon's, Luq's, recommendation of surgery for hip joints and fingers . . . a recommendation that was now a year old. Why had nothing further been done?

The information, as might be expected, was purely clinical and it told Dene precisely nothing about her patient's personality or state of mind, which Gerald Harvey had always impressed upon his staff as being an important aid to treatment.

'The mental condition is always important,' he had told Dene. 'A happy patient responds far better to treatment.'

And Luq had tossed aside her remarks on the psychological aspects.

Dene shrugged her shoulders. Drawn as she was to Luq, she was not going to be influenced by his disapproval, his unhelpful manner; somehow she would find out more about Isobel Travers as a person and determine the best way to be of help to her. She hadn't liked to ask about the manner of Belinda's death . . . had it been illness, accident? She was certain Luq wouldn't approve of her gossiping with servants, but if that was the only way she could find out what she wanted to know, Lucia was her best bet, Dene decided. The girl had already shown an inclination to chatter. In the meantime, she had better return the Travers file to Luq.

His study was bleakly functional. Evidently, for his personal use, he did not subscribe to the stifling clutter that characterised the parlour. He was seated at his desk, immersed in some paperwork, and he looked up impatiently at her entry. Then his features relaxed slightly, as he indicated that she should be seated on the leather chesterfield, the only other piece of furniture.

'Come in sit down. I thought you were one of the servants. There is no peace in this house . . . constant comings and goings.'

Privately, Dene considered the Villa Venganza to be unnaturally quiet and dull. The servants moved about soft-footedly and though Teresa Mañara had a heavier tread, she was not much in evidence; and even when she was, she could not be said to improve the atmosphere. She placed the file on Luq's desk, then faced him squarely, determination in every line of her gamine features.

'I've read Mrs Travers' notes, but they tell me nothing new. I've nursed a dozen such cases. I need to know more about Isobel Travers herself . . . the woman . . . if I'm to help her.'

'I am the last person to tell you such things,' he said brusquely. 'For I confess, I do not wholly understand her myself. If *you* wish to do so, then you must enquire of the lady herself. For some reason, she wishes *me* to treat her malady. As a doctor I can scarcely refuse. A year ago, I asked her to come to Seville and place herself in the hands of one of my colleagues. Once recovered from the operation she could have returned to England. But she refused to leave the villa, and since then . . .'

'Perhaps it's a question of money,' Dene suggested diffidently. 'I understand she's not very well off, and . . .'

'The Rivera Hospital in Seville is a private hospital,' Luq said stiffly, 'endowed by my late mother. There would, of course, be no question of charging Señora Travers.'

'Then perhaps it's the thought of being handed over to one of your colleagues . . . a stranger,' Dene persisted. 'She knows you, would trust you. If she would rather . . .'

'*Señorita!*' he interrupted. 'I provide for the support of Mrs Travers, even though I am not bound to do so. I supply her medication. Further than that I am not prepared to go, personally. It is my considered opinion that an operation would alleviate her condition, restore her to physical self-sufficiency, but I am not prepared to carry out that operation myself . . . to supervise her recovery.'

'But *why?*'

His face darkened.

'Your curiosity drives you too far, *señorita*. Suffice it to say that I have my reasons . . . reasons which *I* consider valid.'

'I can't think how you ever came to be a doctor!' The angry words welled up out of her thwarted attempts to understand her patient. It was almost as if no one *wanted* her to do her best for Isobel. 'In England, doctors *care* about their patients. You don't seem to care. I suppose you're just in it for the money!'

He rose from behind his desk, his face a cold, angry mask.

'Do not make me regret still more that I allowed you to come here. A good nurse is objective, unswayed by emotions. Furthermore, I find your insinuations insulting in the extreme.' He tilted his head arrogantly. 'For your information, I do *not* depend upon the income I receive from the Rivera hospital, nor do I have to justify my decisions regarding my patient to you.'

'Oh, to hell with it!' Dene did not usually resort to bad

language, but this man was enough to make a saint swear. How *could* she be so fascinated by him and yet find him the most irritating man she had ever encountered? 'She may be *your* patient, but while I'm nursing her, she's *my* patient too . . . and she's family . . . your mother-in-law, for heaven's sake, or have you forgotten that her daughter was your wife?'

She knew from recent experience that to mention his wife's name was dangerous, but she was too annoyed to care. She had only seen *his* anger cool, controlled . . . now she witnessed the snapping of that control, the unrestrained, fierce heat of his fury, and she was suddenly frightened of the strength and force of him, as he rounded the desk with his uneven stride, to tower over her, his hands gripping her slight shoulders with no consideration for her gasp of pain.

'Like all very young and silly women, you are too outspoken, letting your emotions rule your head. I did not want another immature female in my household, but against my better judgment, I . . .' He paused, then: 'I know now that I should have held to my resolution . . . your presence is only causing further complications, which I . . .'

'*Is* it because I'm young, *señor*,' Dene demanded, 'or because I refuse to defer meekly to your supposedly superior judgment? You may be a good surgeon; you may know all there is to know about breaking and re-setting deformities, but have you any idea how a woman's mind works? Sometimes a woman's emotions, her intuitions, guide her better than all the cold reasoning power of a man's brain.'

'You think so?' His grasp of her tightened and there was a strange edge to his voice, a dangerous glitter in his dark eyes, which was suddenly unnerving. 'And do your emotions, this intuition, tell you why I was reluctant to bring *you* here?'

He was too close and she had only anger with which to fight him.

'There wasn't much need for me to be intuitive, was there? The moment you set eyes on me, you began thrusting all your reasons, real or imagined, down my throat . . . all based on your belief, mistaken in my opinion, that youth and incompetence naturally go together!'

'So do youth and impulsiveness,' Luq said softly, and somehow there was more menace in his lowered tone than in the normally crisp authoritativeness of his voice. 'Impulsiveness . . . and inexperience.'

'Inexperience? What kind of inexperience?' Dene's voice rose on a note of indignation. She was not a child; she had been well educated; she was widely travelled, well read . . .

'Of the ways of people, the kind of people you have perhaps not encountered before . . . certain types of women, of men . . .'

Certain types of men. Did he mean himself? Dene tensed, aware suddenly, just how close he was . . . aware too that his closeness was demolishing her anger. His hands were very warm through the light material of her dress and he emanated an aura which was a pleasant combination of scrupulously clean skin and hair, of masculine cologne. She swallowed.

'May I remind you, *señor*, I *am* twenty-three and I haven't been immured in a convent . . . or behind barred windows.'

His laugh was edged with bitterness.

'Neither are Spanish girls these days, believe me! It would be refreshingly pleasant, just for once, to meet a woman who *had* retained her innocence of mind and body, not become sullied by worldliness, promiscuity.'

'*I* don't consider myself to be either . . . worldly or promiscuous. Experience of life isn't confined solely to acquiring faults.'

'But you do have a fiancé,' he said slowly, 'which would presuppose . . .'

'You needn't suppose anything of the sort,' she interrupted him crisply. 'In spite of your opinion of women in general, Barry and I have never . . .'

'He must be one of those cold, reserved Englishmen one hears about, with no warmth in the blood of his veins . . . no passion. A Spaniard would not permit his *novia* so much freedom, so long a separation.'

'And that's probably why mixed marriages don't work,' Dene retorted wrenching herself free of him. 'It isn't that Englishmen are cold, or women either . . . but they *are* treated as equals, allowed to have lives of their own. Not incarcerated in some dreary house at the back of beyond. No wonder Belinda . . .'

'We will not speak of Belinda.' Heavy lids narrowed his eyes, giving him a predatory look. 'I have warned you before not to pry into my affairs.'

Dene was unused to being put down in this manner . . . could not resist an attempt to have the last word.

'And I've told you, I think it's unnatural, not to speak of the poor girl, not to allow other people . . . especially her own mother . . . to speak of her. You accuse *Englishmen* of being cold. That's rich! You . . . *you're* solid ice!' She laughed. He could not know it was a laugh at the death of her own illusions. 'And I always believed that Spaniards would be hot-blooded, passionate, romantic. How wrong can you be!'

'*Caramba!*'

The expletive was as forceful as the hands which recaptured her . . . not her shoulders this time, but the upper part of her arms, steely fingers cruelly bruising the soft flesh.

'Is it not enough that you constantly query my judgment, flout my wishes? Do you now seek to insult my *virilidad*?'

'No . . . no, I didn't . . . I . . .'

The words died on a strangled gasp, as she was ruthlessly pulled against the lean, hard muscularity of his chest, her ineffectual struggles overcome by an invincible strength, and she knew with a terrifying certainty that she would not be released until Luq had wiped out what he considered to be the slur upon his masculine pride. There was no gentleness in his conquest of her; his embrace was brutal, holding her immobilised, completely helpless, subject to whatever form of punishment he might decide to inflict upon her. He was forcing his body against hers, every muscle of him hard and unyielding, the thin material of her dress no barrier, and again she felt that strange tensing within herself, which signified a physical attraction, felt the beginnings of a dangerous yielding sensation, as his mouth made short work of her attempts to evade it. His kiss was a blazing, consuming demand, that seemed to drain the strength from her limbs, as it bruised her lips open, pitiless, invading.

She had wanted him to kiss her, some day, but not like this . . . for the wrong reasons. Somewhere within her, anger mingled with despair, anger that he could arouse her by savagery alone, that it should be his own savagery that *prompted* the kiss; despair that it was only pride which drove him . . . fierce pride, which had launched him upon a course of action the results of which he could not possibly have foreseen. He had wanted to punish her, to inflict pain upon her, as retribution for her insulting taunts.

Had he but known it, the punishment had taken a far more
subtle, insidious form; it had confirmed without doubt her
earlier fears of her own susceptibility to his magnetic attraction
. . . a hot awareness, which was destroying all her former calm
belief . . . that a man would have to attract the rational side of
her nature, before he could exert any physical pull upon her.
This was an obsession of the flesh, she told herself, not of the
heart and mind. She must fight it. She *must*.

The heat which engulfed her now was not of passion, but of
shame . . . shame that she could not disguise her response, and
yet she experienced a paradoxical feeling of relief and frustration
when, unexpectedly, Luq thrust her from him so roughly that
she had to grasp at a chair to prevent herself from falling.

Somehow she forced herself to look at him, tormented uncer-
tainty in the sapphire blue eyes.

His lean face was twisted with hatred.

'*Sí*, you are like all the others . . . deliberately provocative, not
satisfied until you have driven a man to the end of his patience.
Now you know how a Spaniard masters his *novia*. Do you now
consider that we are cold-blooded?'

She could not answer him, one trembling hand pressed to her
ravaged lips.

'Let this be a lesson to you, *señorita*. Perhaps, in future, you will
not seek to meddle in things that do not concern you, or to pass
judgment without full understanding of what it is that you
censure!'

In her sombre bedroom that night, Dene fought an uncomfortable battle between her instincts and her sense of duty and of fair
play. All her instincts were urging her to give in her notice, to
leave this dark, mournful house, to put as much distance as
possible between herself and Luquillo de Léon. Only the
thought of Isobel Travers' plight, if she should leave, held her
back; that lonely suffering woman needed her, not just as a
nurse, but as someone in whom she could confide.

She managed to convince herself that his behaviour had been
a momentary, uncharacteristic lapse, unlikely to be repeated,
and if, contrarily, her senses protested at that thought, she
resolutely ignored them. Hadn't she vowed that she would have
no complications in her life? She hadn't left England, the

restrictions imposed by living with staid parents, escaped from a possessive boy-friend, merely to be caught up in a far more complex relationship.

It was a relief, therefore, when she went in to breakfast next morning, to find that José Mañara had returned overnight, full of himself and his successful encounter with a bull in this, the new season. Already his breezy presence had lightened the whole atmosphere of the house.

Asunción's rich, fruity chuckles could be heard whenever he invaded the kitchen; there were frequent excited squeals from Lucia, as he slyly pinched her, or stole a kiss in the shadowy corridors. Even Doña Teresa was seen to smile at her son's boisterous antics, although Dene thought she detected a shadow of anxiety in her manner. The Golden Spaniard had brought a light to the villa which embodied his sunny pseudonym.

Only Luq de Léon and Isobel Travers seemed not to share in the general rejoicing at José's return. Luq was barely civil to him, and Isobel made no bones of her displeasure, in conversation with Dene.

'Such a noisy young man . . . and such a trouble to poor dear Luq. He sets the house in an uproar, distracts the servants from their work . . . particularly Lucia. He positively encourages her familiarities!'

Dene did not argue with her patient, but nor did she pretend to agree; she did not like to indulge in such hypocritical currying of favour. Tactfully, she always managed to change the subject. Personally, she was thankful for José's lighthearted presence, finding his badinage, his flirtatious compliments a refreshing foil to Luq's cold, impersonal manner.

For she had been right about Luq. There had been no reference to, or repetition of, his behaviour. It was as if it had never happened, she thought wistfully . . . as if he had never held her in his arms; and only the faint traces of bruises upon her shoulders confirmed that his momentary loss of control had ever taken place.

He seemed able to put the incident from his mind. But try as she might, Dene could not erase the incident from *her* memory. It was infuriating that he should be able to arouse such a flaring response within her, leaving such an impression that she must continually relive the moment, like any impressionable school-girl, experiencing her first crush.

Since José had arrived, the days seemed to pass more swiftly and then too Dene found herself extremely busy. The daily routine of looking after her patient was surprisingly time-consuming.

First thing in the morning, Isobel had to be helped out of bed and into a relaxing bath, after which there were exercises to be strictly adhered to. Helping her patient to dress was followed by breakfast, and often it was necessary for Dene to cut up the food into manageable pieces. At present, Isobel found it impossible to descend the steep stairs to ground level, so her daily exercise was taken upon the colonnaded verandah which ran around the three faces of the rambling old house. Dene's only free time was in the afternoon, when bed rest was prescribed, and in the evening, after Isobel had retired.

Luq was punctilious about making a daily visit to the sick woman, but his remarks to Dene did not go beyond discussing her patient's progress. She wondered how much longer he intended to remain at the villa . . . and so, apparently, did José.

'Luq is hanging around the old family home longer than usual,' he commented to Dene one afternoon, joining her as she sat on the patio, throwing crumbs to the monotonously murmuring pigeons.

'Probably keeping an eye on me,' Dene said drily, 'making sure I can be trusted to carry out his orders. I'm only here on trial, you know.'

'Hmm, maybe. How do you like La Travers?' he added casually. '*She* does not like *me*, you understand?'

'I like her,' Dene replied truthfully. She sought for some way to answer his final comment. 'I think pain, perhaps, makes her a little less tolerant . . . and you're not the only person she makes remarks about. It's just her way and harmless enough.'

'You think so?' José was unwontedly serious. 'But forgive me if I contradict you. I do not intend to rake up the past, but it is my experience that speaking ill of people can lead to much trouble. Do not let *la Inglesa* influence you against others, Dene.'

He had begun to use the diminutive of her name, while she had long ago dropped the 'Señor' for the friendlier 'José.'

'Don't worry, José,' she said now, her blue eyes laughing at him. 'I've witnessed some of your misdemeanours, but I promise you it hasn't turned me against you.'

He remained grave, however.

'I hope that is so, Dene. Not everyone is so forbearing. *Dios sabe*, I am no saint. But you will hear much against me that is ill, and not only from *la Inglesa*. I should like . . .' he hesitated, 'I should like to have your good opinion, your friendship. I have been rash, thoughtless in the past, but . . .'

Dene was touched. He really meant it. She had always been certain that, despite his wild ways, he was not altogether bad . . . just a little slow in maturing to his responsibilities . . . this trait emphasised perhaps, by comparison with his grave, sensible cousin.

'You have my friendship,' she assured him.

'*Gracias!*'

He took her hand and raised it to his lips. Dene found the courtly gesture oddly moving, and one part of her brain marvelled that she, ordinary Dene Mason, should be sitting here, in a Spanish courtyard, with a real live bullfighter actually kissing her hand.

When she had first discovered José's profession, she had remarked enthusiastically upon it to Luq, but had received a quelling reception.

'Another impressionable young female, seeing only the glamour, not the true worth of a man.'

And now again the moment of illusion was shattered by Luq's harsh voice, as he came upon them unobserved; only the pigeons, more sensitive to atmosphere than the couple by the fountain, scattering at his approach.

'Up to your old tricks, José?'

The young man's face reddened beneath his tan, as he dropped Dene's hand and rose, his manner defensive. How it must annoy him, she thought with her swift perception, to have to look up so far in order to meet his cousin's dark, angry eyes.

José's tone was truculent.

'My conversation with Dene is none of your business, Luq.'

'Is it not? You have a conveniently short memory. What about those other occasions, when your behaviour has given rise to concern? When it *has* been my business to interfere.'

There was some deep significance in Luq's tone, which was

lost upon Dene, but which caused José's lips to tighten, as he turned upon his heel and strode away with his lithe, almost balletic steps.

'Why do you have to upset everyone?' The words burst from Dene's lips. 'What harm is there in José talking to me?'

'*Señorita*, must you always seek to know the why and the wherefore? Can you not accept occasionally that others know better what is good for you?'

'No. Because I have a mind of my own. I'm accustomed to making my own decisions about people, choosing my own friends . . . and I *like* your cousin. I've promised to be his friend,' she finished defiantly.

His expression as he looked at her was strangely bleak.

'Others before you have been misled by that ingenuous manner of his. I thought to save you from similar folly. But I have come to know enough of you in these last weeks to realise that you least of all will be guided. You are headstrong.' He spread his hands in a gesture of defeat. 'So be it. Go your own way. Learn by your own mistakes. But remember, you are still on trial here.'

'My two months' trial relates to my work, my care of Mrs Travers,' Dene retorted. 'It doesn't include censorship of my private life.'

'Oh, but you err, *señorita*. Your probationary period depends as much, if not more, upon your personal circumspection as upon your efficiency as a nurse.'

'And how much longer do you intend to stay around to spy on me?' she enquired furiously.

'As it happens, I am leaving this afternoon.'

'Oh!'

For the first time, Dene realised that he had abandoned casual slacks and shirt for a formal suit. A moment ago she had been longing for his departure . . . now she felt suddenly bereft.

'And before you begin to rejoice,' he continued, 'let me tell you, I shall know exactly what transpires in my absence.'

'Oh, I've no doubt you have your spies,' she retorted, 'Señora Mañara for one. Don't think I haven't noticed her disapproval, every time José speaks to me.'

It seemed that, on this occasion at least, she had won the verbal battle, for, with a brief look at his wristwatch, Luq turned away, leaving her . . . without even a word of farewell, she thought indignantly.

With his departure, indignation was succeeded swiftly by acute depression. There was no satisfaction, after all, in having had the last word. Her confrontations with Luq had been extremely irritating, with her inability to confound him. He was so arrogantly certain that his was the correct reading of every situation. But now she realised that the cut and thrust of their arguments had been exhilarating, adding spice to the day-to-day routine of nursing, lightening the tedium of life at the villa. But most depressing of all was the fact that she had no idea when Luq would return. With his departure went her last link with the outside world and . . . she admitted it to herself . . . a vital part of her, which, judging by the ache in that area, must be her heart.

In spite of her determination not to become emotionally involved, despite her knowledge that there was no future in it, because Luq just wasn't interested in her as a woman, she had been stupid enough to fall in love with him. She had fallen in love, in spite of, or perhaps because of his total unsuitability.

Now Dene knew why, to date, she had felt no urge towards marriage. All her friendships with men had been too mundane, the men boringly ordinary, totally lacking in romance. It might be infuriating, not to be able to fathom Luq's complex nature, to penetrate the air of mystery with which he surrounded himself, but all this was a challenge to a girl of Dene's spirit; and she knew that her meeting with him had been a fateful one . . . which had spoiled her for any other, lesser man.

CHAPTER FIVE

THE only other member of the household who seemed to regret Luq's departure was Isobel Travers, and Dene supposed she missed the reassurance of having her medical adviser close at hand.

Isobel's reaction showed itself in an increase of irritability, a sharpening of her criticism of the Mañaras . . . mother and son . . . and the servants.

Dene, who had seen what pain could do to the sweetest of natures, was gentle and forbearing, but she was finding the seclusion at the villa, her own despondency at Luq's absence, combined with Isobel's continual complaints, wearing to her nerves. Normally bright and cheerful, she became subdued, her cheeks pale, her eyes shadowed.

'Have you left these grounds at all since you have been here?' José asked Dene at the end of her second week.

She admitted that she had not.

'There just doesn't seem to have been time.'

'Today we will *make* time. No!' firmly, as she opened her mouth to protest. 'You must not allow yourself to become a prisoner behind these walls. Time enough for that when winter closes the valley.'

'It gets *that* bad?' she asked.

'In the depths of winter, it is quite impossible to leave the village,' José confirmed. 'You will have noticed that Asunción and Lucia keep the storeroom filled. That is in preparation for the months when no food can be brought in from outside.'

Dene shivered slightly. She had almost become accustomed to the dark, oppressive atmosphere of the Villa Venganza, but at least it was summer and there had always been the knowledge that if at any time it became unbearable, she could leave, return across the Sierras and from there back to England.

But that was defeatism, she told herself sternly. If Isobel Travers had endured two winters here, in *her* bad state of health, surely *she*, fit and healthy, could do no less. Besides, to give up and go home would be to admit that Luq and his forbidding aunt were right . . . that she could not cope with her job and its situation, and that was one concession she was definitely not prepared to make.

However, it was with gratitude that she accepted José's suggestion that they should leave the grounds and take a walk up the mountain slope behind the village. It would be wise, she decided, to know her way around the surrounding area. Then, if she should ever feel an irresistible urge to shake off the confining walls of the villa, to get away on her own, the outside world would not be completely unfamiliar.

The track was not too steep at first, though the terrain was rugged, networked with little bubbling streams. Poplar trees lined the watercourses and grew in small clusters on the mountainside. But as they moved higher up, the trees ceased and a wilderness of grey unrelieved rock began. It was a sultry afternoon and they had left the rest of the household enjoying the customary siesta.

'I can't get used to the idea of wasting a whole afternoon sleeping,' Dene said breathlessly, as they reached a small plateau and flung themselves down upon the sunbaked rock.

The unaccustomed exertion had shaken her from her lethargy, brought a flush to her pale cheeks.

'The custom of the siesta is dying out in the cities,' José told her. 'It interferes too much with business. But here, life follows very much the tempo of the old days.'

'So I've noticed,' she said drily. 'How do you endure it? It can't be a very lively existence for someone who is used to a public life . . . to being fêted?'

'Unfortunately, my lifestyle is also somewhat extravagant. Oh, I admit it freely,' he said at her look of surprise. 'There are many calls upon my purse. One does not just *earn* popularity on the bullfighting circuit . . . one also pays for it. Everyone expects a matador to be free with his money . . . and there are other expenses. A suit of lights is not cheap, and one cannot appear constantly in the same outfit.'

'So you live here out of season to *save* money?' she hazarded, remembering Isobel's less charitable interpretation . . . that José frittered his cash and then sponged on Luq.

'And between the big corridas . . . with my cousin's gracious permission!'

'But surely, it's *your* home too? Your mother lives here . . .'

'La Madre is Luq's housekeeper . . . a paid dependant.' His tone was bitter. 'And I am a dependant . . . but unpaid.'

So Luq didn't actually give him money. Dene was glad. She didn't want any cause to think badly of José.

'Have you never thought of doing anything else?' she asked curiously.

'Earning an honest living, you mean?' He smiled wryly. 'There is nothing my mother and Luq would like better than for me to settle down, to remain here in the valley and run the estate. But, Dene, since I was a small boy and my father took me to the big bullfights, in Seville, Madrid, I knew there was nothing else for me. It is in my blood, you see. My father and my grandfather before me were matadors.'

'I've never been to a bullfight,' Dene said wistfully.

'Then you shall come to my next engagement . . . in Madrid!'

'I'd love to, if I'm allowed to . . . if I'm still here.'

'Why should you not be here?'

'Because, as your cousin keeps reminding me, I'm still on trial.'

'Ignore him!' José dismissed her words with a grandiloquent gesture. 'Luq will not so easily find someone to replace you. You are the first one who . . .'

'Yes?' she prompted.

He seemed reluctant to continue, then shrugged, as if fatalistically.

'The first one who has not walked out within the week.'

'There have been other nurses here . . . before me?'

'In two years? *Ciertamente!* An endless succession of them.'

'All . . . young?'

'All? *Dios,* no! Some of them have been as old as sin . . . and as ugly. You are the first young woman to cross this threshold since . . . since . . .'

'Since Belinda died?' Dene finished for him. 'José, why *is* everyone so reluctant to speak of Belinda? It . . . it isn't natural. People usually want to express their grief.'

'Perhaps,' he said slowly, 'because no one grieves for Belinda.'

Dene stared at him in shocked disbelief. He couldn't mean it! But it was scarcely a subject for jest. She had to ask him, had to know.

'But, José . . .' she began.

He turned towards her and the usual humour was missing from his good-looking face, the blue eyes were bleak, their expression silencing her.

'I do not want to talk about her either, Dene.' He jumped up. 'Shall we take a look at the village on the way home?'

It was so obviously a deliberate change of subject that Dene realised she must respect his reticence . . . for the moment. But she was even more determined that eventually her curiosity should be satisfied. It wasn't just *idle* curiosity . . . she despised people who pried just for the sake of sensationalism. She truly felt that she would understand so much more about her patient . . . about Luq too . . . and somehow that was equally if not more important, if she could unveil this conspiracy of silence about Belinda de Léon.

She had only seen the village in darkness, on the wild night of her arrival. It was not a large settlement . . . twenty or so two-storeyed houses of uncut stone and earth, faced with mortar, the roofs of heavy stone slabs, laid horizontally and covered with clay. The single, unpaved street was crooked, narrow and steep, the houses strung out along its length. Incredibly, there was a church, small and ancient, its thick, old, ochre-hued walls apparently falling down. Across the lower end of the street ran a stream, where, José told her, the women still slapped out their laundry as their mothers and grandmothers had done before them.

There seemed to be no one about. Most of the villagers, José explained, would be working the farm, further up the valley . . . a farm which belonged to the Léon family, comprising some fifty head of cattle, a flock of goats and sheep.

'The farm Luq would have *me* manage,' he added, then, with some bitterness, 'In my grandfather's day the land was devoted to the breeding of fighting bulls.' Some of the land apparently was given over to crops. 'Thus, you see, we are surprisingly self-sufficient, with little need for the outside world.'

'Lucia and Asunción live in the village, don't they?'

'*Sí* . . . Lucia's home is next to the church.'

'Why on earth does your cousin keep on this dismal old place?' she asked José, as they passed under the archway and the gate clanged shut behind them, with a finality that made her think of prison bars.

He shrugged.

'It has been in the Léon family for centuries and Luq is a great traditionalist. No doubt he will have told you of the Léon who seized the original land in retribution?'

Dene nodded. She wondered if Luq had inherited also the ruthlessness, the unforgiving nature of his ancestor.

'The house was not always as you see it.' José's tone became wistful, nostalgic. 'Once it was a place of light and laughter . . . when Luq and I were children.' His face twisted into a reminiscent smile. 'Even then I was determined to become a famous matador. Poor Luq! The hours he has spent, playing the bull for me, while I practised the art of the cape.'

Dene smiled too, imagining the small boys, in the broiling sun, playing their games with some old discarded cape, kicking up the dust around their small, tanned bodies, with shouts of *'Huh, toro!'*

'It is only these last two years that the villa has become so sombre. Believe me, Dene, if it were not for my customary penurious state and the fact that *mia madre* lives here, wild horses would not drag me to Pajaro.'

'Or wild bulls,' she teased.

'As you say!'

'Your cousin doesn't spend much time here either, does he?' she ventured, as they mounted the stairs to the gallery.

'Not these days.' José's face was grave. 'Once he spent every holiday, every weekend here, but not any more . . . not since . . .' He stopped, then began again hastily, seeing the unspoken question in Dene's eyes. 'Lately, I have thought that Luq might be willing to sell up, but for one thing.'

'Oh?'

'The Villa Venganza is also my mother's childhood home; you will have gathered that Luq's father was Madre's brother? She is much attached to these scenes of her youth . . . she sees her memories, not the reality it has become. I do not think he will dispose of the property in her lifetime at least. Also,' he added, and his voice took on the familiar note of bitterness, 'it is a useful

retreat, to which Luq can banish his more troublesome depend-
ants.'

Did José dislike his cousin or not? Dene could not be sure.
Sometimes, when he spoke of him, his voice was natural, affectionate, but from time to time these undertones crept in, which
made her recall Isobel Travers' statement that Teresa Mañara
coveted the Léon estates on her son's behalf. Did José also wish
he were the heir? With Luq's money, he could certainly cut the
necessary dash befitting a national hero of the bullring.

'You say that, as children, you were playmates,' Dene
began carefully. 'Yet somehow, one receives the impression
that . . .'

'That we are enemies?' José shrugged. 'We have much to
disagree over, Dene. I do not deny it would be of inestimable
value to Luq, should I agree to run the farm here. Obviously, *he*
cannot give it the attention it needs himself. He is surgeon, not
farmer. Also, he wishes that I face up to . . . to certain . . .
responsibilities.'

Infuriatingly, he did not enlarge upon this aspect.

'But you *do* like each other?' she persisted.

He stopped to look at her.

'Dene, *querida*, have you never observed that one always
resents him whom one has injured?'

He strode on, along the verandah, leaving Dene more in-
trigued than ever. Who had injured whom? And why?

They entered the house through the kitchen, to be met by a
trio of enquiring gazes from the women seated at the large table.
The plump Asunción's face showed only mild curiosity, but
Dene detected a glitter in Lucia's eyes which she did not
understand, while the expression of Teresa Mañara's yellowish-
complexioned face was unmistakably hostile.

'Where have you been these past hours?' She looked from one
to the other, suspicion implicit in her gaze.

'*Descuidase usted, mia madre,*' José said impatiently. 'Do not
worry! I have merely shown Dene the village and the hills
beyond.'

'All this time?' Teresa Mañara's voice was harsh.

'We rested for a while, on the plateau.'

His mother broke into rapid Spanish, rising as she did so to
advance upon her son, and though Dene could not understand

the words, it was obvious that her dramatic gestures threatened him.

She glanced at José. His face revealed an anger as violent as his mother's, though unlike hers, his was strongly repressed. But as Teresa continued her harangue, his expression became sulky, defiant.

'What is it, José?' Dene dared to ask after a while, when Teresa had lapsed into simmering silence. But before he could answer her, the Señora's wrath was redirected, her words difficult to distinguish as anger slurred her normally precise diction.

'And *you, señorita?* Are you lost to all sense of responsibility of propriety? You leave this villa, secretively, with my son, telling no one where you are going . . . your patient left unattended. How will this sound to my nephew when he comes again?'

After the first sense of shock at Teresa's vituperative attack, which seemed unnecessarily violent, Dene rallied, determined not to be cowed. She had done nothing wrong, merely taken the time off to which she was entitled.

'The afternoons are my own, to do as I please,' she retorted. 'Mrs Travers is supposed to rest. As for Señor de Léon, I don't care what tales you bear to him, since I have done nothing to be . . .'

'Enough, *señorita!'* Doña Teresa drew herself up to her full height. 'This is my home, by my nephew's favour, and you are an employee here, and as such not expected to consort with my son. Most certainly I shall report your behaviour to my nephew, for it seems you have misled him concerning your character. Have you no . . . *lealtad* . . . loyalty . . . to your *novio* in England? Would *he* approve of your behaviour?'

Dene stared at Teresa, as realisation dawned.

'Good lord! Just *how* narrow-minded can you get? Because I take an afternoon walk with José, in order to familiarise myself with the countryside, you're implying that I . . . that we . . .'

'I hold certain views, *señorita*. My son may hold others. I may deplore the life he leads in Seville . . . that I cannot remedy, but while he is in my home, in Luq's home, he will observe *our* standards.'

'We only went for a walk,' Dene repeated, her blue eyes still indignant, as she faced the elderly, implacable Señora.

'It is my nephew's express wish that, in his absence, I should act as chaperone . . .'

'This *is* the twentieth century, for heaven's sake. I don't *need* a chaperone, I . . .'

Teresa Mañara moved swiftly towards Dene and she shrank back nervously. Surely the older woman didn't intend . . . wouldn't dare . . . to strike her? But it seemed she had only moved closer to emphasise her words.

'Señorita Mason, you are a foreigner. Your ways are different to ours. This we know. We have had experience of the ways of Englishwomen.' Her tone was scornful, condemnatory, and Dene had no doubt as to the identity of the women concerned.

'One doesn't have to be brought up in Spain to know how to behave decently,' Dene pointed out. She was struggling to keep her temper.

Teresa Mañara drew a deep breath, as though she too fought an internal battle, and when she spoke again her tone was more moderate, conciliatory.

'Señorita, I have no wish to quarrel with you. But there are matters of which you are ignorant . . . must remain ignorant, not only for our sake but for your own. Please to be guided by me. If you wish, you may question my nephew. Should *he* see fit to explain . . .'

'To explain? To explain why his cousin shouldn't befriend me?'

'Your family, *señora*,' she said, her tone bitter, 'is an anachronism . . . arrogant, full of pride. I thank God I *am* English. We've a few snobs back home, but nothing on *this* scale. Well, for your information, and Señor de León's, I am *not* setting my cap at your son. As an employee, a paid servant, I can well imagine that the Señor would not consider me a suitable . . .'

'*Señorita*, I too am a paid employee,' Teresa reminded her quietly. 'I do *not* seek to insult you. This arrogance, this pride of which you accuse us . . . you misunderstand . . .'

'Oh, I know your precious nephew actually condescended to marry an English girl himself, but look how *that* worked out!'

'What do you mean?' Teresa asked sharply. 'Who has been talking? What have you learnt?'

'Nothing,' Dene snapped, 'precisely nothing. Your wretched secrets are quite safe. But it's obvious from everyone's behaviour, including the Señor's, that his marriage was not a success. Well, you needn't worry . . . any of you. As you pointed out, I'm engaged to be married . . . and even if I wasn't, I wouldn't marry into your family for all the . . .'

'No!' Teresa agreed. 'There is certainly no question of marriage. Which is why I warn you, *señorita* . . . *cuidado*! Take care! And you, my son, you also have a care!'

With this parting shot, she swept out of the kitchen.

Dene gave an incredulous look at José, who all this while had stood by silently, allowing his mother to hurl these unfounded accusations at her . . . and in front of the servants too!

He met her gaze, his expression shamefaced; yet she felt that amusement lurked in the blue eyes and he raised his shoulders in an expressive shrug.

'You are surprised, no, that Madre can silence me with her tongue? You are thinking it is not becoming to a bullfighter to submit to a woman so? But I tell you this, Dene . . . in Spain, we believe that the best bulls are bred from the most courageous cows. Madre, she is something else . . . no?'

His tone, as he spoke of his mother, was so obviously admiring, the analogy he drew so amusing . . . for what Englishman would dare to compare his mother to a cow? . . . that Dene could not help laughing.

'That is better,' he observed complacently, 'and you will still be *mia camarada*?'

She nodded, then sighed.

'But no more walks, it seems.'

Before going to her own room to change for the evening meal, Dene looked in on her patient and stayed for a few minutes' conversation.

'Do you realise,' she asked Isobel after a while, 'that tomorrow will be my second weekend here? I've been here two full weeks now.'

'Have you really?' Isobel too seemed surprised. She sighed. 'Frankly, the days all seem alike to me now. Once upon a time one could look forward to the weekends, to Luq coming home, to a little stimulating company, but now we are lucky if we see him more than once in six weeks.'

'Why don't *you* go to Seville?' Dene asked impulsively. 'I know he asked you once to go to the Rivera hospital and have an operation. He'd be able to keep an eye on you during your convalescence and I could come with you.'

Isobel put her head on one side, her expression thoughtful.

'I must say the idea has its appeal . . . to get away from this dreadful place. If I could just persuade him to operate himself . . . and your presence *would* solve a problem, which in the past has been insurmountable.'

Dene looked at her enquiringly.

'Yes, dear. You see, I couldn't possibly stay at the Casa de Léon alone, unchaperoned except for that dour housekeeper of his. After all, there *are* only four years between Luq and me . . . and these days it isn't considered unusual for a man to be attracted to an older woman.'

Dene strove to keep the incredulity out of blue eyes, which, sometimes embarrassingly honest, made it difficult to dissemble her true feelings. She wouldn't hurt Isobel for the world, but did the other woman honestly consider that people would suspect Luq of having an affair with her, if she moved to Seville? Surely Isobel was fantasising. True, she must have been very attractive once, perhaps right up until the onset of her illness, but now, with her awkward shuffling gait, her deformed hands and her increasing tendency to overweight . . . Besides, she was Luq's *mother-in-law* . . . the idea was ludicrous. But patients must be humoured and Dene swiftly smothered her thoughts.

'I see your problem,' she said tactfully, 'and my offer holds good. If you can persuade Luq to take you to Seville, I'll willingly play propriety.'

'But how long could you stay, Dene dear?' Isobel asked doubtfully. 'It could be a lengthy business . . . and after all, you *are* engaged. You'll be wanting to go back to England and get married some time?'

Dene looked at her consideringly. She could understand Isobel's anxiety. Dared she trust Isobel with her secret? She decided that she could. After all, in the long run, her lie had benefited her patient and would continue to do so, if she could be transferred to Seville. If only Luq could be persuaded to perform the necessary operation himself, or she could persuade Isobel to accept a substitute . . .

'Isobel,' she began, 'I'm going to tell you something . . . just between the two of us . . . because it *may* set your mind at rest on one point. I can stay with you for as long as you need me. You see, I'm afraid I told a lie. It seemed a fairly harmless one, to be sure of getting this job. I don't know *why* it was so important, but Señor de Léon seemed much more willing to employ me when he thought I had a fiancé back in England.'

Isobel's bronze eyes narrowed slightly.

'You mean you're not engaged?'

'No. I didn't want to be tied down . . .'

'You've never been in love with anyone?'

'No.' Dene looked anxiously at Isobel. 'You don't think too badly of me . . . for deceiving Luq . . . I mean, Señor de Léon,' she corrected herself hastily. Just lately, she had found herself thinking of him by his first name.

Isobel smiled brightly.

'Of course not, dear. What's one little lie, if it gets you what you want?' She gave a little laugh. 'Forgive me if I seem personal, but I couldn't help noticing that, like me, you rely on luck as well to see you through.'

Dene was puzzled for a moment, then her face cleared, as Isobel indicated the pendant around her neck.

'Oh, my lucky black cat . . . I see. Yes, I never go anywhere without it. Some people think it silly, I know,' she shrugged deprecatingly, 'but . . .'

'Oh, I don't think it's at all silly.' Isobel was grave now, lowering her voice. 'These days one needs all the protection one can get.' She gave a little shudder. 'Especially in *this* house. No, my dear, you keep your lucky charm handy at all times.'

Though Dene was relieved at Isobel's calm acceptance of her news, pleased that it seemed to have set her patient's mind at rest, it did not make her feel any happier about the deception itself. Until her encounter with Luq de Léon, she could not remember ever telling a deliberate lie in her life.

'And . . . you . . . you won't tell anyone, especially Señor de Léon?'

'Certainly not,' said Isobel. 'It shall be *our* little secret.'

'I'm glad that's settled,' Dene said. 'I'm glad somebody knows the truth. I hate lies. I must go and change for dinner now, or I'll be late . . . and I'm in enough trouble with Doña Teresa as it is. Next time the Señor is here, I'll do my best to persuade him that you should go to Seville . . . in *his* care.'

'Oh, I think you can safely leave that to me, dear,' Isobel said. 'I've known Luq a long time and I think I know best how to handle him.'

Isobel could be right, Dene reflected ruefully. *She* certainly had been singularly *unsuccessful* in *her* dealings with him. It would be interesting to observe Isobel's methods. Her heart gave a little skip of excitement at the thought that perhaps, before long, she would be going to Seville.

She stepped into the corridor, just in time to see Lucia whisking away round the corner. Had the girl been listening to their conversation, and if so, just how much had she heard? Suppose she revealed Dene's secret? Obviously Lucia would bear watching. Dene shrugged fatalistically. She would deal with the problem if and when it arose. The doors in the Villa were thick and heavy. She doubted if the maid could have overheard more than the murmur of their voices.

Dinner, served unfashionably early for Spain, was a tense meal, with only Teresa Mañara, José and Dene at the table, in the claustrophobic aura of the parlour . . . the only meal taken there. Isobel's meals were served in her own room.

José tried valiantly to keep a conversation going, but his mother's replies were monosyllabic and Dene dared not support his efforts for fear of incurring further censure from the Señora. She wished she dared suggest that she take all her meals with her patient.

Since the afternoon's expedition, a dramatic change had taken place in the weather, with stormclouds threatening rain. It would not be an evening when she could stroll around the patio, making the most of the last of the daylight; and the prospect of a long evening spent indoors was not appealing.

There was nothing at the Villa Venganza in the way of entertainment . . . no television, though Dene believed that Doña Teresa had a radio in her own quarters. But in any case, neither radio nor television, had they been available, would have been of use to Dene, with her very basic understanding of Spanish, the most commonly used phrases. This was what it must have been like for Belinda . . . no modern conveniences of any kind, not even a telephone to link her with the outside world. What on earth did they do if they ever had any kind of emergency?

Dene wished fervently that she had thought to bring some books from England. Normally an avid reader, she could spend hours happily oblivious to her surroundings, particularly when immersed in travelogues, adding to her list of places she longed to visit. A sudden thought occurred to her. It was more than likely that Isobel would have books of some kind. Dene didn't much care what they were, so long as they were in English and would help to fill in the long, dull evening ahead of her.

As soon as the uneasy meal was over, she excused herself and hurried along the corridors to Isobel's room. It was Lucia's final task of the day, before returning to the village, to settle Mrs Travers for the night, Dene looking in last thing to make sure that her patient was comfortable and had taken her medication.

Lucia was just leaving Isobel's bedroom. When she saw Dene approaching, she shut the door behind her and laid one finger on her full lips.

'Is Mrs Travers asleep already?' Dene was disappointed. She had been counting on Isobel having some books she could borrow.

Lucia nodded her dark head vehemently. She spoke in a low voice.

'Me, I think it would be as well if *la Inglesa* returned to her own people . . . her own country. She is *antipatica* . . . bad for this house, for the Señor, for everyone. She will be bad for you too, *señorita.*'

'Nonsense!' Dene felt moved to protest. 'She's just a sick, lonely woman who, understandably, gets a bit grumpy now and then. Personally, I find her charming, and she always speaks very highly of Señor de Léon. I'm sure she's very grateful for all he's done for her . . . for what all of you have done.'

Lucia shrugged with Latin grace.

'Nevertheless, she is in a very strange mood tonight. Never is she a nice-tempered lady, but this evening, I think she is *loca!*'

'Perhaps she's in more pain than usual,' Dene said anxiously. 'Maybe I'd better . . .'

'*La Inglesa* is asleep, most sound,' Lucia assured her. 'It is not the pain, *señorita*; that much I know. Something has displeased her. This mood I recognise, I have seen it many times before.'

'Well, if you're sure she's asleep,' Dene said doubtfully. 'I'll come back later . . . before I go to bed myself.' She sighed. 'It's a pity, though. I was hoping she might have some books she could lend me.'

'You want the English books?' Lucia said eagerly. 'The love stories?'

Dene grimaced.

'I'm not especially fond of novels, but at the moment I'd read anything. Do you know where I can find some?'

Lucia drew close to Dene, looking over her shoulder, lowering her voice.

'There are shelves and shelves of the English romances in the late Señora's room. All the time she read . . .' Lucia sniffed, 'nothing better to do. If you like, I will show you.'

'I don't know,' Dene demurred. 'I don't like to just help myself. Shouldn't I ask permission first, from Doña Teresa, or Mrs Travers, since they belonged to her daughter?'

Lucia shrugged.

'Is not necessary. The room it is in the Señor's wing of the house . . . and he is not here to be asked. Is kept locked except for cleaning.' She shivered dramatically. 'Is not often cleaned . . . is *mal ángel*, that room.'

Dene felt a responsive quiver of her own nerves, her hand going for reassurance to the chain about her neck. Had she not sensed something wrong with this house . . . did it all stem from Belinda's room? But she forced herself to speak scathingly.

'Rubbish! H—how can a *room* be sinister?'

'Come,' said Lucia. 'I will show you. I do not mind to go there at night, if you are with me.'

Dene hesitated, then succumbed to temptation. It wasn't just the prospect of obtaining some reading matter. She preferred biographies and travel books to fiction, but she *was* curious to see Belinda de Léon's room.

'There is Don Luquillo's bedroom . . . and here is that of the Señora.'

From a capacious pocket in the rusty black dress, Lucia drew a large bunch of keys. She removed one and inserted it into the lock; it turned smoothly and Lucia extracted it, handing it to Dene.

'Please to lock up, when you leave . . . and return the key to me *mañana*. No one will miss it.'

'But aren't you going to stay . . . while I choose a book?' Dene faltered. She assured herself that she wasn't the least bit nervous about entering Belinda's room, and yet . . .

'*Por Dios*—no!' Lucia said emphatically. 'Me, I do not remain in the villa after dark. I will light the lamps for you, yes? Then I go.'

The primitive oil lamps had barely spluttered into life, their smoky golden haze scarcely sufficient to relieve the gloom of the large, square apartment, before Lucia was gone, softly pulling the door shut behind her; and Dene was left alone to look about her.

Belinda had obviously tried to modernise her room. That much was evident at first glance . . . but why had she not left her influence upon the rest of the villa, upon the *casa* in Seville? This room was totally un-Spanish in character. The rough-cast walls had been painted a soft shade of pink, the floor carpeted in a deeper shade, while the coverings of the divan bed and the curtains were a subtle combination of lilacs and blues.

The room looked as if its occupant were only temporarily absent. A dainty negligee was flung carelessly over the back of a chair, beneath which reposed a pair of fluffy mules . . . and on the chair itself lay a guitar, casually placed, as if the owner had just set it down . . . a guitar! Dene sat down suddenly, legs shaking, mouth dry . . . was this what Asunción had meant . . . Belinda's guitar? Did Belinda . . . ?

Pull yourself together, she instructed herself angrily. You're imagining things. Determinedly, she continued to look around. The modern dressing table bore an assortment of cosmetics, which Dene recognised as being extremely expensive . . . and there were books . . . To one side of the bed an alcove, shelved from floor to ceiling, was crammed with paperbacks.

As she took a final survey of the room, which spoke of wealth, of indulged tastes, Dene's eye was arrested by a painting, which hung behind the door, facing the bed . . . a portrait of a young and beautiful girl. Dene had no doubt whatsoever that this was Belinda, and she moved closer, studying the painted face.

A fall of silvery hair framed a pointed, heart-shaped face, from which blue eyes seemed to stare straight into Dene's. The paint had been delicately handled, as though the artist had lovingly attempted to capture the fragile femininity emphasised by the almost insubstantial negligee ... the one, Dene recognised, which now lay across the chair. Automatically, her eyes moved in search of the artist's signature, not that the name of a Spanish painter would mean anything to her. But it did. Incredulously, she peered more closely, but she had not been mistaken. 'L. de Léon, Seville' and the date. Luq! Luq had painted this picture.

Dene drew a deep breath. This portrait had not been executed in an atmosphere of hatred ... even dislike. When Luq had painted Belinda it had been with tender, loving care in every stroke of the brush. She studied the pictured face more intently. What struck her with some force was the superficial but unmistakable similarity to herself. It was a likeness of colouring rather than feature ... the hair and the sapphire-blue eyes; and now that she looked more closely there were slight but unmistakable signs of petulance in the lovely face, a dissatisfied droop to the pouting lips. Maybe the artist hadn't been conscious of what his brush was recording, but it was there, nevertheless. It must have been painted before their marriage, for the delicate hands were ringless, yet Belinda did not exactly embody Dene's idea of a radiant bride-to-be.

As she looked at the portrait, she had been aware of something else bothering her ... something upsetting the artistic symmetry of the work. She leant forward, as she became aware of an area of paint applied more thickly, giving a slight distortion. Then she realised that the painting had been restored. At some time it had been damaged ... a long, jagged tear, that started by the right eye and then slanted diagonally down across the bosom, then back across the seated figure's knees.

For some reason which she could not fathom, a shiver ran down Dene's back. Ridiculous to imagine that the painting had been deliberately disfigured. It must have been an accident, perhaps during redecorating, or removal perhaps ... from Seville to this villa.

Determinedly she moved away from the portrait; she knew now what Belinda de Léon had looked like, and as she had suspected, the girl had been very lovely. Why then had José hinted that nobody mourned her death? Just what was it about this house that filled her with a sense of foreboding. If ghost there was . . . Belinda's ghost . . . Dene felt it would be a quiet, tragic soul; and it was not just Lucia's superstitious terror that was influencing her, though goodness knows she was superstitious enough herself. There were too many mysteries . . . perhaps that was it. Dene did not like unsubstantiated hints, things left unexplained. The unknown was always worse than the known. Mentally, she listed the questions that disturbed her. How had Belinda died? Why was she beginning to have this feeling that it had not been a natural death? Why was everyone so reluctant to mention her name? Had it been suicide . . . a disgrace to the family? What *had* Lucia meant when she said that the members of the household rarely slept well, and why did the servants prefer to return to their own houses every night? Did they really believe the Villa to be haunted?

Anxious all at once to leave the room, with its locked-away memories, its contents which only added to the enigmas which troubled her mind, Dene took a random handful of books from the shelf, not even bothering to study her selection. She extinguished the lamps and had almost gained the door when it was thrown violently open, a tall figure being silhouetted against the poorly-lit corridor.

'*Madre de Diós!* What are *you* doing in this room?'

CHAPTER SIX

'Luq! I . . . I mean . . . Señor de Léon!'

After the first heart-stopping moment of shock, Dene had recognised him. His low-pitched voice was an ominous rumble of anger.

A lean, strong hand shot out, grasping her by the wrist, catapulting her into the passageway, so that the pile of books flew from her grasp and scattered about her. She was about to bend down and pick them up when he spoke once more.

'How did *you* gain admittance here? Have you the key?' And, as she nodded, 'Give it to me.'

Fingers shaking, she put the key into his outstretched hand and watched as he locked the door, putting the key into his pocket.

'Now, *señorita*, you will come with me . . . immediately!' as she made another futile attempt to retrieve the books.

To make sure of her compliance, steely fingers grasped her arm just above the elbow, making her flinch, and she found herself being ignominiously dragged towards the next door but one . . . that of Luq's study.

The lamps here were already burning, but suitcases and a briefcase, flung negligently on the floor, indicated that Luq had just this moment arrived at the Villa, and Dene cursed her luck. Fewer moments spent studying Belinda's bedroom, the portrait . . . and her intrusion would have remained undetected. Now that she had seen the portrait, she could not help wondering what Luq thought of her own shadowy resemblance to his late wife. She could not believe that he had not noticed it, in fact it explained quite a lot . . . and not only Luq, but the others . . . José, his mother, Lucia, and Isobel . . . what had their reaction been? Very varied, as she remembered. But why had none of them *mentioned* it?

With unceremonious force, Luq thrust Dene down on to the leather chesterfield which occupied one corner of his study, then stood over her, legs astride, hands thrust deeply into the pockets of his well fitting trousers, an unrelenting scowl upon his handsome face.

'Explanations, *señorita*!' he said grimly.

Dene spread her hands in a gesture of helplessness.

'It's quite simple really. I wanted something to read and I . . .'

'And who gave you permission to enter that room?'

'Well, no one, actually. I . . .'

'Exactly! As I thought! You had the impertinence to suborn a servant, to enter a room in my house . . . a room which was deliberately locked against intrusion . . . to poke and pry . . .'

'I was *not* prying!' Dene interrupted stormily. 'I was desperate for something to read. This isn't the liveliest of houses and . . .'

'You were the one so set on coming here,' he reminded her. 'I warned you that it was no suitable place for a young, irresponsible . . . But that is beside the point. Why do you think that room is kept locked?'

Dene stared at him wordlessly. It did seem unforgivable now, to have deliberately entered Belinda's bedroom, when it was so obvious that Luq did not wish anyone to have admission.

'Well?' He was waiting for an answer.

'I . . . I don't know.' Dene studied the high polish on his shoes, with unnecessary intensity, willing back the tears that welled in her eyes. 'I . . . I suppose because you want to keep your m-memories s-sacred . . .'

He swooped so suddenly that she had no time to win her battle for self-control, his hand beneath her chin forcing her head up, revealing the betraying moisture on her cheeks, the trembling of soft lips.

'*Por Dios!*' he swore. 'Have I not told you, I am unmoved by tears?' Yet somehow the expression in his eyes belied the words.

She swallowed.

'I'm sorry. I . . . I'm tired and l-lonely, and I only wanted s-some books. I . . . I didn't mean any harm . . . didn't mean to intrude on your . . .'

'*Santos!* Spare me this sentimental claptrap. There are other reasons why a room may remain locked.'

Luq released her chin and took an irate pace or two around the room.

'I knew it was a mistake to bring another young, impressionable girl here. After the first two left, I . . .'

'First two?' Dene looked at him, the tears drying on her cheeks. 'Do you mean you've had young nurses before?'

'*Ciertamente!* Why do you think I . . . ?'

'But José said . . .'

He rounded on her.

'What has José said . . . and when?'

'He said there hadn't been any young women here since . . . since Belinda . . .'

It did not occur to Dene that *she* had finished José's sentence for him, that she had assumed his concurrence with her interpretation.

'*Madre mia!* Is it impossible for anyone in this house to speak the truth?' He began to pace again. 'I knew I should not bring you here, under the same roof as . . . as . . . But I . . .' The words were muttered almost to himself.

'You needn't disturb yourself on that account,' Dene broke in, her voice sharp with anger. 'I've already had my lecture from Doña Teresa on that score . . . on my unsuitability as a companion for her son.'

'When was this?' His voice was tense.

'This afternoon. He . . . José . . . showed me the village, and we climbed up to the plateau. We . . .'

'You were on the mountainside, alone, with José?'

'Yes!' snapped Dene, her tone defiant. 'And I can't think what all the fuss is about. I . . .'

'Can you not?' he said grimly. 'Then it seems it must be my unpleasant task to enlighten you.'

'If you're going to tell me to remember my place . . . remind me that I'm just an employee, not good enough for the Léon family, save your breath,' Dene told him. 'I told Doña Teresa, and now I'm telling you, I've no designs on your cousin. I like him very much, but that's all. Besides . . .' she hesitated, then took the plunge. After all, once you had told the initial lie, the number of repetitions scarcely seemed to matter. 'Besides, I do have a fiancé to consider.'

Luq seemed to relax a little, though his face still retained its frowning intensity.

'Yes . . . yes, that is so. But will that make any difference, I ask myself?'

Dene bristled.

'Difference? To whom? If you're implying that I'm . . .'

'Señorita!' The bass voice sounded weary as he interrupted her, and indeed there were signs of strain around his eyes . . . his mouth. 'My cousin is a young man . . . *muy macho*. He is accustomed, wherever he goes, to be the object of female adulation. You claim to be immune. Does it not occur to you that a man of José's type might see that as a challenge?'

'Do you mean José would . . . ? Oh no! I don't believe it. You're probably just jealous, because . . .'

'Jealous?' he snapped. 'Jealous of whom . . . and why?'

'Well, of your cousin, of course. He's younger than you, famous, a romantic figure, and you say the girls flock round him . . .'

'And you think I am no longer capable of attracting a woman . . . is that it?' His black eyes were dangerous.

'I . . . I didn't say that. I only . . .'

'But that is what you meant *señorita*,' he said softly, 'despite your protestations of innocence, it occurs to me that you lie, that you *have* indulged in flirtatious behaviour with my cousin.'

'No, I . . .'

'Oh, it may have been harmless in intention. But engaged or not, a woman still likes to prove her powers.' He paused, then added bitterly, 'who should know better than I? Yes, Señorita Mason, I think that you have found my cousin desirable. You are away from home, away from the restraining influence of your parents, your fiancé, the natural satisfier of your sexual appetites . . .'

'How dare you!' Dene gasped. 'I never . . .'

But he continued, as if she had not spoken.

'It is tempting to play a little game, yes? To see if you still have the power to draw a man to your side, even if you do not want him? But with José, you are playing with fire.'

With a swift, unexpected movement he pulled her up to face him.

'You might find it safer to conduct your little experiments upon me . . . safer and, who knows, just as satisfactory?'

'Let me go,' she whispered, as the fire in his eyes, the movement of the long, sensual mouth betrayed his intentions. If he kissed her there was no way she could hide her response to him.

'I think not, *señorita*,' he said, and the calm matter-of-factness of his words was belied by the throatiness of his intonation. 'You tell me there is little diversion in this house, and I am inclined to agree with you. Why should we not divert each other?'

Dene sought to resist, but he had anticipated the attempt, pulling her to him with unnecessary roughness, so that she felt the breath knocked from her body, as his arms clamped round her and his lips quested for her own, remorselessly stopping her mouth from giving utterance to its faint protest.

His mouth was hungry, the sensations he was arousing as familiar as if that other, earlier kiss had only just taken place.

She knew she should deny this invasion, attempt to thwart his possession of her mouth . . . a man of his experience would be bound to recognise and correctly interpret her reactions. But the touch of his lips seemed to paralyse every nerve of her body. She had remembered his earlier kiss so often, dwelling upon it, recalling the response it had evoked in her . . . that now his onslaught seemed almost right, inevitable, a result of her longing for its repetition; her very blood cried out to him, so that she felt the pounding of her pulses must be audible; and after the first few seconds of resistance, her lips quivered and softened.

As he sensed this, his kiss became more caressing, less brutal, more questing, probing, sensual . . .

Stung by desire, Dene pressed against him, clinging, yielding, as he edged her backwards, until she felt the cold leather edge of the chesterfield once more behind her knees and they sank down, still closely entwined, into its upholstered embrace. Dene was conscious that the arousal was not just confined to her own body, as Luq pressed against her, his breathing hard and fast. A small part of her brain was aware that this had gone far enough, that it was only vengeance he intended, and though her body cried out in protest against her brain's saner counsels, she was just about to thrust him from her when the door opened without any preliminary warning knock.

Startled, they moved apart Luq's hand going up to smooth the dishevelment of his dark hair, Dene straightening her skirt.

'*Lo siento mucho*, Luq,' José apologised. 'It seems my visit is inopportune?'

Introducing

Harlequin Temptation™

Have you ever thought
you were in love
with one man...only
to feel attracted to another?

That's just one of the temptations you'll find facing the women in new *Harlequin Temptation* romance novels.

Sensuous...contemporary...compelling...reflecting today's love relationships!

The passionate torment of a woman torn between two loves...the siren call of a career...the magnetic advances of an impetuous employer–nothing is left unexplored in this romantic new series from Harlequin. You'll thrill to a candid new frankness as men and women seek to form lasting relationships in the face of temptations that threaten true love. Begin with your FREE copy of *First Impressions*. Mail the reply card today!

First Impressions
by Maris Soule

He was involved with her best friend!

Tracy Dexter couldn't deny her attraction to her new boss. Mark Prescott looked more like a jet set playboy than a high school principal–and he acted like one, too. It wasn't right for Tracy to go out with him, not when her friend Rose had already staked a claim. It wasn't right, even though Mark's eyes were so persuasive, his kiss so probing and intense. Even though his hands scorched her body with a teasing, raging fire...and when he gently lowered her to the floor she couldn't find the words to say no.

A word of warning to our regular readers: While Harlequin books are always in good taste, you'll find more sensuous writing in new *Harlequin Temptation* than in other Harlequin romance series.

® ™Trademarks of Harlequin Enterprises Ltd.

Get this romance novel FREE as your introduction to new

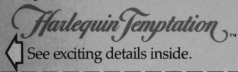

Harlequin Temptation ™

◁ See exciting details inside.

'Perhaps . . . perhaps not,' Luq said grimly, his voice just a little unsteady, and Dene knew instinctively that he was regretting his loss of control. The kiss, begun as an angry attempt to prove his assertion that she was a flirt . . . promiscuous even, had carried him farther than he was prepared to admit, even to himself, but Dene knew just how much their embrace had aroused him and she blushed at the recollection at the flood of feeling the knowledge had caused to swamp through her.

'However,' Luq continued, his tone becoming censorious as he rose to face his cousin, 'it *would* have been a courtesy to knock before entering.'

'Better think yourself lucky it was me and not the fair Elena,' José retorted.

'*Por Diós!*—Elena! I had forgotten!' Luq looked harassed, disordering again the hair he had just smoothed into place. 'Where is she?'

'With Madre,' said José, his blue eyes mischievous, 'in the parlour, and the atmosphere is *muy difícil!*'

Luq turned to Dene.

'Kindly gather up those books from the passageway. Since you have them and since, apparently, your taste runs to such trash, you may as well read them. But I warn you, I will not tolerate a repetition of this evening's ill-mannered intrusion.'

He took the key from his pocket, swinging it from his forefinger.

'I shall return this key to Lucia myself. *La mujer* needs reminding of her station in this house. Just because . . .'

'Please, you mustn't blame Lucia,' Dene pleaded. 'She was only being kind . . . trying to help me.'

'You think so?' He lifted an ironic brow. 'As I told you before, *señorita*, you are no psychologist. In this house, take no one's actions at face value.'

'Not even yours?' she asked sarcastically.

'Mine least of all,' he agreed. With his uneven stride, he moved to the door, turning on his heel to address her once more. 'When you have cleared away the books, kindly report to me in the parlour. I wish you to meet Dr Pareja.'

'What was all that . . . about books?' José asked curiously, following Dene into the passageway.

'These!' She indicated the scattered paperbacks. 'Lucia let me into Belinda's room, so I could look for something to read.'

José whistled as he bent to help her.

'You mean you actually entered the holy of holies?'

'It is a bit like that, isn't it?' Dene agreed ruefully.

José's face was sombre.

'I wonder Luq didn't murder you!' He paused, then: 'That room should be cleared . . . the contents burnt,' he said violently.

Secretly, Dene agreed. She felt that it showed an unhealthy obsession to cling so persistently to relics of the dead.

'But not the portrait, surely?' she demurred. 'I'd no idea Luq was an artist.'.

'He dabbles in his spare time,' José said shortly. 'And the portrait most of all should be destoryed. While it hangs there . . .' He shivered, crossing himself. 'This house is haunted, Dene.'

She took the rest of the books from him, a frisson of fear tingling along her spine, as the oil lamps flickered, making the shadows of the corridor leap and quiver. If José had not been with her she had the idea she might have fled to lock herself in her own room.

'Haunted?' she whispered, her blue eyes wide. 'By . . . by Belinda?'

He nodded.

'José, the . . . the guitar? Something Asunción said . . . ?'

'Señorita Mason, have we to wait all night for you?' It was an irate Luq returned in search of her.

Hastily she thrust the books into José's arms.

'José, please, would you leave these by my door? I . . . I'd better go.

Seething with mingled frustration . . . for she felt she had been on the verge of some discovery . . . and annoyance at Luq's peremptory manner, Dene made her way to the parlour.

Obviously, Doña Teresa had decided that the niceties of hospitality had been sufficiently observed, for there was now no sign of José's mother. Luq had seated himself at the table, a sheaf of notes before him and a file, which Dene recognised as Isobel's cases notes. Then her eyes went to his companion . . . a woman in her middle thirties . . . and her breath caught in her throat. She had never encountered a Spaniard, male or female, with red hair; and there was no doubt that the colour was natural.

Though Elena Pareja was also seated, it was obvious to Dene that she was daintily built, slender and graceful. Somehow her dark complexion seemed enhanced by the flamelike aureole of hair; but as she turned to look at Dene, the younger girl felt she was not going to like Dr Pareja. Normally she prided herself on keeping an open mind during the early stages of a new acquaintance, but something seemed to be warning her against this woman. The green, almond-shaped eyes on either side of a long, finely chiselled nose were coolly appraising, their expression becoming first startled, then venomous, as the Spanish woman took in Dene's fresh, youthful beauty.

'But you did not tell me . . . she is like . . . Luq *querido*, is this wise?'

Once Dene would have been mystified, but now she knew exactly what the other woman had been going to say. So she too had noted the superficial resemblance to Belinda de Léon.

Dr Pareja had made no attempt to rise, as Luq performed the introductions, acknowledging Dene's greeting with the perfunctory nod she evidently accorded to those she considered to be in a position of subservience.

'I have asked Dr Pareja to come here, to give me her opinion of our patient,' Luq explained. 'Dr Pareja is an expert in her field.'

He did not explain what branch of medicine Elena Pareja practised, and Dene could only conclude that it was connected with rheumatology. She wondered why on earth he hadn't taken this step two years ago, when Isobel had first contracted the disease, especially in view of her previous reluctance to go to Seville.

'Dr Pareja and I will be here for the next week,' Luq continued. 'We shall be making continuous observations and tests, so you will have more free time at your disposal.' He turned to Elena Pareja. 'Is there anything you wish to ask Señorita Mason?'

Elena Pareja gestured dismissively.

'*Nada . . . nada . . .* you may go, nurse.'

She had not even been invited to sit down, or asked for a progress report on Isobel Travers; and they had continued their conversation . . . in Spanish, of course . . . before she had even left the room. Seething at Elena Pareja's contemptuous dismissal, Dene made her way to her own room. It was really late now. By the time she was ready for bed, she would not feel like reading.

Nevertheless, before she put out her lamp, she could not resist looking to see what type of fiction had appealed to Belinda de Léon. As she had suspected, all the books were novels of a sensational kind. Had Belinda been an incurably romantic person, or had all this devouring of love-stories been some form of compensation for an unsatisfactory marriage? Had the Léons always occupied separate rooms? She did not know enough of Spanish ways to be sure if this was a customary arrangement. That room had certainly been a woman's room, with no evidence that any man had ever entered it . . . shared it. She recalled José's remark, his apparent conviction, that Belinda haunted the villa. She had heard that bullfighters were superstitious, and who was *she* to scoff at that . . . but did he really believe it, or had he been putting it on, to scare her? Highly superstitious herself, Dene felt a sudden urge to have a locked door between herself and the rest of the villa. She turned the key in the lock, extinguished the lamps and climbed into bed, feeling more secure. Though what use you think a door would be against a ghost, she told herself, with ironic self-contempt . . .

Something had disturbed her! But what? Dene sat up in bed, feeling the perspiration of fear trickling down between her breasts. Had she been dreaming, or had she really heard the strains of guitar music? No, not music even, but discordant, jangling sounds, as though the instrument were being played by an unpractised hand. But the house was silent now . . . uncannily so, after the sounds she had heard . . . imagined? She was on the edge of sleep once more, when a sound in the passageway disturbed her . . . a faint shuffle, as of feet, just outside her door. She shot up in bed, heart pounding, mouth dry. She had left her window shutter very slightly ajar and the moonlight shafting through them illumined a section of her door. Before her fascinated gaze, the handle began to turn, first one way, then the other.

Dene swallowed the nervous lump in her throat.

'Who . . . who's there?'

There was no reply; only the handle abruptly ceased its movement. Dene sat for a moment or two, a chill shiver traversing the length of her spine, then:

'This is ridiculous,' she told herself . . . aloud, as if the sound of a voice, even her own, would reassure her . . . would exorcise the ghosts, if ghosts there were.

Dene might be superstitious, open to suggestion, but she did not lack courage. She forced herself to get out of bed and walk to the door. With a sudden movement she unlocked it, threw it open and looked out into the passageway. It was empty.

Only then did she realise that she was holding her breath. She expelled it on a sigh of relief, re-locked the door and got back into bed. It had been a trick of the tremulous moonlight, she told herself firmly. There had been no one in the passageway, just as there had been no guitar music. There were no such things as ghosts . . . were there?

Next morning, Dene found her patient silent and inclined to be sulky, already having received her first visit from Elena Pareja.

'I can't think why Luq had to bring this Dr Pareja here,' Isobel, complained to Dene, as the girl supervised her bath and exercises. 'I don't *like* the woman. I don't like the way she looks at me.'

Dene knew exactly how Isobel felt. She had felt her own hackles respond to that supercilious glance, but it would be unprofessional in a nurse to join in criticism of a doctor, so she tried to placate the irritable woman.

'I'm sure Señor de Léon is only doing what he thinks is best for *you*,' she murmured soothingly. 'Sometimes two opinions are better than one.'

Isobel snorted.

'Luq has no parallel in this field . . . that woman can only be inferior to him. Who is she? I've never heard of her before.'

Remembering the telephone call she had taken at the Casa in Seville, Dene shrugged.

'All I can tell you is that Señor de Léon referred to her as a colleague.' She recalled a thought which had occurred to her the previous night, after seeing the portrait of Belinda de Léon, and hesitated, wondering whether she should mention it. But perhaps it *would* give Isobel something else to think about, other than the detested Dr Pareja's presence.

'Isobel,' she began diffidently, 'I . . I was in your . . . your late daughter's room last night . . .'

'Oh! Who with?' The older woman seemed to stiffen and Dene hastened to explain the circumstances.

'Of course I realise now that I should have asked first and I won't intrude again, I promise. But . . . about the portrait . . .'

'The portrait?'

'Yes . . . of Belinda, the one Señor de Léon painted . . .'

'What of it?'

'Oh dear, this *hadn't* been a good idea. Isobel still seemed annoyed at her temerity in entering that room uninvited.

'J-just that I couldn't help noticing she . . . she looked a bit like . . . like me,' she ended lamely.

Isobel seemed to draw in a deep breath and her face relaxed into a smile . . . twisted, but nevertheless a smile.

'Oh yes . . . yes, I noticed the likeness, of course.'

'But you didn't say anything,' Dene pointed out. 'No one said anything . . . but they must *all* have noticed. In fact, looking back, I *know* they did. So why . . . ?'

'That is what I have asked myself,' Isobel said musingly. 'Why they brought you here, knowing . . .'

'Knowing that I would remind you of your daughter,' Dene finished for her. 'It . . . it does seem a bit . . . well, thoughtless.'

Hastily she reviewed the circumstances and had to admit to herself that Luq had *not* wanted to bring her here. If it had not been for her own persistence . . . and surely *he* would scarcely relish a constant reminder of his late wife; she might have been disappointed still, if he had refused to employ her, but at least she would have respected and accepted a reason like that. So *why* hadn't he told her? Why had nobody told her? It was very puzzling; and it didn't seem as if Isobel intended to explain her own silence on the subject, for she began to talk rapidly and rather wildly about other things. So, after making sure that Isobel had everything to hand for her breakfast, Dene made her way to the cheerful, homely kitchen for her own meal.

José and his mother were already seated at the large, well-scrubbed table, waited on by Asunción, and as Dene entered, Lucia was setting out two breakfasts upon a large tray.

'This Dr Pareja,' she announced to the room at large, 'is so proud that she must be served in the parlour.'

'It is not for you to comment on your betters,' Doña Teresa rebuked, but her tone was mild and from José's comment of the previous night, Dene knew that she too held no brief for Elena Pareja.

'Luq is breakfasting in the parlour also,' José pointed out. 'And if they are talking surgery over their meal, I for one am glad they eat separately.'

'*E'un bravo!*' Lucia said teasingly. '*El matador* is squeamish!'

As she passed the table, she ruffled José's wavy blond hair and Dene saw a slight frown on Doña Teresa's brow, though she made no comment.

'Have you plans for today, Dene?' José asked as, the meal concluded, they rose from the table.

She shrugged.

'Just routine, I suppose.'

'A pity,' José observed. 'I would have liked to invite you to come with me to the next village. It is the last day of the local *feria*.'

Dene sighed.

'I wish I could . . . but even if I were free, you know your mother and Luq would disapprove.' She looked at her watch. 'It's time for Mrs Travers' walk around the veranda.' She frowned. 'I wonder what she does for fresh air and exercise in winter.'

'The winters are not long in duration,' José assured her, following her into the passageway. 'January and February, when the tiger wind blows and snow closes the village are bad, but for the rest the air is still and mild.'

'If you *are* going to the *feria*, I'd be grateful if you'd put a letter in the collection box there,' said Dene. 'I've written to my parents, but I haven't been able to post it yet.'

There was no local service. All letters had to be despatched from and collected at the store-cum-post office in the nearest village.

She encountered José again, a few minutes later, lounging gracefully upon the verandah, as she and Isobel made their way slowly along its colonnaded length. José held out his hand for the letter.

'*Buenos días, señora,*' he greeted Isobel, his manner subtly mocking, 'so now you have *two* doctors to attend you, no?'

'I was quite content with one,' Isobel said coldly.

José laughed. It was a cynical sound and Dene looked at him in surprise.

'Do not concern yourself, *señora*. The doctor Elena, so *guapísima*, will not be here solely for *your* benefit.'

'What do you mean?' Isobel's voice was sharp, impatient, and Dene knew her rheumatism must be troubling her more than usual.

'You English have a saying for it, *si*? Luq is killing the two birds with the one pebble? The beautiful Elena *may* study your ills, but there will be time also for the more . . . interesting pursuits.'

'Such as?' Dene asked, her curiosity aroused.

José looked from one to the other, his good-looking face alight with mischief.

'You have not guessed? Luq may be a cold, clinical devil, but he is also *muy macho*! Elena is Luq's *amante*, of course.'

'His . . . mistress?' Dene asked, not quite sure if she had interpreted the word correctly, and hoping very much that she had not.

'*Sí!*' José laughed. 'Did you think *you* were the sole recipient of his favours?'

Dene flushed, furious at José's indiscreet words and aware of Isobel's curious eyes upon her. Whatever would her patient think? She would be imagining all kinds of unprofessional conduct.

'Say what you like about Dr Pareja. You obviously know your cousin better than I do. But leave me out of it. What you saw last night . . .' She faltered, her voice trailing away, at a loss for words as she realised she was only making the whole thing sound worse.

Isobel's bronze eyes were intent.

'What *is* all this?' she asked lightly. 'You're talking in riddles, both of you.'

'Oh, just an interesting little encounter I witnessed last night,' said José, 'between our ice-cold Luquillo and Dene . . . not that I blame him, you understand. I too find Señorita Mason *encantadora*!'

'José, stop it!' Dene couldn't help laughing. It was impossible to be cross for long with this engaging young man. 'Now please let us get on with our walk, or you'll have Luq down on both our necks.'

'So you call him Luq, then?' Isobel enquired casually, as they continued their slow progress.

'No, not really. It was just a slip of the tongue . . . with everyone else referring to him that way.'

'Do you believe what José said . . . about Dr Pareja?'

'You mean that she's Señor de Léon's mistress?' Dene considered the matter, remembering again the telephone call to the Casa, Elena's assured, peremptory manner . . . the words '*caro mio*' spoken before she had realised she was not addressing Luquillo de Léon. 'It's possible,' she said at last, 'and I suppose José would know if anyone does, since he spends a lot of time in Seville himself.'

They walked on, and Dene found herself considering the idea of Elena Pareja as Luq's mistress with violent distaste, and what did Isobel think of Luq having a mistress? Surely she would be distressed on her late daughter's account; and yet it *had* been two years. One could scarcely blame Luq for seeking such happiness as he could find. In fact, she wondered that he had not married again. But then, she told herself, if his heart *was* buried with Belinda, he would not want such a permanent commitment; perhaps it was purely physical assuagement that he sought from Elena Pareja. Did the other woman realise just how lucky she was even to have that much of him? What would it be like, she wondered, to be made love to by Luq de Léon . . . and by love she knew that she meant more than kisses. The very contemplation of the idea caused such a pang, somewhere deep and inaccessible inside her, that she was forced to banish the thought. It was too painful.

As they turned at the end of the verandah, Dene remembered something she had intended to ask Isobel.

'I suppose you didn't come to my room last night?'

Isobel looked so startled that she hastened to explain.

'I thought I heard someone at my door . . . I thought the handle turned. But when I got up and looked, there was nobody there. I . . . just wondered if you needed me.' No need to mention the guitar music, Dene decided, if indeed music there had been. Isobel had admitted to being as susceptible to nervous suggestion as herself. It would be cruel to alarm her needlessly.

'No, dear.' Isobel shook her head. 'For a wonder, I slept right through last night. It's not often I have an undisturbed night. The pain, you know . . . but last night I was lucky.'

Dene was troubled to think of Isobel having restless nights.

'If the pain is ever too bad and you think I can help, you will call me?' she begged. 'I don't mind being woken, honestly.'

'You're very kind, my dear. I'll remember.'

Isobel was silent for a moment as they retraced their steps, then she asked:

'You don't suppose it could have been José, trying your door? That young man . . .'

'No . . . oh no!' Dene was shocked at the very idea. 'I'm quite sure he wouldn't dream of doing such a thing.'

Isobel shrugged.

'I suppose you know best, my dear. But I'd be inclined to keep your door locked at night, if I were you.'

As they neared the end of their walk, they found Luq and Elena Pareja waiting on the verandah, and Dene felt her cheeks burning at the sight of Luq, so recently had her thoughts been of him . . . and with such intimate connotations.

'Dr Pareja wishes to examine Señora Travers . . . and to spend the day with her, making observations and discussing her case,' Luq told Dene. 'You may consider yourself at liberty until tonight.'

Dene's face lit up.

'Then have I your permission to leave the Villa?'

'*Ciertamente!* You wish to go somewhere in particular?'

Dene hesitated. If she told him, would the plan be prohibited?

'José is going to the next village. He said if I'd been free, I could have gone with him. As . . . as I am free, I don't suppose . . . ?'

'To the cattle fair?' Luq raised quizzical black brows. 'You are interested in such things?'

'Anything would be better than sitting around here twiddling my thumbs,' she told him with feeling.

He looked at her consideringly.

'Yes, one tends to forget that a nurse has needs, as well as her patient. Very well, I permit.'

Dene could scarcely believe her luck. She had expected an outright refusal, particularly since José was to be her companion.

She hastened off in search of him, hoping that he had not already left. After a search of the villa, she eventually found him in the kitchen, cajoling Lucia into preparing a packed lunch. He was delighted to hear that Dene was able to accompany him after all.

'Make that two packed lunches, Lucia!' he commanded.

'No, make it four!'

Dene swung round to find Luq at her shoulder; the noise and activity of the kitchen had drowned the sounds of his approach.

'Four?' she enquired with a sinking heart. Surely he hadn't changed his mind? Did he intend to take Elena instead of spending a day observing their patient. In that case who would look after Isobel?

'Four!' he agreed. 'Lucia, it is your birthday!'

'No, *señor*.' The girl looked puzzled.

Luq laughed.

'It is an English expression, Lucia. It means you are about to have a treat. You will come to the *feria* with us, *si*?'

'*Si* . . . Oh *si, señor*!' The girl's dark, vivid face was alight immediately. '*Muchas gracias, señor*.'

'Run along and change, then.' Indulgent amusement softened Luq's features beyond belief, Dene thought, as she watched him, strange sensations rioting within her at the rare sight of his handsome face transformed by laughter. She wished he would look at her like that . . . half teasing, half affectionate.

'Asunción will make the lunches,' he said, as Lucia hesitated. 'Hurry up, girl. We will call at your house on the way to the car.'

He turned to Dene, assessing the white nurse's dress.

'Do you not wish to change also, *señorita*?'

'Oh, yes . . . yes, of course.'

'We will wait for you on the patio.'

It was not the exertion of running along the passageways to her room which made Dene breathless, or brought the sparkle to eyes that anxiously regarded her appearance in the mirror. Nor was it just the thought of a whole day away from the villa, she told herself, as she rattled through the contents of her wardrobe. Nor would the prospect of accompanying José throw her into such disorder, such anticipatory excitement. The outing had taken on a whole new dimension, now that Luq was coming too.

A full day in Luq's company! But then Lucia had been excited too ... and *Luq* had invited *her* to make up the foursome. But even that thought could not totally extinguish Dene's high spirits.

She was torn between practicality and vanity. Should she wear a shirt and jeans? A cattle fair scarcely sounded the right venue for a good dress, and yet Lucia would scarcely be likely to possess trousers. Vanity won the day.

She settled on a rather stunning twosome, which she had been saving for a special occasion ... something of which she had begun to despair. The dress itself, long-sleeved and V-necked, was powder blue, the colour intensifying the deeper shade of her eyes. A sleeveless, multi-coloured jacket in delicate toning shades completed the outfit. After much deliberation, she settled for white shoes with a medium heel and a matching white handbag.

Her make-up freshened and her hair set free from its severe, workaday style into a fall of gleaming blonde silk, she was ready, guiltily conscious of having taken fifteen minutes to change. Would Luq be growing impatient? She did not even stop to consider José's reactions.

She descended the curving stair to the patio, selfconsciously aware of two pairs of eyes assessing her appearance; dark eyes coolly enigmatic, sparkling blue ones frankly appreciative.

'*Muy guapa!*' José exclaimed, stepping forward to take Dene's hand, spinning her round with a waltz-like movement. 'Is she not *estupenda*, Luq?'

'Very attractive,' Luq said gravely. 'Almost worth waiting for.' Ostentatiously, he consulted his watch. 'Shall we go?'

Dene did not know whether to feel pleased or annoyed by his double-edged reply. Still undecided, she slipped her arm through José's, ignoring Luq, as they crossed the patio towards the arched gateway.

A movement on the verandah caught her eye and she looked up to see Isobel, with Elena Pareja in attendance, watching their departure. She waved to Isobel and was rewarded with a slight gesture of a frail hand. Isobel's face was expressionless and, in the midst of her own enthusiasm for the outing, Dene could spare a sympathetic thought for the other woman's restricted, uneventful life. What wouldn't Isobel give, she thought, to be able to accompany them.

Down in the village of Pajaro, Lucia's house stood close by the dilapidated church.

'Is the church ever used?' Dene asked Luq, as José rapped on the ill-fitting door of the stone dwelling.

He shook his head.

'There is no resident priest these days. The villagers walk to the next village for Mass every Sunday and on holy days. An hour's walk is not far in good weather.'

'And in bad weather?'

He shrugged.

'They are good Catholics. They go!'

Meanwhile, Lucia had appeared in answer to José's summons, and Dene gasped in admiration. The girl's black workaday dress had not disguised her dark, flamboyant beauty, but in the full, flounced polka-dot dress of flaming red, she was sensational.

A sturdy figure hovered in the shadowy doorway behind her, a broad-shouldered man with tanned skin and prominent cheekbones, the grizzled hair as thick on his chin as on his head. In his arms he carried a small child . . . a boy, Dene thought . . . whose arms stretched out in entreaty towards Lucia's departing backview.

'Is that Lucia's husband?' Dene asked doubtfully. The man looked too old.

'Pedro . . . her father,' Luq said shortly.

'And the child?'

'Lucia's son . . . Mateo.'

'So she *is* married, then?'

'No.' Luq sounded exasperated and obviously wanted to change the subject.

Dene was embarrassed, feeling as though, by her curiosity, she had been guilty of a faux pas of some kind. She seemed fated to ask Luq the wrong questions. She was relieved when the elderly man and the child disappeared back inside the house and Lucia ran towards them, full skirts swaying, her lovely face alight with anticipation.

'What a beautiful dress, Lucia,' said Dene with genuine admiration.

Lucia acknowledged the compliment gravely, her festive clothes giving her a new dignity, which her servant's garb had masked.

'The Señorita too is *muy bonita*.'

'Call me Dene, Lucia,' Dene said impulsively. 'I really want you to,' she insisted, as Lucia looked doubtful.

'Is not respectful.'

'Oh, come on, Lucia!' José tucked an arm companionably through that of the servant girl. 'Today is a *fiesta*. We are all on first name terms . . . eh, Luq?'

'*Cómo nó!*' his cousin replied, but his eyes were on Dene. 'You permit that *I* call you Dene?' he asked.

'Yes . . . yes, of course,' she replied, aware of a certain breathlessness. It was strange how the sound of her name on his lips carried such an implication of intimacy . . . purely a fiction of her heightened sensibilities where he was concerned, she knew.

'And you will call me Luq?'

'If . . . if you wish.'

'I wish!'

'All right, then . . . Luq.' She flushed as she used his name for the first time and her lids fluttered down before his quizzical smile.

They took Luq's car, larger and more comfortable than José's sports model; and though José had issued the original invitation, somehow Dene found herself in the front passenger seat beside Luq, while José and Lucia occupied the rear, Lucia chatting almost non-stop about anything and everything.

Dene was surprised that Lucia should be so excited over a cattle fair, until José explained that this was the most important occasion in the Alpujarras.

'Today,' he said, leaning forward to speak to her, 'is the last day of the *feria* . . . and also the feast of the Virgen de los Alpujarras.'

'A special day . . . on which one may pray for one's heart's desire,' Lucia added, her voice unwontedly grave.

What did Lucia most desire? Dene wondered. As for herself . . . she drew a deep breath . . . could the deity these people worshipped be expected to grant the prayer of an unbeliever? Suddenly she wished desperately that she believed in something other than the efficacy of her little lucky charm; it seemed a shallow trifle on which to depend, after the fervid faith she had witnessed during the Semana Santa in Seville. Nevertheless, as always, her hand went to it, then stopped, surprise and then dismay engulfing her. It wasn't in its usual place about her neck. Then she remembered—to avoid breaking the fragile chain, she had removed it when she changed her dress for this outing, and had forgotten to replace it. Well, it would still be on the dressing table when she returned. She was not likely to come to any harm because, just for once, she was not wearing her little black cat.

The cattle fair was held just outside the village, on the dry, stony river bed, the pebble river with its golden sand running between poplars and rose-flowered oleanders, while, in the background, rose smooth red cliffs. There were barrel organs, vociferous hawkers, snack vendors cried their wares . . . shrimps! crayfish! bonbons! peanuts! Stalls and drinking booths had been constructed of green branches; moustachioed, swarthy, swaggering gipsies in brightly coloured, ragged clothes showed the paces of their horses, asses and mules, trotting them up and down, the sound of their hoofbeats mingling with the cries of the vendors.

They did the round of the booths, watched with amusement the haggling over the livestock, then joined other parties, picnicking under the shade of ancient orange trees. There was much conversation and badinage over the meal, instigated mainly by José, but Dene found herself responding in kind, the exhilaration of the day loosening her tongue, setting free her normally exuberant spirits and sharpening her ready wit.

'Is Dene not an asset to our household?' José demanded of his cousin, after one particular duel of sparkling repartee. 'Never have I encountered so many qualities in one woman. In Seville she devours culture; she has the sense of humour. This is no brainless blonde, not like . . .' He stopped, a look of horror crossing his handsome features.

What had he been about to say? Dene thought she could guess, looking from one face to the other, José's dismay would have been comical, but for the cold, set expression of Luq's features; and Lucia looked decidedly sulky. Dene reflected that it was rather tactless of José to sing one girl's praises in front of another.

'You make me sound an unbearable blue-stocking,' she said, in an attempt to lighten the atmosphere. 'I'd far sooner be beautiful, like Lucia.'

After an hilarious attempt on her part to explain to José the derivation of the expression 'blue-stocking' good humour was restored and the conversation, to Dene's relief, became general . . . uncontroversial.

'It *is* good to have a holiday,' Lucia said to Dene later, when the men, amity restored, had wandered off to inspect the horses. 'Mateo wanted to come with me,' she said wistfully. 'He does not see very much of his mother, that little one.'

'I saw your little boy,' Dene said. 'How old is he?'

'Nearly three,' Lucia told her. 'He was born just before Don Luquillo married.' She sighed deeply and seemed to fall into a reverie.

A horrible premonition made Dene feel as if someone were squeezing the breath from her lungs. Luq had said that Lucia wasn't married, he had seemed embarrassed by her persistent questions. Was it possible? Could Lucia's son be . . . Luq's? She *could* not ask, and even had she possessed the necessary impertinence to do so, she would not ask. She didn't want to know.

How *could* she be in love with this man, Dene asked herself, on the strength of no more than two kisses? But she knew it was more than that. Right from the very first moment of their acquaintance, there had been something about him that had menaced her peace of mind. Then, she had thought it was because he held her future career in the palm of his hand. But now she recognised that it had been an instinctive knowledge that this man was subtly different to any other, in so far as *she* was concerned. Her thoughts depressed her; for to be in love with Luq de Leon was such a hopeless, profitless emotion. Even if it were not for her suspicions regarding Lucia, her almost certain knowledge that Elena was his mistress, there would always be a barrier between Luq de Léon and love . . . the memories of his dead Belinda.

Though the sun was still shining as brightly as ever, Dene felt that a shadow had been cast across her day, and she joined only perfunctorily in the other's conversation.

Later they drove into the village, to watch the procession of the Virgin, and Dene was able to post her letter herself. She wondered what her parents would make of her descriptions of the Villa Venganza and its inhabitants. It had been difficult to describe it in words which would bridge the gulf between the life they lived and this totally unknown foreign atmosphere. It would all be so much outside their limited experience. They would not even begin to understand, would be puzzled, apprehensive even, and certainly disapproving, if they knew the whole of her life here.

The procession was an impressive sight, very elaborate for a small village occasion. The dumpy Virgin, a glittering figure, was carried from the church to the accompaniment of ringing bells, the firing of rockets and shotguns.

Immediately following the statue came the priests of the surrounding districts, then the Civil Guard and finally the municipal authorities. The vanguard was made up of ordinary folk, bearing guttering candles, many of the women deliberately shoeless.

'A self-imposed penance,' Luq commented, when Dene exclaimed, for the roadway was rough and stony. 'Or an offering . . . in order to obtain something they really desire.'

For one insane moment Dene felt like shedding her fashionable shoes and following the procession, if it would bring her what she now knew was *her* heart's desire. Then her sense of humour came to her rescue and she giggled inwardly, imagining the reactions of her companions, if she had given in to her impulse.

It was growing dark, before the procession had completed its tour of the town and the Virgin re-entered her sanctuary, when, once again, bells began to ring, rockets shot into the sky and shots were fired. The night had come quickly, the hills purple, the valleys shadowed and as suddenly as it had begun, the noise ceased and with astonishing rapidity, the crowds of people melted away into side streets, houses, or . . . in the case of visitors . . . their cars.

The lovely hours of escape were over and though the two men seemed unaffected by the necessity of returning to the Villa, both Dene and Lucia were silent on the homeward journey.

Dene guessed that the other girl did not get many occasions for frivolity, the boundaries of her life set by the village on the one hand and her work at the Villa Venganza on the other.

The car once more garaged next to José's in the primitive lean-to, they strolled through the village and at Lucia's door, José turned to Luq.

'I have some business with Pedro. Don't wait for me.'

Pedro, Dene recalled, was the name of Lucia's father. What possible business could José have to conduct with *him*? She thought she sensed displeasure in Luq's acknowledgement, as José followed Lucia into the rough and ready dwelling. Did he resent being left to escort *her* back to the villa? Would he have preferred a chance to remain behind with Lucia?

'Pedro has a cousin who works at a stud . . . where the fighting bulls are bred,' Luq explained as they walked on. 'The bulls will be used in forthcoming *corridas* and José hopes to visit the ranch, to assess the potential of the bulls he will meet. Once,' he added reminiscently, 'bulls were bred here, on our own land, in my grandfather's time. José still remembers and regrets those days. I think if he were not a matador, he too would breed bulls, but . . .' He shrugged, leaving his sentence unfinished. But Dene remembered the almost wistful note in José's voice, when *he* had told her of his grandfather's stud. Perhaps, some day, the bullfighting circuit would lose its glamour and José would settle down to become a farmer as his cousin and his mother wished.

They walked on . . . alone now . . . the darkness giving an illusion of intimacy to their solitariness and Dene was acutely aware of the man at her side, the brush of his arm against hers.

'You have enjoyed your day?' Luq spoke again, as they gained the narrow track which led up to the villa.

'Very much, thank you, *señor*.'

He paused, looking down at her, only the silhouette of his head visible against the night sky.

'I think we might dispense permanently with such formality, no? At least when we are alone?'

Dene was glad that the darkness hid the warm tide of colour his words had evoked. There had been a secret pleasure today, in being able to speak his name aloud . . . the name that was never out of her thoughts.

'Do you agree?' He had not moved on and waited now for her reply.

'I . . . I don't mind, if you don't?' It was impossible to control the slight breathlessness in her voice.

'*Bueno!*' He sounded pleased. 'Come, you must be tired.'

In the darkness, his hand sought hers. Dene knew it was an impersonal gesture, intended only to guide her steps up the twisting, uneven route to the villa, but the feel of his warm, lean fingers enclosing hers, was a subtle ravishment of her senses and she had to control an impulse to tighten her own grip, to sway closer.

The track, which had seemed unpleasantly endless on the night of her arrival, was traversed all too quickly and as they sighted the lights of the villa, Dene anticipated the moment, when he would release her hand; but it did not seem to occur to him to do so, and their fingers were still linked as they entered the grounds and crossed the patio towards the outer stairway.

Despite the lateness of the hour, the air was still warm and scented with perfumes from the neglected garden, which lay behind the villa and Dene felt reluctant to go inside. Insensibly, her pace slackened, until, at the rear entrance, she paused, looking back wistfully at the shadowed landscape, visible only as a series of shapes of varying intensity.

Luq seemed unusually sensitive to her mood.

'What is it, Dene?'

'It seems such a pity, when a wonderful day like this has to end,' she said sadly. 'I always feel that once I let it escape in sleep, the next day has already taken over and things can never be the same.'

He laughed. It was a low, attractive sound of sympathy . . . not mockery as once she would have expected.

'You are superstitious, no? And has your black cat brought you luck in my country?' His fingers brushed her neck where the chain usually rested and she quivered uncontrollably at his touch.

'It . . . it isn't there,' she told him, her voice shaky. 'I forgot to put it on today.'

He mistook the reason for the little shudder.

'Do not be alarmed, *chica*. As you see, no harm has come to you without it. But tell me, this has been *such* a wonderful day, *si?* A cattle fair? A religious occasion?'

Dene was silent for a moment. She couldn't tell him that it had been, not the occasion, but the company, which had given the day its significance. But some answer was required of her.

'It was nice to . . . to get away from the house for a few hours,' she said at last.

'You find the villa so oppressive?' He sounded anxious, and Dene thrilled to his apparent concern for her feelings.

'Sometimes,' she admitted. 'It . . . it has a strange atmosphere, especially at night, when the servants have gone home.' She hesitated. 'José said . . . said it was haunted!'

'*Cual estupidez!*' The answer was violent. 'What a nonsense!'

'But . . . sometimes, I've thought he was right,' said Dene, diffident in the face of his scornful denial. 'There . . . there *are* strange noises sometimes, and . . .' Should she tell him about the guitar music? She decided against it. Guitar music was associated with Belinda, and that was forbidden territory. Instead she said: 'It . . . it doesn't seem to be a . . . a happy house.'

'*You* are unhappy here?'

'Not exactly unhappy, more . . . more uneasy.'

'All old houses make strange noises in the night,' Luq said firmly, and then, with emphasis, 'any sounds you hear, Dene . . . any sounds at all . . . remember, they are entirely due to *natural* causes.'

He linked his arm in hers, walking her along the verandah, away from the entrance, as though granting her a reprieve from the final conclusion of her day.

'It was a happy house once,' he said reflectively, 'a home. When we were children, the house was filled with laughter . . . and love. Despite the difference in our ages, José and I were always *amigos*.'

'But you're not now?' Dene ventured to ask him the same question she had put to José. She sensed rather than saw his shrug.

'*Quién sabe?* who knows?'

'Sometimes I think you are . . . sometimes I think you're not.'

'Perhaps that is the way it is. Occasionally, it is possible to forget, and then . . .' He stopped, and Dene held her breath, hoping he would go on, but he seemed to have checked himself, as though he had been about to commit an indiscretion.

Their strolling pace had brought them to a window, through whose partially closed shutters enough light filtered for him to be able to see her face. He halted, resting his hands upon her shoulders, turning her towards him. She looked up at him expectantly, a fluttering sensation at the pit of her stomach. Was this to be the perfect end to a perfect day? Was he about to kiss her? Twice he had kissed her in anger, but now that there seemed to be a truce between them . . . She swayed slightly.

'Do you wish to leave the villa?'

It was not at all what she had expected, hoped . . . and she had to take a moment to steady herself, to command her voice . . . a moment in which she felt his grip tighten on her shoulders.

'I warned you, it would not be an easy post for someone as young as yourself. If you wish to resign . . . ?'

'Are you giving me the sack, before my two months' trial is up?' Dene felt apprehension well within her.

'No.' His voice was grave and she expelled her breath in a silent sigh of relief. 'I am prepared to keep to the terms of our agreement . . . if you are?'

'I want to stay,' she said firmly.

'Even though the daily routine is tedious . . . though the house makes you uneasy?'

'Yes.' Dene could not tell him that she was prepared to bear these twin trials, in order to stay within the orbit of his life . . . even if his visits *were* infrequent. If only she and her patient were in Seville . . . which reminded her . . . 'Luq!'

'*Si?*'

'I think Mrs Travers would be willing now to go to Seville, to have the operation you recommended, if . . . if *you* would operate personally, let her convalesce at the Casa de Léon. If I could accompany her . . .'

'Dene!' He spoke abruptly. 'Do you trust me?'

She caught her breath.

'In . . . in what way?'

He gave a short, cynical laugh.

'Not in the way you perhaps imagine. I am aware that I have been less than a gentleman in our previous encounters. But . . .' his voice was suddenly husky, 'I am a man, and besides being very exasperating, you are also very lovely.' He ran a finger along the curve of her jaw. It was a light, fleeting caress, yet she shuddered at its impact upon her. 'This apology is long overdue. I regret my behaviour . . . especially so as you are affianced . . .'

'And if I weren't?' she couldn't resist asking.

'But you are.' His voice was suddenly harsh. 'You would not

be here if that were not the case. No . . . when I ask if you trust me, I refer not to my integrity as a man, but as a doctor.'

Thank goodness she had not revealed her deception to him. It would look as though she were inviting him to . . . But *why* was it so vital that she be engaged? What possible difference could it make? Had it something to do with José, perhaps . . . his mother's disapproval of her friendship with him? Was she one of these possessive mothers, who thought no girl was good enough for her son . . . or was it *her* nationality? Was Teresa afraid José might marry an English girl, as his cousin had done? But Luq was waiting for her answer.

'Yes, I trust you.'

'You mentioned the possibility of transferring Señora Travers to Seville. True, there was a time when I urged this upon her. I had thought that, with the restoration of her mobility, she would be able to return to her own country, that I would be relieved of a . . . a responsibility. There is nothing here for her . . . since . . .'

'Since she lost her daughter?' Dene said softly.

'Yes!' He snatched at the suggestion so eagerly that Dene had the distinct impression that it was not what he had intended to say.

He was silent for so long that she moved slightly, in an attempt to see his face. As she did so, she caught sight of a flicker of movement behind the partially closed window shutters. Someone had been watching them . . . listening? Some uneasy instinct prompted her to move away from the lighted window. The old house was so rambling that it was not always possible to relate the interior geography to its exterior; and for some reason, Dene felt that it was not politic for their conversation to be overheard.

Luq moved with her, unaware, still talking, his hand at her elbow, making it difficult for her to concentrate intelligently upon his words.

'For the present, I feel it would be more . . .' he hesitated, 'more suitable for the Señora to stay here, at least until Dr Pareja has completed her observations and given me her findings. That is why I ask you to give me your trust, in my capacity as a physician. I know we have disagreed before, as to what is best for our patient, but . . .'

'But you're the doctor,' Dene said quietly, 'and you've been attending Mrs Travers for a long time. I understand. Besides,' she added, 'of course you would want to do what is best for your own mother-in-law.'

'Yes . . . of course.' But there was a reservation in his tone she did not quite understand. 'So you will help me . . . to persuade her to stay here, for the present at least . . . to co-operate with Elena?'

His use of the doctor's first name jarred upon Dene, but she steeled herself to reply calmly.

'Yes, Luq, I'll do whatever I can to help.'

To herself, she added, 'because I love you and I want to have a part in your life . . . however small, however insignificant.'

They had reached the heavy door once more and again Luq paused.

'Thank you, Dene . . . and in my turn, I promise that nothing in this house shall harm you. You need feel no unease.'

'I know.' She attempted a little laugh. 'It's just a silly superstitious feeling I have, that . . .'

'Yes, that is the way to regard it . . . only superstition.'

He opened the door for her, then, on the threshold, raised a lean hand to tilt up her chin, his lips brushing hers in far too brief a caress.

'I am most grateful, *querida*.'

She did not move, willing him to repeat the kiss, to prolong it this time, but a voice broke into the hushed pause of expectancy.

'Goodnight, Dene . . . Luq!' José with his catlike tread had come up the outer staircase, unseen, unheard, his business with Pedro, evidently, concluded.

Dene thought he gave them a curiously penetrating glance, before turning in the direction of his own quarters.

The kiss, the endearment had meant nothing, Dene told herself firmly, as she made her way along the gloomy corridors to her room. He had merely been expressing gratitude for her co-operation; but she could not resist savouring the sound upon her tongue. '*Querida*'. It must be the liquid sweetness of the Spanish word, which imbued it with so much more meaning than its English counterpart, so lightly and casually used.

Her first thought, having gained her room, was to retrieve the lucky charm she had uncharacteristically left behind. But there was no sign of it, even though she searched behind the dressing table to see if, perchance, it had slipped down. At last she gave up the attempt. Perhaps Teresa, ever the conscientious house-keeper, had made her daily check of the rooms, seen it and put it somewhere for safe keeping. Dene yawned. She would ask Teresa in the morning.

It was an effort to remove her make-up, but she performed the nightly ritual, before donning the scrap of chiffon that did duty as nightwear in warm weather. Tired now, she extinguished the lamps and slid gratefully between fresh, crisp sheets.

Then she screamed, and having once screamed, seemed un-able to stop, the sound interspersed with choking hysterical sobs of pure fear.

CHAPTER SEVEN

'*POR DIOS! Qué pasa?*'

It seemed like hours to the terrified girl, but in reality it was only minutes, before the door opened and José, still fully dressed, burst in, immediately relighting the lamps Dene had just extinguished. He was followed immediately by Luq, pulling a short towelling robe about him, while seconds later, Elena Pareja entered, glamorously dishevelled, followed more slowly by Teresa Mañara.

Luq's arrival seemed to restore strength to Dene's limbs, until then paralysed by fear, and leaping from the bed, she flung herself into his arms, heedless of the presence of others, or her scanty, revealing attire.

'*Qué pasa?*' Luq repeated, holding her tightly, as she clung frantically to him, her face buried against the hair-roughened chest revealed by the open V of his robe.

'There . . . there's something in my bed. S-something horrible!'

She felt Luq tense suddenly, heard him mutter.

'*Cristos*—it has begun again! José . . . *por favor!*'

She turned shudderingly in his grasp to watch half fascinated, half afraid, as José strode to the bed, flinging back the covers.

'*Una paloma muerta!*' he exclaimed in tones of deep disgust.

Dene watched, as he picked up the dead pigeon, its buff feathers bloodstained, the head hanging limply awry, then she looked up at Luq's grim, swarthy face.

'Who . . . who on earth would do such a thing?' A small sob escaped her. 'Who in this house dislikes me *that* much?'

She looked around at the others watching her . . . José troubled, Teresa expressionless, Elena maliciously amused.

'*Madre mía*, what a fuss about a small practical joke!' she scoffed.

'It is scarcely that, Elena,' Luq said grimly. 'But come, all of you . . . back to your beds. José, remove that . . . *thing*! Tia Teresa, *por favor* . . . clean sheets?'

Doña Teresa nodded reluctantly.

'And the bed it was only changed this morning,' she grumbled. 'The only task Lucia has completed today . . . since *you* saw fit to deprive me of her services.'

Dene gave Teresa Mañara a startled look. Was she implying that Lucia might have done this? Oh, surely not! Lucia had always seemed so friendly . . . and yet . . . hadn't Luq warned her never to take anyone's motives at face value . . . even his own?

José, after a speculative look at his cousin, left the room, but Elena Pareja lingered.

'Shall I be needed . . . to administer a sedative, perhaps?' Her tone was still mocking.

'Thank you, Elena, but no. *That* will not be necessary.' Luq's tone was polite but determined.

With obvious reluctance the Spanish woman left the room and Dene knew that the other did not relish leaving the two of them together. Alone for a moment, Dene repeated her question, glad of Luq's arms still firmly about her.

'Luq, who would do such a thing? and why?'

'Perhaps Elena was right,' he said with an attempt at lightness, 'maybe it *was* just a joke?'

She shook her head, sapphire blue eyes still reflecting the horror she had felt.

'It was too beastly for that. A practical joke is meant to be . . . well, funny. We used to play jokes on each other at the nurses' home . . . a hairbrush in somebody's bed, a damp sponge. But this . . . this was sadistic . . . a dead bird!' She shuddered again at the remembrance and a gasping sob broke from her as reaction began to set in.

'Perhaps you *should* have a sedative?' Luq suggested, one hand smoothing her hair, as she leant tremblingly against him.

'No . . . no, I'll be all right. J-just don't leave me alone . . . not yet.'

Perceptibly, his clasp tightened and she felt him draw a deep breath, as though to speak, then gently but firmly he released her, as Doña Teresa returned, a set of clean sheets across her arm. Silently, her face grim, she began to strip the bed, removing the soiled, bloodstained linen; and Dene shivered, as a few beige feathers fluttered to the floor.

'*Gracias*, Tia Teresa,' said Luq, 'but you must be tired. I will help Dene to remake her bed.'

Dene thought the older woman was about to protest, but then she set her lips and left the room, shutting the door behind her with the suspicion of a bang. She looked doubtfully at Luq.

'I don't think your aunt approves of you staying here.'

He was showing surprising deftness, as he tucked in the fresh sheets.

'I am here in my capacity as a doctor,' he said, 'you have just suffered an unpleasant shock. Now . . . into bed, *por favor*.'

As he turned towards her, Dene suddenly realised just how inadequate was the protection afforded by her nightdress and saw her realisation mirrored in the depths of his dark eyes. Selfconsciously, she scrambled into the bed, pulling the covers up to her chin.

'Would you like a warm drink?' Luq suggested, half moving towards the door.

'Oh no!' Dene held out one pleading hand. 'D-don't leave me!'

To make her a drink, he would have to go to the kitchen, at the other end of the villa, leaving her alone, and her nerves did not feel steady enough yet.

'Please, Luq . . . we *have* to talk about this. I have to know who it is in this house who hates me. Do *you* know? It can't be any of the servants, can it? It . . . it has to be a member of the family, or . . .' She hesitated, fearing to annoy him.

'Or?' He was quick to take her up, his voice sharp.

'Or Dr Pareja,' she mumbled.

'*Dios!*' Dark eyes widened. 'Why should Elena do a thing so *estupido?*'

'I . . . I don't know,' she faltered.

She couldn't very well reveal her belief that the other woman was his mistress . . . say that perhaps Elena had done it in a fit of jealousy, because Dene and not the doctor had been invited to go to the *feria*.

'I think it would be better if you slept now,' Luq said decisively. 'You are tired . . . not thinking clearly. We are all tired. Lock your door behind me. Nothing more will happen tonight, and tomorrow we will discuss that further, *si?*'

'I . . . I don't think I *could* sleep,' Dene whispered, 'not even with the door locked.' She began to tremble once more at the idea of being alone with her thoughts, remembering that moment when she had thrust her feet down into the bed and encountered . . . that . . .

'Perhaps you would sleep more easily if I stayed here with you?' Luq's voice sounded strangely hoarse, unlike his usual smooth, deep tones.

She stared at him, sapphire-blue eyes widening, cheeks warming at the direction of her own thoughts. What exactly did he have in mind.

'You . . . you mean . . . ?'

'I *mean* that you should lie down and *go to sleep*,' he said, speaking more firmly, but avoiding her gaze. He drew a chair close to the bed. 'See, I will sit here. Give me your hand.'

Obediently she did so, her eyes still wonderingly on his handsome, swarthy face. A new Luq had been revealed to her today . . . a Luq who could think of the pleasures of others, who could be lighthearted and, now, gentle and understanding.

'Close your eyes,' he commanded, and she obeyed him . . . at first supremely conscious of the warm, strong clasp of his hand, then, as fatigue overtook her, drifting into a healing, restoring sleep.

She woke only once during the night, thinking she heard the bedroom door softly open and close, but when she looked, all was quiet Luq was still on guard, though himself in a deep sleep.

When she woke again, the oil lamps had guttered out, but the early light of dawn was filtering through her shutters. Luq's grip had slackened and he was slumped sideways in the chair, his normally austere expression relaxed, looking younger in sleep. Dene lay on her side, content just to study his face, itemising every feature, as though she would imprint his appearance indelibly upon her memory.

An overnight shadow blurred the edges of the square-cut jaw and the firm mouth was gentler in repose, revealing the full sensuality of the lips. His hair, usually immaculately groomed, was tousled, and she studied the blue-black thicket, searching for any traces of grey. There were none.

But then, as he slept on, she began to think about the reason for his presence and a little of last night's horror returned. She would be uneasy, she knew, until she discovered who had placed the dead pigeon in her bed and why.

Eventually Luq stirred, his dark eyes opening slowly, reluctantly, looking about him as if bemused, wondering where he was. Then he was alert, turning to look at Dene, relaxing again, as he registered her safety.

'*Buenos dias*, Dene.'

'Good morning,' she said shyly. 'Th-thank you for staying with me. But you must be terribly stiff, sitting in that chair all night?'

'The bed would have been more comfortable,' he agreed, a faint smile curving his mouth at her furious blush.

He rose, stretching, yawning, like some great cat, she thought, unable to drag her gaze away from his lithe muscularity, barely concealed by the short robe . . . realising, as she had not done last night, that he wore nothing else beneath it.

As though conscious of her fascinated scrutiny, he tightened the belt of the robe and limped briskly towards the door.

'Luq,' she began, 'I . . .'

'You will feel more at ease now it is daylight, and we will meet again at breakfast, *si?*' He seemed suddenly anxious to be gone.

Dene was disappointed that he should be so eager to leave her—and yet what reason had he for wanting to stay? she thought bleakly. Remaining in her room last night had only been, as he had pointed out, the act of a doctor, concerned for someone shocked and distressed. She meant nothing more to him than an employee, someone for whose welfare he felt responsible. He would do as much, no doubt, for Asunción . . . or Lucia. Nevertheless she had to talk to him.

'Luq, you know I have to help Isobel with her bath before breakfast, and I wanted to ask you, while we're still alone, to tell you . . .'

He frowned, interrupting her once more.

'Possibly you do not feel equal to your duties this morning? Would you like me to ask Lucia to . . . ?'

'Oh no!' It would never do to neglect her patient. 'It's not that. I've quite recovered from last night, really.'

And indeed some of her fear *had* vanished with the darkness, and though the incident of the dead bird had been unpleasant it

hadn't actually harmed her. It was just the thought that someone could want to do such a thing to her.

'Then I will see you at breakfast,' he repeated firmly. 'Now is
not the time to talk.'

After his departure, Dene relaxed for a moment or two longer,
knowing that Lucia would be in shortly, with the warm water for
her wash. For an instant she thought longingly of luxuriating in a
deep, warm bath, but there was no bathroom as such at the Villa
Venganza . . . only a rather primitive shower arrangement,
which emitted cold water, piped straight from a mountain
spring.

The water for Isobel's morning bath had to be heated in the
kitchen and lugged along to her bedroom in massive cans, a task
performed every morning by a grumbling Lucia. It would
certainly be more convenient to all concerned, Dene thought, if
arrangements could be made for Isobel to be transferred to
Seville, and she wondered, not for the first time, why Luq, once
in favour of the move, was anxious now to postpone it. But she
had promised not to question his decision.

Lucia had dark shadows under her eyes this morning, eyes
that were also slightly red-rimmed.

'Is something wrong, Lucia?' Dene asked.

'*Nada . . . nada, señorita*,' said Lucia, but she spoke so drearily
that Dene did not believe her.

'Are you sure?' she pressed. 'Is everything all right at home?
Your father . . . your little boy?'

'*Si*, they are both well, *muchas gracias, señorita*.'

'Oh, come on, Lucia . . . it was Dene yesterday!'

'And today you are Señorita again . . . as *he* is Señor once
more.' Lucia's tone was bitter. 'Yesterday, for a while, I thought
that at last he . . . but no, I am a servant . . . good enough to
share the Señor's bed on a lonely winter night . . . to be taken on
an outing like a child. It is not enough that I love him. *I* am no
English *señorita*. I am not good enough to . . .'

Lucia's voice had become more and more indistinct and now
she ran from the room, her sobs still audible, as she fled down the
passageway.

Dene sank back against the pillows, all urge to get up and
begin a new day evaporated, like Lucia's happiness of yesterday.

'Good enough to share the Señor's bed', Lucia had said and, 'I love him'; and there was no doubt as to whom she referred. Her mention of an English *señorita* confirmed that. Luq had fathered Lucia's child, but he had *married* Belinda Travers. Suddenly all the brightness was gone from the day; and it was an effort to make the best of her appearance and put on a cheerful face for her patient. But it had to be done.

She found Isobel agog with curiosity.

'My dear, what *was* all the commotion about last night? I thought I heard someone screaming, and then the sound of running feet.'

Dene had no wish to alarm the older woman, in her handicapped state, but she knew it was no good trying to pretend that nothing had happened, so she adopted her briskest, no-nonsense manner, as she helped Isobel out of bed.

'Just someone playing a very childish practical joke, I'm afraid. I'm sorry if all the noise disturbed you.'

'But what *was* it? Who screamed?' Isobel was not to be diverted, and as Lucia trudged to and fro with her bathwater, her eyes still red and swollen, Dene recounted the previous night's adventures, essayed a laugh, trying to play down the horror of the moment.

Even so, Isobel shuddered.

'My dear Dene, how macabre! Oh, if it had happened to me, I just know I should have died of fright!' Pointedly, she lowered her voice, so that Lucia should not overhear. 'Mind you, dear, you don't surprise me. There have been some very strange happenings in this house ... some particularly nasty tricks played, especially on young girls like yourself. It makes me wonder if *someone* ...' Her eyes flickered towards Lucia ... 'if *someone* isn't jealous.'

'You surely don't mean ... not Lucia? Oh no, I'm sure *she* wouldn't do a spiteful thing like that. What possible reason could she have ... ?'

Dene's voice faltered away, as she remembered her own brief suspicion last night, remembered Lucia's bitter words only a while since. *Did* Lucia resent the presence of other young women at the villa ... seeing them as a threat? She had always seemed perfectly friendly, and yet there it was again ... the recollection that Luq *had* told her not to take anyone's actions at face value.

'These isolated country communities trouble me.' Isobel was

still speaking confidentially. 'So much inbreeding in the old days, you know . . . there still is in villages like Pajaro. Way back, Lucia's family were probably closely connected with the Léons . . . and I'm sure you've heard the story about Luq's ancestor . . . the one who gave the villa its name?'

'Villa of Vengeance,' said Dene. 'Yes, I've heard the story.'

But then, she thought, if Isobel's theory was valid, the characteristics of that ancestor could be in the blood of *anyone* at this villa, not just Lucia's. She shuddered and her hand went to her neck in the old gesture of superstitious propitiation . . . until she remembered . . .

Isobel was quick to notice.

'Oh dear—how unfortunate! You've lost your charm. How did that happen?' And when Dene explained, Isobel looked grave. 'You may be certain, someone has deliberately removed it, for their own reasons, knowing how you depend upon it.'

Dene helped Isobel into the portable bath.

'You said *other* nasty things had happened here?'

Isobel nodded.

'It always begins in the same way . . . harmless enough at first, though distasteful, like your dead pigeon, and then . . .'

'Go on . . .'

'No, dear, I don't think I should. You see, I don't want to alarm you, because then you'd leave, just like the others.'

'The others?' queried Dene.

'The first two nurses I had . . . such sweet, pretty girls. One lasted a fortnight, the second only a week. After that . . .' she sighed, 'Luq hired a succession of dull, elderly women. But they didn't like it here any more than the youngsters, but for different reasons . . . too many inconveniences, no bathroom, no shops, no cinemas.'

'I see,' Dene said slowly, 'but nobody played these . . . unpleasant tricks on the older women?'

'No dear, definitely not.'

A thought occurred to Dene and she wondered if she dared to broach the subject. Would it touch too sensitive a nerve? She helped Isobel out of the fast-cooling water.

'If you'd rather not talk about it, I'll quite understand, but what about when . . . when Belinda was here?'

'*What* about it?' Isobel asked sharply.

'Did ... did *she* have any nasty experiences, like ... like mine?'

'Oh, I see. Yes, there were one or two occurrences ... nothing too bad at first, but the last one ...' Isobel drew a long shuddering breath, 'the last one proved fatal.'

Dene blanched.

'You ... you mean ...' She couldn't bring herself to say it.

'They said it must have been an accident, but it wasn't. Perhaps it wasn't intended as murder, but it had the same effect. Belinda was expecting a child. She was to have gone to Seville for the confinement, but the fright caused premature labour, and she died in childbirth.'

'How absolutely dreadful!' Dene was appalled. She sank on to a chair and looked at Isobel's averted profile. 'I'm *so* sorry ... for all of you. Poor Belinda, poor you, and poor Luq ... losing his wife and his child.'

Isobel was dressed now and she motioned Dene towards the window, pointing out at the concrete balustrade that ran around the verandah.

'You see the space ... there ... where one of the large urns is missing?'

The remaining urns held geraniums, in many different glowing shades.

Dene nodded wordlessly.

'Belinda was strolling on the patio one evening. It was almost dark. The urn fell. It missed her by inches, but ...' Isobel shrugged expressively.

Dene had been certain that Isobel would speak to her of Belinda's death some day, but now that she had there was no pleasure, no triumph in being proved right, only a clammy fear ... fear of what? Her own safety?

Dene was very silent at breakfast and she was aware of veiled, anxious glances from her companions. Doña Teresa was unusually quiet and preoccupied, while Luq and José made desultory attempts at conversation. Asunción served the food; of Lucia there was no sign; possibly she was serving Elena in the parlour.

Doña Teresa broke her silence, bursting suddenly into impassioned speech, her Spanish too rapid for Dene to catch more than a word or two, and for once Luq did not adjure her to speak

English; in fact he and José joined in what soon appeared to be an extremely acrimonious discussion. But she might be mistaken, Dene thought, accustomed as she was now to the extravagant gestures which seemed automatically to accompany their native tongue. Finally, with a defiant look at her nephew, Teresa leant across the table to Dene, pointing her remarks with one stabbing finger.

'Señorita Mason, it would be as well if you left this house, returned to England, before harm comes to you.'

Dene stared at her. It was a warning; but was it a friendly one, out of real concern for her welfare, or had it a more sinister import? The horror of last night brushed her spine once more with icy fingers.

Luq spoke impatiently, his lean features drawn into lines of irritability.

'Take no notice of Tia Teresa, Dene. Have I not promised that no harm shall touch you?'

'How can *you* hope to protect *me*?' Dene burst out, fear giving vehemence to her words, 'when you couldn't even protect your own *wife*?'

The stillness around the table became tangible. Uneasy looks passed between the family. Luq broke the silence first.

'What is this you are saying?'

Dene met his gaze squarely.

'This morning, Isobel wanted to know what all the noise was about . . . she told me about Belinda's 'accident'. She also told me about the two young nurses . . .' Her voice rose an octave. 'Why did José lie to me? Why did he say there had been no other young women here since Belinda? Why did no one play tricks on the older nurses? Who's got it in for young women . . . and why?'

Again the family exchanged glances, closing ranks, she thought, in a conspiracy of silence. Then, with a muttered, unconvincing excuse, José left the table and his mother rose to follow him, casting a darkling glance at Dene as she did so.

'Take my advice, *señorita*. Go, before it is too late.'

Dene looked at Luq.

'Well?' she said sharply, 'are *you* going to explain or are you going to walk away too?'

Luq hesitated before replying, his dark eyes holding hers in an intent stare.

'I asked you once if you trusted me, and you said you did.'

'But that had nothing to do with . . .'

'Please!' He raised one lean hand. 'Hear me out. If you can trust me in one respect, surely it is only logical to trust me in all things?'

Was it? Did that necessarily follow? Could she trust anyone in this house? Doubtfully, she studied his swarthy face, noted the integrity implied by the firm chin, the steady gaze, and remembered that she loved him. Surely her heart, her intuition, could not play her false? Then, slowly, she nodded.

'Yes, I trust you, but I suppose that means you don't intend to tell me anything?'

He sighed.

'Believe me, Dene, I deplore deceit . . . lies for whatever purpose. José *did* mislead you . . . or rather you made an assumption concerning his words and he did not disagree with you . . . but his motives were good. I hope some day to be free to unravel some of our mysteries for you but in the meantime . . .' He leant across the table, covering her hand with his. 'I don't *want* to have secrets from *you*, Dene.' Suddenly his voice was unsteady, the expression in his eyes disturbing. If she had not known that it was impossible, she would have thought . . .

'You expect *me* to trust *you*,' she pointed out, suddenly anxious to relieve the tension which had sprung up between them . . . 'can't *you* trust *me*?'

'Implicitly!' he said with conviction. 'But . . .' and he seemed to choose his words with care, 'there are secrets which it is safer not to possess . . . safer for you, that is. Trust me a little longer, Dene, *por favor?* Some day, I hope . . .' But here he stopped, as if fearing to say too much, and with a rapid change of subject, he added: 'Once again your time is your own today. Elena and I are now ready to discuss the best treatment for Señora Travers.'

Dene came down to earth with a bump and withdrew the hand he still held. Fancy reading any deeper meaning into his touch, his expression, his words. This was as good an excuse as any, she thought bitterly, to closet himself with his mistress, with no fear of being disturbed.

'What will you do?' he asked.

She shrugged. What did he care?

'It looks like a nice morning. I may take a walk.'

'Alone?'

She thought his tone held a hint of suspicion and she supposed he and Doña Teresa still did not trust her where his cousin was concerned . . . and it annoyed her. That was probably the only reason he had joined the outing to the *feria* . . . to play propriety.

'Maybe I'll go alone, maybe not,' she said lightly, turning her shoulder on him, deliberately concentrating on finishing her breakfast, as if it required all her attention.

But she was aware of him, lingering for an instant or two in the doorway, then she heard his uneven tread as he moved away and she relaxed. For a moment she had thought he meant to forbid her to leave the villa. She stacked her plates and carried them over to the sink, where Asunción was up to her elbows in water. An idea was forming.

'Do you know where Lucia is?' she enunciated carefully.

Asunción looked blank, and Dene regretted her meagre knowledge of Spanish.

'Lucia?' she repeated on an upward inflection, and this time a smile of understanding crossed the pump features. '*En casa . . . con* Pedro.'

So, like a wounded animal, Lucia had made for home with her troubles, and Dene's idea became resolution. She would go in search of the other girl. She might just be in a mood to answer questions, particularly if she was aggrieved at something.

As she crossed the patio towards the gateway, she wondered if Belinda had known about Lucia's child. Had she been in ignorance of Luq's treatment of the servant girl, or hadn't she cared . . . had she married him in spite of it? Dene found herself debating a hypothetical case, as she descended the steep, stony track to the village. Just suppose . . . and it *was* the wildest of imaginings . . . just suppose Luq were to ask *her* to marry him. How would *she* feel about his earlier dealings with Lucia? Would she be able to overlook them?

She came to the conclusion that she *could* . . . if only there had not been a child . . . if only Lucia were not in love with Luq. She would not form a third in a tangled triangle of relationships, with Lucia . . . with Elena Pareja.

She wondered if she should go away. There were plenty of excuses she could make . . . elderly parents, her fiancé. Yes, that would be a logical reason . . . her future husband's growing impatience at her absence; and yet, her conscience reminded her, there was Isobel to be considered. Isobel seemed to like her, and she'd had so many disappointments, with a long string of nurses, none of whom had lasted very long. Besides . . . and this really destroyed the only excuse she could concoct . . . Isobel knew she was *not* engaged.

By now she had reached Lucia's house and she postponed the consideration of her own problems.

The door opened to her knock and the stocky Pedro stood there, the expression on his swarthy face decidedly hostile. He said nothing, waiting for her to speak, and she wondered if he understood English.

'Lucia?' she began.

He broke into a torrent of angry speech, and as she had feared, she could not understand a word. But she gathered, more from his manner than anything, that his anger was directed at herself. But why?

'Please . . .' she began again, when he paused for breath, '*por favor*, Señor Pedro. I am a friend . . . *amiga* . . . I only want to help Lucia . . . to help, she repeated, desperately racking her brains for the word, 'to help . . . *ayudar*,' she said triumphantly.

He continued to regard her with suspicion, but perhaps the habitual expression of honesty in her sapphire-blue eyes convinced him, for he gestured towards the crumbling facade of the church next to his house.

'*La iglesia!*'

Then, quietly, firmly, he shut the door in Dene's face.

The grounds surrounding the church were untended, the earth uneven and stony, and looking at the drunken tombstones, Dene wondered how the villagers had ever managed to bury their dead in this hard, uncompromising soil. Before she entered the church, curiosity prompted her to seek out Belinda's grave, for she supposed Luq's wife must have been buried here.

At last she found the grave, in a corner of the churchyard, recognisable by the more recent, unweathered stone of its simple memorial, the inscription being brief. Apart from the date, it simply said 'Belinda, daughter of the late John Travers.' Strangely, there was no mention of a husband, or of the child whose untimely birth had caused her death. The plot was separate from the rest, forming neither a part of the Léon sector, nor of the villagers'.

Poor Belinda, outcast in death, her grave inconspicuous, her name avoided by everyone. No wonder José had claimed that she haunted the villa! Dene felt that its unfeeling inhabitants *deserved* to be haunted . . . and by something far more sinister than this poor defenceless ghost.

Somewhat depressed by her discovery and these thoughts, she turned away and retracing her steps, entered the church, with a doubtful, upward look at its crumbling masonry. She hoped the edifice was not dangerous, not likely to tumble down about her ears.

Inside, it was cool, shadowy and musty with age, the sun filtering through murky, leaded panes, to highlight the outlines of worn flagstones, dusty benches and memorial tablets. Here Dene found more long-dead Léons, and here too was an effigy, lying upon a tomb, its stone garments those of an earlier age, but the features, though crudely carved, were so like Luq's that Dene caught her breath, anguish stabbing at her heart, as she imagined *him* dead. He was not hers, and yet she could imagine the sense of loss.

'He is like the Señor, no?' It was Lucia, moving from the shadows, her face pale, resigned now, as against its earlier, tear-stained rebelliousness. 'He is the ancestor who named the Villa.'

'The one who killed his wife's lover?' Dene could not forbear a shudder at the recollection. She wondered if Luq had been a jealous husband. Dene herself had always resented any possessiveness on the part of her boy-friends, the trait having been very pronounced in Barry's case, and yet if Luq were to become possessive . . . of her . . . she knew she would welcome it, revel in it.

She looked at Lucia, standing silently, staring down at the effigy. Did she come here to brood over this carved replica of her lover, to console herself by dwelling on the stone features as she could not upon their living duplicate?

'The *señorita* likes old buildings?'

'I do,' Dene agreed, 'but I didn't come here to look at the church. I was looking for you.'

The other girl elevated surprised eyebrows, but said nothing.

'Lucia,' Dene said impulsively, 'I know you're unhappy, and I don't mean to pry . . . but let me help you, if I can.'

'How can *you* help *me?*' The words were spoken in a dull monotone, which expressed more convincingly Lucia's sense of despair than had her earlier, dramatic outburst.

'Look, let's get out of this gloomy place into the sunshine,' said Dene, 'and walk . . . the fresh air will do you more good than moping in here.'

'I come here to pray,' Lucia said with simple dignity. 'Man does not use this building any longer, but God and His Blessed Mother are still here.'

However, she followed Dene and moved beside her, their steps turning towards the mountain path, which once Dene had taken with José. The quickest way led back through the unkempt churchyard, past Belinda's solitary resting place . . . and Dene stopped for a moment, to give expression to the thought that troubled her.

'Lucia, why is this inscription so brief? Isn't it normal here to have the husband's name, and *both* parents?'

Lucia shrugged.

'The Señor arranges these things. He did not, apparently, wish his name inscribed, and he did not know the name of the Señora's mother.'

'Isobel, surely?' Dene said.

'Oh no, *señorita!*' Lucia sounded surprised. 'Did you not know? *La Inglesa* was not the mother but the stepmother of Doña Belinda.'

Dene had forgotten Isobel's mention of having lost two husbands.

'Still, Mrs Travers was as fond of Belinda as if she *had* been her own daughter. She still grieves for her.'

'*La Inglesa* grieves for no one but herself,' was Lucia's cryptic reply, and she steadfastly refused to be drawn further, much to Dene's frustration.

As they climbed in silence, she brooded over the Villa and its inhabitants. Did no one in the house like anyone else? She couldn't remember hearing any of them bestow anything but criticism upon each other. Villa of Vengeance, she thought fancifully. *Did* the spectre of Luq's implacable ancestor still hang over the house he had wrested from his enemy, imbuing everyone that lived in it with his own restless, vengeful spirit?

'Lucia, did . . . did you like Doña Belinda?' Dene ventured after a while.

Lucia shrugged.

'It is hard to *dislike* where one pities. She should never have come to Spain, the young *Inglesa*. She did not understand Spanish ways, Spanish men. She liked the men . . . *ola*, *how* she liked them! . . . but to understand is difficult.' She sighed. 'Is difficult even for Spanish girl sometimes.'

'What was she like?'

Don't let her clam up on me, Dene begged inwardly as Lucia gave her an odd look.

'Like? But you know . . . the young *Inglesa* was like you . . . pretty, with the blonde hair, the blue eyes . . .'

'I meant as a person, her . . . her character?'

'Pah!' Lucia blew out on a breath of disgust. 'Me, I did not see what all the fuss was about. She was pretty, *si*. But there was nothing behind the face, no *cerebro* . . . brain, you comprehend?'

Dene nodded.

'She was no wife for Don Luquillo. How could she share the life of such a one? All she think about was the clothes, the perfume, and the books. Never did she dirty the hands, and all day long she strum that guitar, until me, I think I shall go *loca*!'

'But she and Luq got on all right?' Dene prompted.

Lucia's lips tightened and Dene knew that she would learn no more.

'*That* you must ask the Señor . . . if he will tell you.'

They reached the sheltered vantage point of the plateau and Dene sat down, gesturing to Lucia to join her.

'Lucia,' she began diffidently, 'perhaps there *isn't* much I can do to help you, but I *am* a good listener, if you'd like to talk about your troubles. I promise to regard anything you tell me as a confidence.

'You *could* help me,' Lucia's voice was unlike her normally bright cheerful tones, and she almost muttered the words, 'by going away!'

CHAPTER EIGHT

DENE looked at her, startled. She had not expected anything like this. Had Lucia actually sensed her growing attraction towards Luq? She could have sworn she had never revealed it to anyone, either by tone or expression.

'You want me to go away . . . you mean, back to England?'

Lucia nodded, avoiding Dene's eyes.

'But why?' Dene asked, her voice revealing her hurt. 'What have I ever done to you?'

Lucia looked still more uncomfortable. Springing up, she began to pace the rocky ledge.

'Nothing, *señorita*! I admit it freely. It is not your fault. But while *you* are here, I know he will not look at *me*. It is always the same with him . . . the beautiful girls, and especially the English girls, it seems. Why cannot he be content with his own kind? Marry the mother of his child? I have told him, I would be willing to stay here, to make a home for him when he chooses to visit it. I would not want to go to Seville, to embarrass him before his fine, rich friends. I *know* that he loves me, loves our son . . . and yet he makes the excuses . . . always the excuses . . . and I do not believe one of them!' She stamped her feet emphatically, dark eyes flashing.

Dene was temporarily speechless. The implication of Lucia's words left her quite stunned. She had been prepared to hear that he was the father of Lucia's baby, but that he was also an unprincipled philanderer? That was what, in effect, Lucia was saying. Since his wife's death there had been two young English nurses at the villa, both of whom had left after only a short period of time . . . to evade Luq's attentions? That was the only interpretation open to her.

Shame mantling her cheeks, she recalled the two incidents when Luq had made advances to *her*. On both occasions he had been angry, his lovemaking violent, and on the second occasion only José's unlooked for intervention had saved her from . . .

from . . . Yet latterly, Luq had been gentle with her, almost . . . respectful; and she had sensed that he was holding himself in check. Which *was* the real Luq? she wondered miserably. Did she love a man created by her imagination. Did the Luq she loved not even exist?

'You are offended, *señorita*. I spoke clumsily, but I am fighting for what I want . . . for what I love. As a woman, you will understand? You have a *novio* in England. You cannot want *two* men? You are only a *coqueta* . . . a flirt, perhaps?' she suggested hopefully.

'No!' Dene said the word almost violently, then, more gently, 'I give you my word, Lucia, I never intended, never dreamt that anything like this would happen. I'd no idea he had such a terrible reputation . . . that he actually had a child . . . that there'd been other incidents . . . those two young nurses . . .'

'The young nurses?' Lucia queried.

Oh dear, Dene thought. Perhaps she'd put her foot in it, revealed something which Lucia did *not* know. But Lucia *had* mentioned English girls. She hurried on, hoping to cover up any indiscretion.

'I admit I'm attracted to him, but I promise you, it won't go any further . . . nothing will come of it. When I first met him, I didn't even like him very much, but he seems to have a certain . . . I don't know . . . I think you call it "*machismo*"? In any case, for a while I thought he was a married man, until I found out that his wife was dead. And now that I know *you* are in love with him, that he loves you, that your son . . .'

As Dene spoke, her voice becoming more and more agitated, a look of bewilderment replaced Lucia's sombre expression.

'*Señorita, por favor!* I *think* my English it is good, but now I am not so sure. You speak so strangely. Explain more clearly. . . . slowly for me, *si?*'

'What I'm saying, Lucia, is that you needn't have any fears about Luq and me. I . . .' Dene's voice broke slightly on the words, 'I'm going away. I honestly didn't know that you and he . . . that Mateo was his s-son.'

Lucia began to laugh. Her mirth was loud and clear, filling the hillside with its echoes. She jumped up and stood, hands on hips, her lovely head thrown back to show the gleam of faultless, white teeth.

At first Dene was furious that Lucia should find her confession amusing, but then she began to wonder if the other girl were hysterical with relief; and, her training asserting itself, was just about to administer a good hard slap, when Lucia suddenly sobered.

'*Señorita*,' she said and the old sparkle was back in her dark, lustrous eyes, 'I think you should come with me . . . I have something to show you.'

And despite Dene's urgent questioning, Lucia refused to say another word, hurrying down the hillside with a light, sure tread, so that Dene, less familiar with the terrain, had perforce to slip and slither in pursuit. Lucia did not pause until she reached the door of her father's house. Here she did hesitate.

'The *señorita* will not object to entering a humble home?'

'Don't be silly,' Dene rejoined.

'Then please to enter, *señorita* . . . *mi casa*, *su casa*!' The words were said with a quaint, courteous formality.

The living room of the house though sparsely furnished was scrupulously neat, immaculately clean . . . as was its sole occupant.

'*Mi papá*,' Lucia introduced.

Pedro inclined his head stiffly in Dene's direction, then interrogated Lucia in rapid Spanish, to which she replied with much gesticulating, her tone at first placatory, then with increasing humour, until father and daughter were openly laughing, while Dene watched them with growing bewilderment.

At the sound of Lucia's voice, a small boy entered from another room at the rear and the girl swooped upon him, lavishing kisses and embraces upon him.

When Dene had seen the child before, it had been from a distance, his figure shadowed by the doorway and the bulk of the man holding him. But now, as Lucia held out the boy for her inspection, she gasped and a sudden wild elation swept through her, her eyes going to Lucia's for confirmation that they had not deceived her.

The boy, Mateo, a sturdy child, regarded her with brilliant blue eyes, beneath a tangle of golden-fair curls . . . with the eyes of *José Mañara*!

If Dene had any lingering doubts, they were swept aside, as a woman entered the room, taking the child from Lucia, nursing

him against the bosom of her black dress with every sign of
affection . . . Teresa Mañara.

'You seem surprised, Señorita Mason,' the older woman said
drily.

'I am.' Dene admitted it frankly. 'I knew, of course, that Lucia
had a son, but I thought . . .'

'She thought the *papa* was Luq!' Lucia gurgled, then breaking
once more into her own language, she reeled off a spate of words,
amongst which Dene recognised her own name and that of Luq
constantly repeated.

A look of grim amusement crossed Teresa Mañara's sallow
face, but she made no comment.

'He's a lovely child, Lucia,' Dene said warmly. 'You must be
very proud of him.'

She felt so happy that she would have praised the child
whatever his appearance, but he really was beautiful, his features expressive of intelligence and with a trace of the Léon
arrogance already evident.

Lucia spread her hands.

'I am proud of my son, *si* . . . but of me, I have only shame.'

'Because . . . because you're not married?' Dene ventured
gently, 'But *why* won't José . . . ?'

'Because, *señorita* . . .' it was Doña Teresa who interrupted,
'because my son is *malvado*!'

Dene, thinking of José's bright good looks, his friendly, engaging manner, felt bound to protest.

'Oh, surely not a villain, *señora* . . . thoughtless, perhaps, even
immoral, but I'm sure he's not wholly bad?' Her eyes went to
Lucia's beautiful face, luminous with love.

'No, *señorita*,' Lucia said softly, 'he is not *malo*, but nevertheless
he will not marry, will never marry, he says. It is a vow which he
has taken.' The sigh which accompanied her words was as heavy
as the burden borne by her heart, and she took her son from
Teresa's arms, burying her face in his golden curls, as if he alone
was her consolation.

All this time Pedro had been silent, looking keenly from one
face to the other. It seemed now that he had reached a decision,
for he rose, crossed the room towards Dene and bowing formally,
extended his gnarled, weatherbeaten hand.

'*Perdóname, señorita.*'

'*Mi papá* asks your pardon, *señorita*,' Lucia explained. 'I had led him to believe . . . as I did, that you were *enamorada* with José. I realise now that it was my own fears which misled me . . . my fears, and the shadows of the past.'

Dene took the outthrust hand and shook it warmly, her smile expressing for her what her tongue could not.

'*Gracias*, Pedro!' She turned to Lucia. 'You mentioned the past. Lucia . . . the two nurses. Who . . . Did . . . did José . . . ?'

Lucia smiled gently, shaking her head.

'No, *señorita*. The two English girls, they were foolish, empty-headed creatures. Each in turn fancied themselves enamoured of Luq. Let him see their infatuation . . . let all around see it. That is why he refused to employ young women, until you came. He wanted no . . . no . . .'

'Further complications!' Señora Mañara supplied the words briskly, with a look of . . . was it warning? . . . in her dark eyes, as she spoke, and Lucia nodded.

Dene felt herself growing hot with embarrassment. *She* had revealed her feelings towards Luq, knew that Lucia had passed on the intelligence to her father and, worse still, to Teresa Mañara. They would be regarding her in the same light as those two other young women, and knowing Doña Teresa, Dene felt sure that Luq would be told of her indiscretion. The conviction grew within her that now she too would be dismissed. Luq, it was obvious, wanted no more emotional entanglements in his life. Elena Pareja probably supplied all that he wanted from a woman; and it would not suit Teresa Mañara for her nephew to marry again.

Dene could not help remembering Isobel's statement that Teresa coveted the Léon property and fortune for her son . . . and now it was obvious that she approved of Lucia and adored the boy Mateo. She felt that if anyone could overcome José's opposition to marriage, it would be his mother . . . with a view to her grandson's eventual inheritance.

Teresa moved towards the door.

'You will give me your company back to the villa, Señorita Mason?'

Despite Dene's misgivings, Doña Teresa's manner towards her was subtly warmer. But of course, she had forgotten . . . as far as everyone at the villa was concerned, except Isobel, *she* was already engaged to be married. They probably did not consider her a serious threat to their plans. A mild infatuation for one's employer could speedily be dispelled once the employee had been dismissed and returned to the care of her fiancé. At least that was how Teresa's mind would work . . . not knowing of Dene's deliberate falsehood.

'Yes, I'm coming,' Dene replied. 'But there's just one thing I *must* ask Lucia.' She looked the other girl straight in the eyes. 'Forgive me if I'm wrong, but did *you* put the pigeon in my bed?'

Her regard was as steadily returned.

'No, *señorita*. I give you my word.'

Their eyes held in a long, unwavering glance, then Dene nodded.

'I believe you, Lucia . . . thank you.'

This was the first time she had felt at all comfortable in Teresa Mañara's company, Dene thought, as they made their way back, up the hill towards the villa.

'You are wondering about my son, perhaps, *señorita*?' Teresa said abruptly. '*Why* he will not marry Lucia, as he should . . . does not support her?'

'Yes.' With her habitual honesty, Dene admitted to curiosity. 'Though of course,' she added hastily, 'it's none of my business.'

'He *would* support her,' Teresa said slowly, 'so far as his means allow. But Pedro will not permit. He has pride, that one. For his daughter, he demands the justice of marriage . . . nothing less, and Luq and I agree with him. We should like to see Lucia and José married.' She looked at Dene with wry amusement. '*You* find that strange, *si*? You who accused us of arrogant pride?'

'I'm beginning to realise that I've been wrong about a lot of things,' Dene said soberly.

They walked on, each in thoughtful silence. But at the gateway Dene turned to Teresa once more.

'But if you and Luq approve and Pedro wishes it, *why* won't José marry Lucia? She said he would never marry . . . that he had made a vow. Why?'

Teresa's steps slowed to a halt. Suddenly she looked her age, weary, dispirited.

'He has many reasons, *señorita* . . . some have their origins buried amidst things that are best forgotten. Do not seek to know more, I entreat you.' She hesitated, then: 'I meant what I said to you this morning, in all seriousness, and I say it to you again. Go home, *señorita*, to your own people, while you still may.'

'*Señora*,' said Dene, as the other woman turned away, 'I . . . I suppose *you* haven't seen my lucky charm . . . a black cat on a silver chain?'

'I have seen you wear such a thing,' Doña Teresa admitted. 'I cannot approve of such superstitious, irreligious nonsenses . . . our women they wear the medallion, or the Holy Crucifix.'

'Yes, yes, I know, but . . . well, it means a lot to me, and I seem to have mislaid it. I wondered if you . . .'

Teresa shook her head.

'No. If I had found it, much as I disapprove, your property would have been returned to you.' She nodded dismissively and continued on her way.

For the next few days, Dene was embarrassed every time she encountered Luq, feeling sure that his aunt would have told him everything . . . of *her* belief that he was Mateo's father . . . of her unguarded revelation of her feelings for him. But no comment was forthcoming and as there was nothing in his manner to indicate that he knew of her misapprehension, she began to relax once more. Not that she saw a lot of him, she thought wistfully; he seemed either to be working in his study, or in conference with the attractive Elena Pareja.

'You've had no more unpleasant experiences, then?' Isobel quizzed her, one morning two or three days later.

'No, thank goodness,' Dene laughed. 'Whoever it was must have realised that I don't scare that easily. Besides, I've taken your advice ever since . . . I keep my door locked.'

'Very wise, dear,' Isobel approved. 'But you *will* take extra special care at night, won't you . . . don't wander on the patio after dark. I can't help remembering what happened to Belinda . . .'

'Isobel!' Dene interrupted. 'Haven't *you* any idea of who was responsible for . . . for the incidents? You've known these people much longer than I have.'

Isobel nodded.

'Of course I *know* who did it, dear, but knowing isn't the same as being able to prove it, is it? and of course these people would stick together. It would only be my word against theirs.'

'You wouldn't tell me, I suppose? After all, things have begun to happen to me.'

Isobel shook her head decidedly.

'Oh no, dear. As I said, I've no *proof*, and you might be in even more danger if someone thought you *knew*. But just remember one thing . . . jealousy and possessiveness are very dangerous emotions.' Then, with a deliberate change of subject: 'I don't suppose you know what Luq has decided . . . about my case? He and that Dr Pareja come and go, but they never discuss anything in front of me, and they tell me absolutely nothing.'

'I don't know any more than you,' Dene confessed. 'In fact, just lately I've felt as if I'm not really needed here. If it wasn't that I thought you and I had become good friends, that I could still be of use to you, I really don't think I should feel justified in staying.'

Isobel sighed deeply.

'Well, I don't want to be selfish, dear. I wouldn't dream of influencing you in any way, holding you back . . . if you want to be off to pastures new . . .'

Isobel's brave attempt at a smile wrung Dene's always tender heart.

'Of course I wouldn't *dream* of leaving you,' she said stoutly. 'And I'll see if I can find out what treatment Luq has decided on.'

'Would you really, dear? I'd be so grateful. I never see him alone these days. That woman is always with him. Quite honestly, I don't see what useful purpose she serves. Do you know, she's never once examined me?'

Dene sought an interview that evening, after dinner. Hitherto, she had hesitated to go to Luq's study uninvited, especially since she had unwittingly betrayed her feelings to Lucia and through her to Teresa. She was relieved to find him alone, however, for she did not relish questioning him under the supercilious gaze of Elena Pareja.

'This is an unexpected pleasure,' he commented, as in response to her gentle knock he opened the door. 'What can I do for you?' His dark eyes narrowed and he scanned her face intently. 'You are not troubled about anything? Nothing has happened to . . .'

'No, no, nothing like that. I wanted to talk to you . . . about Mrs Travers.'

'I see.'

He reseated himself behind his desk, motioning her towards the chesterfield. The feel of its cool leather against her bare legs brought back a flood of memories of being in Luq's arms on this very spot and she felt herself colouring. But if he noticed, he made no comment. He'd probably forgotten the incident, she thought sadly.

'What about Señora Travers?' His tone was guarded.

'She's anxious to know what conclusions you've reached . . . what treatment you and Dr Pareja intend. She's a little concerned, because she never has an opportunity to discuss it with *you* . . . alone. I . . . I don't think she has much faith in Dr Pareja.'

'But *I do* have faith in Elena,' Luq replied gravely, 'which is what counts.'

'Of course, *he would*,' Dene thought miserably. Naturally he would have no fault to find with a mistress who was both glamorous *and* an intellectual on his own level.

Luq was waiting courteously for her to continue.

'*Have* you decided what to do, because if so, I do think you ought to . . .'

Her voice trailed away as he elevated dark eyebrows, his face taking on an expression of extreme hauteur.

'Since when have *you* been the arbiter of *my* actions . . . *Nurse*?'

It was a deliberate snub, the emphasis on her status, instead of using her name.

'I . . . . I'm sorry, I didn't mean to sound as if . . . as if I was telling you what to do, but after all, it *is* Isobel's future you're deciding, and in common humanity . . .'

'Humanity has many facets,' Luq said repressively. 'Be assured that when we have decided on the best course of action, that decision will be speedily implemented.'

'I don't see why it's taking so long,' Dene argued. 'Either Isobel needs an operation or she doesn't. I should have thought you'd had long enough to . . .'

Again his expression stopped her in mid-sentence.

'Oh, all right,' she said wearily. 'I can see you don't intend to tell me anything; but I think it's a bit unfair. After all, I *am* Isobel's nurse, and if I'm to do my job properly . . .'

'Tell me, Dene . . .' His tone was more friendly now and her heart lifted a little at the sound of her name on his lips once more. 'Tell me, you get on well with Isobel, *si?*'

'Yes, of course.' Dene was surprised. 'Why else should I be so concerned about her welfare?'

'You talk to her . . . exchange confidences?'

'Yes . . . yes, we do. She's a lonely woman, Luq. She needs . . .'

'I recall telling you, on the occasion of our first meeting, that this position would require certain qualities. I mentioned tact and discretion. You remember?'

Dene nodded. She had forgotten none of the incidents of any of her encounters with Luquillo de Léon . . . all were indelibly etched upon her memory.

Luq rose from behind his desk and strolled across the room, seating himself beside Dene with an abstracted air.

She tensed, recalling again the last time they had shared this chesterfield . . . but he was still speaking, looking at her with an intent scrutiny now, that was half analytical, half ruefully amused.

'You have such honest eyes, Dene.'

It was totally unexpected and the nearest he had come lately to paying her a compliment. To her annoyance, she felt her colour rising. What was she supposed to say? Was she supposed to say anything at all? What were her eyes revealing to him? Hastily she lowered her gaze, lashes sweeping warm cheeks.

'And you blush easily,' he continued, heightening her discomfort. 'Could you tell a lie?'

The question was rapped out suddenly, disconcertingly, and she looked at him wonderingly. Had he, somehow, found out that her engagement was a fiction, that she had lied *to him*? Had Isobel . . .? Was that why he'd asked if she confided in her patient?

'I . . . I suppose I could, if there was a good reason for doing so,' she temporised, and waited for him to tell her that he knew of her falsehood.

But he was shaking his dark head.

'I do not think a lie would rest easily on your conscience. You are too transparently honest and if you lied, you would colour up prettily, thus . . .'

One lean hand brushed her still warm cheek, his touch having the quality of a caress, and she tried to disguise as a cough, the shuddering breath that escaped her.

She met his gaze with troubled eyes. If he had not discovered her lie of convenience, what was this conversation all about ... or was he merely trying to change the subject, to divert her from her purpose?

'We *were* talking about Isobel,' she reminded him.

'And we still are,' he assured her. 'You see, Dene, Elena and I ...' a small sick feeling filled her throat at the easy way in which he paired his name with that of the glamorous doctor ... 'Elena and I have almost concluded our deliberations. We think we are in agreement as to our future course of action. But ...' he hesitated, 'but Isobel may not necessarily agree with our findings. If I told you what we have in mind, would you be capable of dissimulation, of pretending that you were in complete ignorance of our plans?'

'You ... you mean ...' Dene's voice rose indignantly, 'you don't intend to tell Isobel what treatment she's to receive? Surely you can't do that ... it isn't ethical? She'd have to sign a consent form for any operation ...'

'Dene ... Dene!' He spread his hands in an exaggerated gesture of despair. 'You see! Already you are fighting me, and you have not even heard what I intend. I am not saying that Isobel will not know *eventually*. As you say, it would be unethical to perform an operation without her consent, but it may not come to that ...'

'No operation, you mean?'

'Perhaps not. Elena thinks, and I agree with her, that we should have Isobel in hospital for ... for more tests and observation before any final decision is made.'

'Hospital ... in Seville?' Dene's face brightened. 'But that's exactly what she ...'

'Not necessarily in Seville,' Luq interrupted. 'It may be that other, more suitable facilities can be provided elsewhere.'

'But I know she'd rather go to Seville, be under *your* care ...'

'Dene, in your years of nursing, haven't you learnt yet that the patient does not always necessarily know what is best for him or her?'

'Yes, but ...'

'Well, in this case, we feel that the Rivera hospital is perhaps not the answer.'

'All right,' Dene said slowly. 'I suppose I must accept that you know best.'

'Thank you,' he said drily.

'But I *will* be able to go with her, won't I?'

'No!'

'Why not?' Dene was really dismayed now. If she was not to accompany her patient, that meant there would no longer be any need for her to remain in Spain. It meant she would be sent back to England, that she would never see Luq again.

'The hospital we have in mind has its own trained staff, far better equipped to deal with . . . such cases . . .'

'So when do I have to leave, then?'

Dene had to swallow hard to keep back the threatening tears. She wished she had never come to Luq's study, pressed him for an answer. At least she would have had a few more days of her fool's paradise . . . believing that the truce he had initiated might grow into something else. What an idiot she'd been! Just because she'd discovered that José and not Luq was the father of Lucia's son it didn't mean that Luq was necessarily available. There was still Elena Pareja. She turned her head away, so that Luq would not see the unnatural brightness of her eyes.

She felt his hand rest on her shoulder, his voice oddly tender as he said:

'No dates have been settled yet. It is a question of availability of hospital space, you understand? This problem is common enough in England also, I believe?'

'Yes . . .' she nodded, her voice muffled, unsteady.

'You would be *so* unhappy to leave Spain?' he queried, the hand that had touched her shoulder now touching her damp cheek, turning her head towards him.

Wordlessly, she nodded, unable to meet his eyes.

'Why *is* this? Have you not a good family to return to . . . a fiancé eagerly awaiting you?'

'No!' She choked on the word. Suddenly it was important that there should be no more lies between them. Before she left, he *had* to know the truth about her.

'No home . . . no family?'

'No fiancé!' she said flatly, and was appalled by the ferocity of his expression.

'What is this you tell me? No fiancé? He has broken off the engagement?'

'There never was any engagement.'

The eyes on either side of the arrogant nose were dark, twin fires of anger.

'Explain this to me, *por favor?* Am I to understand that you have *lied* to me?'

'I suppose you're shocked,' she said, lifting her head defiantly to face him. 'It must be quite a shock for you to be proved wrong. You were so certain that I couldn't tell a lie.'

'You are *proud* of this?' he asked incredulously, 'that you are capable of deception?'

'No . . . no, I'm not proud of myself. I didn't intend to lie to you, but when you refused to employ me, threatened to send me back to England, I wanted to impress you with the inconvenience I'd gone to in order to come to Spain . . . to work for you; and when I mentioned a fiancé, it . . . it seemed to make some sort of difference. You . . . you seemed to change your mind. So then I *couldn't* tell you that . . .'

'I see! So why have you chosen this moment to enlighten me?'

'I've never been happy about it,' Dene said earnestly. 'I've always felt guilty, and when you . . . you said I had honest eyes, I . . . I felt so ashamed, I had to tell you the truth. When you asked me if I could tell a lie, I thought at first that Isobel had told you, though she promised . . .'

'Isobel! Isobel? *What* did you think Isobel had told me?'

'That . . . that I wasn't engaged . . .'

'*Caramba!* You told *Isobel?* When?'

'Only . . . only recently,' she assured him, 'and only because she seemed concerned that I might not be able to stay with her after her operation. That's why I . . .'

'There is no question of your staying with Isobel when she leaves here. I thought I had made that clear.'

'But I didn't *know* that when I told her,' Dene said reasonably. 'I'm sorry if you're annoyed because I told her and not you, but I was afraid you'd send me away . . .'

'Ah yes, now we come full circle. *Why* are you so anxious not to leave Spain?'

Impossible to think of a convincing reason, which did not involve telling the truth.

'I just don't want to,' she mumbled, 'that's all.'

'You are *happy* here?' His tone was incredulous. 'I understood that this place made you uneasy, that you were bored . . . ?'

Dene shrugged.

'I . . . I suppose I've got used to it.'

'There is someone here, perhaps, that you are attached to . . . is that it?'

His dark gaze was penetrating and she felt herself colouring. Oh, surely Doña Teresa hadn't told him after all? It would be too humiliating, when he wasn't the slightest bit interested in her.

He gave a short, humourless laugh.

'As I observed before, you have a transparently honest face.' He looked at her broodingly. 'This was one of my objections to employing a young, impressionable girl.'

He was thinking of the two nurses who, according to Lucia, had become infatuated with him. Dene opened her mouth to deny that she was as foolish, but he forestalled her.

'I am aware, of course, that Europeans find bullfighting immensely glamorous, that silly young girls are apt to have their heads turned by the colour, the spectacle of a handsome young man pitting his strength against the bull.'

What on earth was he talking about?

'Have you ever been to a *corrida*, Dene?'

'No.' She was relieved by this change of subject, however irrelevant. 'But I'd like to. I don't suppose I ever shall now.'

'Perhaps it would be a salutary experience,' he said grimly. 'Perhaps you would see José in a different light . . . particularly if I took you backstage, to see the less attractive aspects of his life.'

Now Dene understood, and she was flooded with relief. Doña Teresa had said nothing. She couldn't have done. Luq obviously thought, as everyone else had done, that she was attracted by José . . . the Golden Spaniard. With the realisation, her face cooled. Since Lucia and Teresa Mañara knew the truth, it would do no harm to allow *Luq* to continue in his misconception, if only to save her own face.

'Could I really go to José's next fight? He *did* ask me,' she said, deliberately infusing extra enthusiasm into her voice.

He shrugged, his tone irritable.

'Who knows? And now, perhaps, you had better look in on your patient . . . and not a word, please, of what we have discussed in this room.' Drily he added, 'If necessary you will have to exercise the skill I thought you incapable of. You will have to lie.'

'Oh!'

With a furious glare at him, Dene swept towards the door. So now he was going to keep throwing that up at her! He caught her before she had time to turn the handle, one lean hand supporting his full weight against the wooden panels.

'I have your promise? You will not discuss my proposals for her treatment with Mrs Travers?'

'How can I,' she returned pertly, 'when I don't even know what they are?'

'That's no answer, Dene. You know enough to disturb your patient, if you should inadvertently . . .'

'All right,' she said irritably, 'I promise. I won't say a word. I'll act the dumb blonde.'

His free hand came up to lift a strand of the silky hair, released from its daytime bondage.

'Like liquid silver,' he said, his voice suddenly husky, 'but *you* are no dumb blonde, Dene. I wish . . .'

She looked at him expectantly, but he did not finish his sentence. It was a habit she had noticed increasingly in him of late, a habit which did not accord with his normal forceful and positive manner. His hand still toyed with her hair as though reluctant to release it and his eyes seemed riveted to the sight of her mouth, as, nervously, she licked suddenly dry lips. He was so close to her, the air between them so fraught with tension, she thought that surely it must end as on those other occasions, when he had kissed her with such hungry ferocity, and she knew she was longing for just that to happen. It even seemed to her that he swayed a little closer, or perhaps her own body moved; but then, frustratingly, he stood upright, removing his hand from the door, no longer impeding her exit.

'Tia Teresa tells me your talisman is lost. Is this so?'

She nodded, her eyes still wistfully upon the sensual lines of his mouth.

'And this troubles you, *si?*'

'A little,' she admitted.

He hesitated, then drew from his pocket an oval medallion, suspended from a heavy silver chain.

'Would you consider wearing this in its place? It is one of my own . . .'

'But . . . but you may need it yourself.'

He smiled.

'I have many such. I shall not miss it and it would please me if you would consent, unless . . . unless you find the symbols of our religion distasteful to you?'

'Oh no . . . no, of course not!'

Dene would have accepted the medallion in any case, knowing that at some time it had hung around *his* neck, been *warmed* by his flesh.

'Then allow me . . .'

She held her breath as he placed the chain around her neck, lifting the heavy hair in order to do so . . . perhaps now he would . . . But he turned away towards his desk.

'Run along, little nurse,' he said. His voice was still throaty, but after a moment's hesitation, while she hoped he would change his mind and call her back, Dene slipped from the room.

Isobel was sitting up in bed, eagerly awaiting her.

'Well?' she said, before Dene had even closed the door. 'What did he say?'

Dene had taken two or three deep breaths before entering, and it seemed to be effective, for her voice was steady and she did not colour up as she answered.

'Nothing really . . . nothing positive.'

'You mean they *still* haven't decided?' Isobel's voice was irritable. 'After all this time?'

Automatically, Dene straightened her patient's pillows.

'I suppose they've got to be absolutely certain,' she murmured, 'for *your* sake.'

'And when they *have* decided, will you be allowed to nurse me?'

'I . . . I don't know.' Surely this was something she could answer without revealing what Luq had said. 'I . . . I've been wondering about that. Surely the hospital will have their own nurses. They wouldn't want me in the way.'

'Oh, not at the hospital,' Isobel agreed, 'but afterwards, when I'm convalescing, at the Casa de Léon. I *am* going to convalesce there?'

'I really don't know.' Dene was suddenly anxious to get away from this awkward catechism. 'Luq doesn't confide in me. He . . .'

'Well, what *have* you been talking about all this time?' Isobel said impatiently. 'It's ages since you said you'd go and talk to him.'

Dene smiled. This was safer ground.

'Well, we did sidetrack a little. I remember we discussed bullfighting. Luq doesn't seem to think much of it, does he? That surprises me, in a Spaniard.'

'So you didn't devote that much time to my case?'

'Oh, we did . . . we did,' Dene assured her hastily. 'We discussed that first . . . the rest came later, just before I left him.'

'So you *did* discuss me!' Isobel said triumphantly. 'I knew you were prevaricating.'

'Well, perhaps discuss wasn't quite the right word.' Dene was beginning to feel flustered. 'After all, it's not as if I'm his equal. He probably discusses you with Dr Pareja. I'm only the nurse. I questioned him, and he said that they hadn't reached any decision yet.'

Isobel's misshapen hand grasped Dene's wrist for a moment, so tightly that it hurt.

'You're not lying to me, Dene? I know you *can* tell lies, remember?'

'Isobel, please, you're hurting me!'

'I'm . . . I'm sorry.' Isobel released the bruised wrist and groped feverishly beneath her pillow for a handkerchief, which she applied to her eyes. 'It's just so awful . . . day after day, not knowing . . . wondering . . . and I *can't* get Luq to talk to me about it. He always has that dreadful woman tagging on . . .'

'I understand,' Dene said sympathetically. 'Really I do . . . and I'm sure they'll make up their minds soon.'

Surreptitiously, she rubbed her wrist, but Isobel noticed.

'Oh dear, did I do that? I'm so sorry, my dear. I wouldn't have hurt you for the world.'

'It's all right,' Dene told her. 'See, it's only a bit red.'

Nevertheless, it was surprising, she thought, as she hurried along the shadowy passageway to her own room, just how much strength Isobel had left in her twisted fingers.

It was quite early, the earliest Dene had been in bed since her arrival at the Villa, and she decided to read for a while. After all the trouble she had experienced, getting hold of some reading matter, she thought wryly, this was her first opportunity to look at Belinda's books.

She locked her door. She had kept up the habit, even though there had been no more incidents . . . locking the door in the daytime, when she was absent, and again at night before she retired. Window shutters tightly closed and the room illumined by the soft light of the lamps, it was quite cosy, and she propped herself up against her pillows and began to look through the books, studying the brief synopsis inside each, to see which one promised the most interesting read. A stiff piece of card slid from between the pages of a book. She picked it up and turned it over, catching her breath as she saw the picture postcard.

It was a photograph of José in the full panoply of a bullfighter. With no Luq to show up his lack of inches, he looked tall, arrogant and elegant, in a turquoise-blue suit of lights, which set off his tanned good looks and crown of golden hair. There was a slight smudge on the otherwise pristine surface of the photograph, and turning it this way and that to catch the light, Dene drew in her breath. The smudge was undoubtedly lipstick. As a bookmark or as a memento of a famous cousin-in-law, the photograph was innocent enough . . . but the lipstick stain imbued it with a deeper significance. Dene stacked the books on the bedside table and extinguished the lamps, then fell asleep still pondering over her accidental discovery.

She had no idea how long she had been asleep, when she was woken, and at first she could not think what had disturbed her. Then she heard it, recognised it . . . those strident, discordant notes . . . guitar music. Dene felt the perspiration start out over her body . . . was this the prelude to something unpleasant? Then she realised she could smell burning . . . not the final guttering odour of oil lamps, but of burning cloth, singeing wood. Hastily she reached for the torch which, nowadays, she kept close at hand. Its beam picked out the steadily increasing grey pall that curled insidiously under her door. The house must be on fire! She must give a warning.

Without pausing to put on her dressing gown, she ran to the door and unlocked it, throwing it wide, then leapt back with a shrill cry of alarm as the smouldering papers and what looked like a charred blanket blazed into flames inches from her feet. She turned and ran for the window, throwing open the shutters. Outside it was light, the night was over, but there was no escape that way. She had forgotten the iron grilles that barred every window in this house.

The flames in the doorway were leaping higher. It would be foolhardy to attempt to jump across them in her flimsy night-dress and she looked around for something with which to beat them out. The bedside rug was the only possibility. She had just begun her frenzied desperate attempt, the thick rug heavy in her hands, when she heard the sound of running feet, and Lucia appeared, followed by Luq, clad only in a pair of trousers, his feet and torso bare, and she heard him swear.

'*Hija de diablo!* Dene, throw me the rug. Lucia ... water, quickly!'

As Lucia turned about to do his bidding, Dene, with the last of her strength, flung the heavy rug through the smoke and flames and stumbled back, dazed and choking with the fumes, as he began a vigorous onslaught. Once Lucia returned with a pitcher of water, the last of the conflagration was soon extinguished and Luq stepped through the door, heedless of the wet ashes adhering to the lower edges of his trousers, clinging to his bare feet.

Somehow it seemed natural to collapse into his outstretched arms, to nestle against the roughness of his muscular chest.

'Oh, Luq!' was all she could manage to say, as he held her closely, and she could feel him shaking with a reaction almost as great as her own. At last he held her away, surveying her closely.

'Are you hurt ... burnt?'

She shook her head.

'No, but I was so scared. Luq, I heard someone playing the guitar again ... I ...' She swayed, and with a muttered imprecation, he swung her up into his arms and carried her along the passageway.

As they passed Isobel's room, her anxious face looked around the door and frightened eyes took in their dishevelled appearance.

'Whatever is wrong? I thought I heard a scream, and . . . and I smelt burning. I was terrified! I thought the whole house was on fire and I should be burnt alive in my bed. I called out, but nobody came,' she said reproachfully.

'Everything is under control,' Luq said brusquely. 'As you are unharmed, I suggest you go back to bed. Dene is the one who has suffered most.'

Dene struggled slightly in his grasp.

'I'll be all right now, Luq, I'm sure I will. If Isobel needs me, I . . .'

But his arms tightened.

'I will send Lucia to Señora Travers. *You* are coming with me.'

She had expected Luq to enter his study, but it was his own bedroom to which he carried her . . . a room she had never entered. He set her down on his bed and began a minute inspection of her hands and feet.

'No burns,' he said at last, and sat down rather abruptly on the edge of the bed, pressing his face into his hands.

'Luq?' She regarded him anxiously. 'Are *you* all right?'

He raised his head.

'*Sí* . . . just for a moment, I was imagining what could have happened, remembering . . .'

She shivered and immediately he was all concern, enfolding her in one of his own blankets, holding her in the circle of his arms. She closed her eyes, relaxing thankfully against him. This was heaven! It was almost worth being nearly burnt alive, to be held in Luq's arms, to know that he was concerned for her. She felt his arms tighten and knew that concern had become awareness. Confidently, she lifted her face to his, knowing that this time he would kiss her . . . and she was not disappointed.

His lips were as feverish and possessive as they had been on other occasions, but with one subtle difference . . . they were not angry, punishing, but sensuously demanding, drawing from her an all too ready response. Her arms escaped from the blanket to encircle his neck, her hands plunging into the thickness of the blue-black hair, pulling his head closer, to deepen his kiss, arching against him, so that the covering he had pulled about her fell away entirely, leaving nothing between his hands and her flesh but the flimsy material of her nightdress.

The warmth of his hands, the feel of his hard body pressed to hers, were arousing sensations she had never dreamt possible until she had met Luq de Léon, and she knew that he was not unaffected by their proximity, the intimacy of their situation. Somehow it seemed more exciting, more disturbing to realise that it was *his* bed upon which they lay together, straining against each other, as though they could never be close enough. Her hands caressed the naked warmth of his upper torso, thrilling to the silken smoothness of the flesh, stretched taut over steely muscles, while *his* fingers made their own voyage of discovery, holding, caressing, stirring into pulsating life the warm, soft flesh of her breasts.

Where their mutual desire might have led them, she never knew, for even as his hands ventured upon deeper intimacies, sounds of a disturbance in the passageway outside reached their ears ... Isobel's voice raised in querulous, almost hysterical enquiry. Teresa Mañara's rather harsh tones formed an accompaniment, while overall could be heard Lucia's voice in excited explanation.

'*Dios!*' Luq groaned, reluctantly releasing himself from Dene's arms. 'What a household this is!' He implanted one final, lingering kiss upon her love-swollen lips, then made for the door.

Unwilling to be left alone, Dene followed him. Their appearance was the signal for further uproar. Doña Teresa's expression was decidedly disapproving, while Isobel, one misshapen hand extended in accusation, gave vent to *her* feelings.

'You see? The house could be burnt down around our ears, and me a helpless invalid, while your nephew amuses himself with *my* nurse!'

Luq stepped into the midst of the affray.

'Señora Travers,' he said firmly, 'the house is *not* on fire . . . a very minor conflagration has been extinguished, and Nurse Mason, fortunately, does not appear to have suffered any ill effects.'

'I suppose you've been examining her all this time?' Isobel asked sarcastically.

Luq ignored her remark, looking beyond her with evident relief to where Elena Pareja, looking glamorously cool, calm and collected in comparison with the dishevelled state of the others, was walking briskly towards them. What her dark eyes made of the situation, Dene could not guess, but she assessed Isobel's hysterical condition immediately and took her firmly in charge, escorting her back to her own room.

With Isobel's departure, Doña Teresa seemed to think she should add her own comments, and a totally incomprehensible, verbal sparring match ensued between her and her nephew, at the conclusion of which he turned to Dene, his lean face pale and taut with anger.

'Go and get dressed, Dene,' he ordered abruptly. 'And then come to my study.'

He turned and followed his aunt, the conversation taking up, apparently, where it had left off, the gesticulations of aunt and nephew adding vehemence to their words.

No one seeing her fifteen minutes later, in her crisp white nurse's uniform, her hair coiled smoothly about her head, would have guessed at the inner turbulence of her emotions.

It took all her courage to push open the door in response to his summons, her heart fluttering with anticipation that was half fear, half excitement. It was a blow to find that he was not alone, but seated at his desk, the very decorative Dr Pareja perched elegantly upon one corner, her head very close to his, as they bent over the papers before them.

'Sit down, Dene,' was all he said, before he continued his conference with Elena.

It was very discourteous of them, Dene decided, to speak in Spanish, when they knew she could not understand a word, especially since, from their occasional glances at her, she was certain she formed part of their discussion. She shifted restlessly in her seat, wondering how much longer they intended to keep her waiting, when Elena would go, leaving her alone with Luq to discuss . . . what?

But Elena seemed in no hurry to depart. In fact it seemed she intended to remain. Dene did not know what to expect of Luq's manner towards her . . . conscious awareness of what had passed between them? Total avoidance of the subject? What she had not expected were his next words to her.

'I want you to go to England, as soon as possible.'

CHAPTER NINE

THE shock was so tremendous that Dene's dry lips could not even form the word 'why'. She could only stare at him, dismay in her eyes for both Luq and Elena to see.

'It may take a few hours to make arrangements.' After one glance, he avoided her eyes. 'I shall have to drive into the next village, to telephone the airline—for the first time, I regret that I have never had the instrument installed at the Villa. In the meantime, I suggest that you remain in your room, do the necessary packing . . .'

'B-but . . . Mrs Travers . . .' she managed to get the words out.

'I think Dr Pareja is competent to deal with our patient,' Luq said impatiently. He looked at his wristwatch. 'The sooner I am gone, the sooner it may be possible to obtain an early flight. I have a letter I wish you to take back with you . . . but that can be written on my return.'

At first Dene was too dazed to think clearly. She returned to her own room and sat on the side of the bed. Luq's words drummed inside her head in an incessant rhythm. 'I want you to go to England.' He was getting rid of her . . . but why? Was it because of this morning's incident . . . the attempt to set fire to her room? Surely it would be fairer to banish the perpetrator of the deed, not the victim? Or was it because of what had followed, because she had responded too willingly, too ardently to his kisses? It was impossible to forget that two other girls had been dismissed because they believed themselves to be in love with Luq.

But did it really matter what the reason was? She was being sent away . . . it was as simple as that . . . and she didn't want to go, in spite of the terror she had experienced that morning. She would rather stay here in the face of any risk.

Slowly, as the first effects of shock wore off, a plan began to form. Initially, she needed to get away from the Villa because, if she were still here when Luq returned, he would hustle her on to the next plane for England and it would be too late for any action on her part.

José! José would help her. She must find him ... explain, persuade him; and there wasn't much time. In Luq's powerful car the journey to and from the next village would not take long. Just let there be a delay on telephone calls to Malaga, she prayed.

As she had hoped, she found José alone, and he did not take much persuading. He was due to leave himself next day, en route for an important *corrida* in Madrid. There would be nothing simpler, he assured her, than to leave a day earlier than planned. There wasn't time to go into all her motives for running away, but fortunately José believed in acting first and asking questions afterwards.

'Never did I expect a chance to make off with you from under Luq's nose!' he teased, as, an hour after what Dene thought of as her sentence of banishment, they drove away from Pajaro on the first stage of their journey to Madrid.

Dene regretted that she had not even dared to say goodbye to her patient, and she hoped Isobel would forgive her desertion. Perhaps she could write and apologise, when she was certain of her next move. At least, she consoled her conscience, Isobel was under a doctor's care. That was a relief, even though it meant that the attractive Elena would be staying on at the villa. Dene hated seeing her and Luq together, and somehow it was even worse to know that she herself would be hundreds of miles away, imagining the two of them in the isolation of the Villa of Vengeance.

'I wonder if I'll ever come back to Pajaro?' said Dene, her voice tremulous.

José shot her a startled glance.

'But of course. Why should you not do so?'

Why not indeed? But then José did not know the full story. She had not told him yet of her impending banishment, merely that she needed to get away for a few days ... and that before Luq returned; and José, bless him, had not wasted time in probing; he had whisked her suitcase out under cover of his own luggage, made airy excuses to his mother for his earlier departure, while Dene had made a surreptitious exit via the garden, in order to meet him at the lean-to which sheltered the family's cars. But she supposed, now that they were on their way, questions were inevitable, and José *was* entitled to some explanation. Sure enough, once he had negotiated the twisting, downhill route and they were on the main road through the valley of the Alpujarras, he shot her an interrogative glance.

'You had a bad fright this morning, no?'

Of course—that was it! She needn't tell him what Luq had said. José himself had provided her with a readymade reason for her precipitate flight.

'Yes, yes . . . someone at the Villa seems to have it in for me. I just felt I had to get away for a bit, to think things over.'

After all, *that* was true enough, and she did not need to simulate the shudder, as she recalled her panic that morning, fighting the flames that barred her way to safety.

It was time to change the subject. José *seemed* satisfied with her answer, but if he probed too deeply, he might find some weakness in her excuse.

'Tell me something about the bullfight, José. I don't know what to expect. I've heard so much . . . some good, some bad. Some people say it's marvellous, others that it's cruel. But I suppose, as a matador, you're prejudiced?'

'No,' he said slowly, 'I do not think so. I can see both points of view. For the bull, yes, it is a tragedy perhaps. But sometimes, you know, it is the matador who dies.' He crossed himself swiftly, then continued. 'I only know it is something I have to do, for as long as I am able. For the matador, the *corrida* is manhood, pride, patriotism.'

'When is the bullfight?'

'You must learn to call it the *corrida*,' José said. Then, after a pause, 'It is in three days' time.'

'Three days!'

So that meant they would be away for several days . . . if she ever returned, a small, chilly inner voice whispered. By now Luq would have discovered her flight. How had he reacted? she wondered. Annoyance because she had disobeyed him, or relief because she had taken the initiative, was off his hands . . . no longer his responsibility. Even now, in his clinical brain, the process of forgetting her might have begun, her name just one of a string of those people who had briefly touched his life. To take her mind off that dreadful notion, she concentrated on the coming *corrida*.

'Are you . . . are you ever afraid?' She asked the question diffidently, wondering if perhaps José would be insulted.

'*Si*,' he said simply. 'Often.'

'Of . . . of being injured?'

'*Si*, that most of all.' He hesitated. 'But there is also the fear of failure. The crowds can be very fickle, Dene. When a matador gives the *aficionados* a good *corrida*, he is a hero. But if it is a poor fight, if he has not shown the skill, the daring they expect, the crowd becomes ugly . . . catcalls, whistles, insults. Even his *cuadrilla*, his crew, standing behind the barriers, will not meet his eye.'

'How unfair!' Dene said indignantly.

José shrugged. 'They have paid for excitement.'

'Even at the risk of a man's life . . . a man who might be married, with a wife and children to consider?'

'No matador should be married,' José said sharply.

Dene looked at him consideringly, then, greatly daring:

'Is . . . is that why you've never married?'

For the lighthearted José, his profile was unusually severe.

'*Si* . . . *mi papa* was a matador. I saw my mother's anxiety each time he went to the *corrida*. I saw her suffering when he died. I swore then that I would never submit any woman to such a life.'

'But . . . but you may not be a matador always.'

His face was bleak.

'As I told you, it is in my blood, Dene. My career will only end if and when a bull ends it for me.'

'And Lucia . . . how does she feel about this?'

'You *know* about Lucia?' His expression softened for a moment. 'Lucia knows nothing of my feelings. She believes that I will not marry her because of her station.'

'But that's unkind!' Dene exploded. 'To let her think you despise her . . . it's cruel!'

'Would it be kinder to tell her that I love her, but that I still will not marry her?'

'Yes,' said Dene with conviction. 'Yes, I think it would. What makes you think Lucia would be any less unhappy if you died *now* than if she were your wife? A woman *needs* to know that she is loved. I think Lucia would understand your principles far better than your present attitude.'

'You speak from experience, perhaps?' His words were teasing, but his voice still held an element of strain.

'Yes . . . at least, I know that if I loved someone, I would rather know that he loved me, even if there *were* reasons . . .' She stopped as her throat closed chokingly over the words.

'You are in love with someone who does not return that love?' José sounded surprised. 'The *novio* in England, *si?*'

'No! I'm not engaged. I never was.'

This time there was no doubt of José's surprise, and was it . . . dismay? The car swerved dangerously, as he took his eyes off the road to look at her.

'I may as well tell you,' she said. 'I told Isobel, and now Luq knows, so it's no secret any more.'

José drew a long breath.

'You *told* Isobel? *Before* you told Luq?'

'Yes.' She smiled ruefully. 'I think he *was* a little annoyed about that, but you see . . .'

Swiftly Dene related the story of her deception. José drove on in silence for some time, and when this became unbearable, Dene touched his arm.

'José, do you . . . do you think it was so wrong?'

'To tell a lie?' His old brilliant smile flashed out once more. '*Por Diós!* Who am *I* to condemn you for that? No, Dene, it was not so wrong of itself, but you could not know, could not foresee the consequences.'

'Consequences?'

'I am not at liberty to tell you more. No . . .' as she drew breath to protest, 'these are confidential, family matters, you understand? Luq has forbidden.'

And Dene was forced to accept his words.

They made an overnight stop at an *albergo*, making an early start next morning. Her second day away from the villa . . . from Luq, Dene thought drearily, as they saw far off, in a bluish haze, the outlines of Madrid.

For two days, José kept Dene busy in a whirl of sightseeing, as much, she suspected, to keep his mind off the coming *corrida* as to amuse her; and it *had* helped her a little too. While not entirely banishing her unhappiness, her problems, it had pushed them to the back of her mind for a few hours.

Once this would have been Dene's dream, a self-indulgent orgy of sightseeing. But what was she *doing* here, she asked herself, for the hundredth time, when all she wanted was to be near Luq?

The day of the *corrida* arrived and now Dene saw a different José. Gone the lighthearted, flirtatious manner. Now he was grave, withdrawn, obviously making an effort to control his nerves . . . refusing all meals.

'A *torero* never eats before starting for the ring,' he told Dene.

Just after five o'clock in the evening, they drove to the arena; the *corrida* would begin at seven. Dene was allowed to wait in an ante-chamber to the dressing room, while José was prepared for the coming event, and now, with the cessation of action, she too began to feel the strain.

At last she was informed that she might, just for a moment, enter José's dressing room, where now he kept the traditional 'vigil of arms'. Dressed in a suit of purple and silver, he knelt silently before a candle and a picture of the Virgin. Somehow this simple scene brought home to Dene the extreme seriousness of what he was about to undertake. She could sense the atmosphere of anxiety in the room, his will to remain calm. Almost she fancied she could hear the beating of his heart, sense the twanging of tight-held nerves. He did not speak. Indeed he did not even seem to notice her presence, and Dene found herself actually tiptoeing from the room, from whence she made her way to the public part of the arena, to find her seat.

A sudden hush fell over the crowd, as the interior gates swung open; somewhere a band struck up. The opening parade was under way, in which all the participants of the coming spectacle took part. First came the mounted *picadores* in their short jackets and chamois trousers, the right leg encased in steel from the waist down, their horses swathed in protective padding; next the *bandilleros*. Immediately behind the mounted escort came the three *matadores*, with proud, strutting carriage, resplendent in their tight-fitting silken hose, knee-length pants and stiff, bullion-encrusted jackets . . . the *traje de luces* . . . suit of lights.

The procession over, the crowd was silent once more,

watching the men below them in the ring, José and his *cuadrilla*, waiting for the first bull of the *corrida*.

'Watch the bull's ears,' José had told her. 'If they are tipped back when he is being shown the cape, he is not concentrating, his charge will be uncertain. But if his ears point forward, his charge will be straight and direct.'

José was unfurling his cape now and with a series of breathtaking passes brought his bull under control, testing him. He teased the beast, waiting for it to come on; then, as the bull failed to respond, he ran straight to it, made a few more passes . . . a series of veronicas . . . a half-veronica, the cape gathered in against his body.

'*E'un bravo!*' exclaimed a man at Dene's elbow. 'He has the gift for capework, the Golden One . . . the devil's own dash!' And Dene felt immensely proud to think that she was acquainted with this man, the hero of the crowd surrounding her.

Then it was the turn of the *picadores*, jabbing at the hump of muscle over the bull's neck, making him know the seriousness of the encounter. After each *pic* José led the bull away from the horsemen, executing intricate passes with his cape. Now the *banderilleros* placed their colourful, decorated, barbed sticks in the bull's shoulders, three separate pairs to be correctly placed. The bull was all José's now, to build up towards the final climax, going through a series of linked, artistic passes. Finally the bull charged . . . the most dangerous moment of the contest, and Dene held her breath. Now José must move forward, sword in hand, to go in over the horn, making his own escape as the thrust plunged home.

The bull sank slowly to its knees, and now Dene found time to sympathise with the noble creature, in these its last moments, feeling herself in complete empathy with the *matador*'s traditional gesture, as he reached out to gently touch his dying adversary between the horns. It had been a perfect kill and the crowd signified their approval; hats, flowers, coins . . . all were thrown into the ring.

With José's exit, Dene sank back into her seat. For the next two contests at least she could relax; and she realised, with a sense of wonder, that she would actually be glad when the *corrida* was over . . . she who had so longed to attend a bullfight.

José's second bull was an enormous beast. Dene was sure it

was almost twice as big as the first. It acted differently too. The first one's behaviour had been almost diffident by comparison. This one entered the ring as though looking for trouble. She knew she was right, when she heard the reaction of the crowd, the indrawn breath, the inaudible muttering. Her immediate neighbour gave voice to similar thoughts.

'E'un bicho!'

Yet the crowd were enjoying their fear, the sensation was tangible, and Dene recalled José telling her that, for the *aficionados*, that was the beauty and grandeur of the bullfight . . . the feeling that the risk of the man being wounded was always present.

The lances of the *picadors*, the *banderillos*, had maddened the beast, its flesh already raw and bleeding.

'It's horrible!' Dene did not realise she had said the words aloud.

'But no, *señorita*!' her neighbour protested. 'Is truth, is beauty . . . a commemoration of the days, when men faced bulls as an act of religious faith.'

With sword and cape, José enticed the beast into the centre of the ring, playing it with the right hand, making passes at the animal's breast. The bull paused and Dene sensed that it was gathering itself for the final charge. Soon . . . soon it would all be over and she could breathe again. There was no preliminary warning snort, or pawing of the ground; the animal just launched itself at the silver and purple figure which tormented it; and José did not move. Instead, he held his rigid stance, allowing the bull to bear down on him, luring it to his right, sword held aloft, where it must pierce the vital spot, driven home by the animal's charging weight.

'He is trying to kill *recibiendo*!'

Dene heard her neighbour's horrified protest, just at the moment when she knew José's ploy had failed, heard her own scream, as the bull, instead of following the movement of the cape, seemed to plunge its horns directly into the gaudy figure of the matador, tossing him contemptuously aside, then turning for another attack. For a moment she sat immobilised, watching as the bull was killed by another man and a stretcher party, bearing the pathetic, crumpled heap of purple and silver material, was closely followed by the horses, dragging the bull's disfigured carcase from the ring. Then she was up and running through the tunnel, backstage, to where the dressing rooms lay. There was no glamour here now, as she tried to find someone who could understand her impassioned pleas . . . only the smell of manure, of urine, blood, the odours of antiseptics, of anaesthetics. At last she found a man who understood her, who showed her into a room where a table, its purpose all too sinisterly significant, stood beneath an arc of powerful lights.

'You are Mañara's wife, his girl-friend?'

'No, just . . . just a friend. José . . . is . . . is he . . . ?'

'They have taken him to the hospital, *señorita*. His wound is not immediately serious . . . no vital organ injured, the doctor thinks.'

'What hospital? Where? How can I find it? I don't know Madrid.'

Oh, if only Luq were here to take charge! He would know what to do, but Luq *wasn't* here . . . didn't know that *she* was here, the trouble she was in. She felt her eyes filling with tears, her legs beginning to tremble, as reaction to shock set in.

Although José's shoulder was still stiff and sore, where the bull's horn had pierced and torn it, he had insisted that he was well enough to drive, on their return journey to Andalusia.

'After all, it is an automatic gear change,' he pointed out. 'I only have to sit behind the wheel and steer.'

'I wish I could drive,' Dene had mourned. 'Wouldn't it be better if we flew, or went by train?'

'I am not leaving my splendid car in Madrid,' José protested. 'We drive. All will be well, you will see.'

José was determined to complete the journey in one day, anxious to be home, and Dene knew why and could rejoice for him, even though she had no reason herself to celebrate.

For the first two days, as José lay in hospital, she had been terribly worried about him. Although the doctors and nursing staff had assured her that he was in no danger, he had obviously been in great pain and, when he was conscious, anguish of mind. For he had been told, categorically, that he would never fight again. Too many muscles had been badly damaged and the weakness would always remain. On the third day, as the pain-killing drugs and his own strong constitution began to fight his injuries, Dene ventured to speak to him of his future.

'What will you do now, José?'

He shrugged, then winced with pain.

'There must be something ... something you've always thought you'd like to do, if you weren't a bullfighter?' Then she remembered. 'José!' she cried excitedly, 'there is something. I remember Luq telling me ... you could do what your grandfather did ... breed bulls.'

For a moment a spark of interest lit the pain-filled blue eyes, but then he shook his head.

'One needs capital ... I have always lived right up to my income.'

'Luq would help you ...'

'No!' There was fierce pride and determination in the denial. 'I have always lived by my own efforts ... I will *not* be an object of charity.'

Dene realised that she must choose her ground more carefully.

'To whom does the farm at Pajaro belong?'

'Technically, to Luq ... but a doctor has no time for farming. *Mi madre* has authority in his absence, but the *peónes* grow slack under a woman's rule.'

'You once told me Luq wanted *you* to run the farm for him. Just think, José ... if it were run properly, it would make a profit ... those dreary houses in the village could be improved, the church restored. Something could be done to brighten up the Villa ... it's a pretty cheerless place.'

'Go on.'

She was holding his interest at least.

'If you were his manager, Luq would have to pay you a salary. It wouldn't be charity, and in time, you might be able to afford your own bulls.'

'Maybe.' His tone was still non-committal, but she thought there was a little more energy and a little more hope in it.

'And,' she added, greatly daring, 'you could ... if you wanted to, that is ... marry Lucia.'

That really *did* rouse him.

'*If* I wanted to! *Madre mia*, Dene, *how* I want to! I want to hold my own son in my arms, to let him know that he *is* my son. I want more sons ... and daughters ...' He sat up in bed, becoming animated. 'And when I breed my bulls, my great fighting bulls, I

will know that there is someone to follow in my footsteps, to carry
on my work . . .' He lay back, exhausted, but looking happier
already. Then his expression clouded once more. 'But it is not
possible. I have sworn a vow.'

'I know you swore not to marry while you were a matador,'
Dene said impatiently, 'but that's all over now, and while you
may be sorry at first, I'm sure it's really a blessing in disguise.'

He looked at her morosely.

'It was a double vow, Dene. It did not just concern myself . . .
the bullfighting . . . but Luq too.'

Dene looked her puzzlement and José sighed.

'I swore that I would not snatch happiness for myself, while
Luq could not . . . after what I did to him . . .' He stopped, then
began again. 'I think perhaps it is time someone told you
the full story of Belinda.'

Dene held her breath. She dared not speak, attempt to
encourage him, in case he changed his mind. But he seemed
almost unaware of her presence, his eyes fixed upon the walls of
his hospital room, as though, like a giant cinema screen, it
presented the past.

'When Isobel and Belinda Travers came to Madrid, they were
immediately accepted into the circle of *aficionados* of the bullfight.
Belinda was a pretty little thing, very much like you to look at,
but without a real brain in her head . . . unlike you.'

Now he *was* looking at Dene and there was a little of the old
mischief in his smile. But he added more sombrely.

'No brains . . . and fewer morals. She found it all so glamorous, to be acquainted with the matadors. She did not hide her
interest in me . . . and I . . .' he pursed his mouth self-
deprecatingly, 'I have never been known to rebuff a beautiful
woman . . . yet. If *you* had been willing . . . but you were different
Dene . . . and besides, I soon realised . . .'

'Yes?'

But he had decided not to pursue that train of thought.

'Then Luq met Belinda. He was fascinated by her at first. He
too only saw the façade. He asked her to marry him and I think
she was flattered. He was a rich man, well known in Seville, and
highly regarded in his profession. Poor, empty-headed little girl!
She thought she could have us both. One night, after a successful
corrida, we celebrated. Luq was down at Pajaro . . . farm busi-

ness. Alas, we celebrated too well. Belinda made a play for me . . . Oh, I do not pretend that I am blameless, but I was too drunk to listen to my very small conscience . . .' He hesitated, looking at Dene, assessing her reaction, then continued bleakly, 'A month later, she was pregnant.'

Dene gasped.

'You mean the baby wasn't . . .'

'The baby *would* have been mine.' He emphasised the past tense. 'She wanted me to marry her, of course . . . she was horrified, terrified. When I told her I didn't intend to marry anyone, that in any case another woman was already expecting my child, she rushed Luq into marriage with most indecent haste.'

'And Luq didn't know?' Dene was angry to think of Luq being deceived, being used.

'Oh, he knew all right,' José said grimly. 'The little *Inglesa* consulted a doctor at *his* hospital, and when he in his turn congratulated Luq upon his premature but happy expectations, Luq knew of course that it was not *his* doing.'

'Then why on earth did he *marry* her?'

'Because,' José said simply, 'he is a fool . . . a chivalrous fool. Everyone knew he was engaged to Belinda . . . everyone thought the child must be his . . . so he married her. But they never lived together as man and wife. The moment the ceremony was over, he despatched her to Pajaro, with her poisonous mother in attendance.'

Dene ignored this unwarranted attack on Isobel in her keenness to know more.

'And you think Luq still holds this against you . . . that he would object if you married Lucia?'

José smiled wearily.

'No . . . as I said, he is a chivalrous fool, my cousin. Did you know that I was also responsible for that limp of his?'

'No, but I've often wondered how . . .'

'It was the bulls . . . always the bulls. As a small boy I wandered into the pen of my grandfather's prize bull. If it hadn't been for Luq, I wouldn't be here to tell the tale. I was small and he threw me from the pen, but in escaping himself, he fell badly . . . broke his leg in three places.' He sighed heavily. 'There are so many ways in which I have injured Luq.'

It had taken Dene many hours of persuasion, of reassurance, but at last she had convinced José that it would be in everyone's best interests, Luq's not least of all, if he married Lucia and settled down to run the family farm.

'You say Luq cannot really spare the time for the farm and his profession . . . and after all,' she pointed out, though it cost her a personal pang to do so, 'Luq obviously doesn't *want* to get married again. He has his Elena Pareja.'

'And heaven forbid he should ever marry *her*!' José returned. 'I wish,' he said wistfully, 'he would marry someone like you. There was a time when I thought . . .'

'I'd be the *last* person,' Dene said hastily. 'I can understand now why he took exception to me at first sight. I only remind him of Belinda.'

'That wasn't the only reason,' José assured her. 'Any love he had for her is long dead . . . but his other motives are for Luq to divulge, if he chooses.'

José's well-meant words had the wrong effect. Now Dene knew that Luq had more than one reason to dislike her; and with this realisation came the long-postponed decision. She had promised José that she would accompany him to Pajaro, as his nurse: the doctors at the hospital had only agreed to release him so soon on this condition. But as soon as that promise was fulfilled, José safely in his mother's care, and Lucia's, she was going back to England.

Some hours later they entered the suburbs of Cordoba and crossed the bridge over the Guadalquivir.

'We shan't make it to Pajaro tonight after all,' José admitted reluctantly. 'It's at least another two hours until we reach Seville and then some hours to the Villa.' His face were beginning to look grey with strain.

'Could we go to the Casa?' Dene suggested. 'Surely, in the circumstances, Luq wouldn't object. He might even be there himself.'

The thought filled her with sudden, choking excitement . . . and apprehension. How would he greet her? Would he be furiously angry since he had not intended that she *should* return? These thoughts occupied her, until a distant red glare announced their approach to Seville.

Luq was not at the Casa in the Avenida de los Santos, but his housekeeper took them in with much muttering and exclaiming over José's state of health. Dene was relieved to see that in spite of her disapproving manner, she *was* quite fond of the young man, and between them they hustled him off to his bed.

At first, Maria was scandalised by Dene's insistence on helping, until Dene pointed out that she was, after all, a nurse and used to caring for male as well as female patients.

Next morning José, though still pale and evidently in some discomfort, was insistent on continuing their journey, and again Dene wished she were able to share the driving. The first thing she would do on arrival back in England was to put her name down for driving lessons. It was obviously a necessary accomplishment in times of crisis, and it would give her a new interest, she thought drearily, something she would certainly need.

How had she ever thought Pajaro a dreary little village? Dene wondered, as they drove slowly up the dry rutted track, dust motes dancing in the sun, beams of which lit up the grey buildings and reflected from glistening windowpanes and whitened steps. The *peons* of Pajaro might be poor, but they took a pride in their homes nevertheless.

Now they had parked the car ... they were walking up the steep narrow mule track to the Villa, José moving too slowly for Dene's eager feet, so that she was forced to slow her pace to match his. Here was the wall, the heavy gate which had once seemed to imprison her, the courtyard with its silent fountain, its noisy, scavenging pigeons. They were mounting the stairs ... soon they would be in the Villa. There would be exclamations, questions, over José's accident, explanations ... recriminations? Then, perhaps, there would be an opportunity to be alone with Luq, ostensibly to ask after her patient, but also so that she could gauge his reaction to her return, though she felt she knew what that would be.

The old-fashioned external bell jangled into silence and they stood, waiting for the door to be opened. Who would be the first person they saw? Dene's nervous apprehension mounted in proportion to the slowness of the footsteps they could hear, approaching within.

CHAPTER TEN

The heavy door creaked open with agonising slowness, to reveal the sturdy figure of Asunción. At the sight of José, still pale with fatigue, the elderly cook broke into rapid speech. Question and answer followed, and when at last the flow ceased, José turned to Dene, a strangely exalted glitter in his eyes.

'Much of interest has happened in our absence. But first I must speak with Lucia . . . if you excuse?'

Dene smiled indulgently, as he strode in the direction of the kitchen, imagining Lucia's surprised delight at what José had to tell her. She only wished she could be as sure of her own welcome.

She tapped on the door of Isobel's room and without waiting for a reply, opened the door and walked in. On the threshold, she stopped in surprise, thinking for a moment that she had come to the wrong room. But there was no mistake; this *was* the bedroom once occupied by her patient. Yet it was as if Isobel Travers had never existed. The room had been completely cleared of the frills and knick-knacks with which Isobel had surrounded herself, leaving it as plain and unadorned as the rest of the house.

Leaving the door ajar, Dene hurried through the villa, making for Luq's wing. Obviously, the decision to send Isobel to hospital had finally been taken; but she must find out to which hospital, whether she would be able to visit . . . how Isobel was.

To her surprise, the door to Belinda's room, usually fast locked, stood wide open, and venturing to look inside, she discovered that this too was in the process of being cleared. Boxes and crates stood in the centre of the floor, filled to overflowing with books, ornaments and clothes. Leaning carelessly against a crate was the portrait of Belinda.

Dene drew in a sharp breath, moving farther into the room, for the painting had been slashed with some sharp instruments, which had not only opened up the earlier disfigurement, but had added new damage. What *was* going on?

She turned on her heel and ran the few steps to Luq's study, knocking frantically on his door. There was no reply and she flung the door open. The room was tidy, as if it had not been used for some time, but at least it looked much as usual. There were no inexplicable changes or disappearances here. Her eye was caught by a glint of silver, something lying on his desk that looked familiar. Moving closer, she discovered that it was her missing lucky charm, though it was scarcely recognisable. The chain was broken and the black cat itself battered and twisted out of shape. José was right: things *had* been happening . . . very strange things.

Grasping the talisman in her clenched hand, Dene made her way back along the corridors, deep in thought. Her own room was as she had left it . . . a few personal belongings on the dressing table, the wardrobe and drawers still filled with her clothes. She had half expected to find them all packed up, ready to be sent back to England.

A small envelope, propped against the mirror, caught her eye. It was half obscured by a box of tissues and she had not noticed it at first. Could it be a message from Luq? Eagerly she ripped it open. But the writing was not in the bold, black, arrogant upright of Luq's hand; it was in a more cramped style, as though the writer had formed the words with difficulty. She turned to the last page; the signature was Isobel's. Dene sat down on the side of the bed and began to read. Perhaps, at last, some of the things that puzzled her were about to be explained.

'My dear friend,' Isobel had written, 'for I feel you are my only friend in this house. I do not know if you will ever read this letter. With your sudden mysterious disappearance, I am so afraid that Luq has got rid of you, as he does with anyone who thwarts him.' Dene began to feel slightly sick and she had to force herself to continue. 'If you read this letter it means that you are still safe and I beg you, go away again, before it is too late. I am at this moment afraid for myself. But my life is just a burden to me now, whilst you are still young. The Léon family has a long history of vengefulness. They never forgive those who have wronged them. Belinda discovered too late what Luq was like and . . . poor innocent creature . . . could not hide her distaste from him. You have only to look at her portrait to see how violently he can vent his feelings. And you, my dear . . . I fear that you too have done something to incur his anger . . . perhaps preferring his cousin to himself? Your poor lucky black cat . . . I found it near his study. Only someone in a violent rage could have done so much damage. And now I must seize my opportunity to place this note in your room . . . if my legs will carry me so far, and if I can avoid that woman . . . she watches me all the time. Do not trust her, Dene . . . she is in league with him. In haste, your unhappy friend, Isobel.'

With trembling hands Dene refolded the paper, then sat petrified, uncertain what course of action to take. Her first incredulity had hardened into conviction. Isobel's letter explained so much that had puzzled her and the older woman had gone to much pain and effort to warn her. But, she thought despairingly, she could not escape unaided. Having only so recently returned, José would not be willing, or able, to make another long drive; and besides, it would be unfair to ask him; despite his disclaimers, she knew his shoulder still pained him. So what was she to do? How was she to face Luq . . . for face him she obviously must some time? Would she be able to bluff it out, act normally, so that he did not suspect what she knew? Her heart wrenched painfully within her. Oh, how could she have been so mistaken in him? How *could* she have fallen in love with the monster of iniquity that Isobel's words painted? And there was nowhere she could turn for help. She dared not trust anyone in this house with what she had learnt. How true was the saying that blood was thicker than water! She had only to look back to see the meaning of those significant silences, the uneasy glances, the conspiracy of secrecy. They were all in it, all knew of Luq's propensity for violence, all covering up for him.

But she could not stay in this room alone. At any moment she might be discovered, by Luq himself. For the moment at least, she would feel safer in a crowd. Thrusting the letter into the pocket of her dress, she stood up and forcing her tremulous legs to carry her, made her way to the kitchen.

There she discovered José, still in animated conversation with a glowing Lucia, while a beaming Asunción listened with every appearance of pleasure. As Dene entered, the girl swung round, her dark good looks brilliant with happiness.

'Señorita . . . Dene . . . you have returned and you have

brought my José back to me! For this I thank you . . . and we are to be married at last . . . the little Mateo is to have a *papa*!'

She must react normally . . . mustn't let them suspect . . . that she knew.

'I'm . . . I'm delighted for you, Lucia, really I am.'

It would be natural . . . expected . . . for her to enquire after her patient. Swallowing the cold lump of fear that clogged her throat, she tried to sound casual.

'I've just come from Señora Travers' room. She . . .'

'Pah!' Lucia spat out the sound. 'We are free of *la Inglesa*. At last the Señor has his revenge!'

Dene paled. Were they not even bothering to hide their deeds?

'F-free of her?' she stammered.

But before Lucia could reply, there came the sound of horses' hoofs on the cobbles below.

'The Señor is back!'

Dene felt herself begin to tremble uncontrollably, as Lucia bustled around the stove, inspecting the contents of the saucepans.

'You were not expected,' Lucia said worriedly to José. 'Here is only luncheon for two.'

Dene had to sit down. Her legs would hold her no longer . . . any moment now she must face Luq.

'Two?' José enquired.

But there was no need for explanation, as the outer door opened and two people entered, dressed in riding clothes, their faces glowing with exercise . . . Luq and Elena Pareja.

Luq looked around the kitchen and as his dark eyes registered the presence of the two truants, his expression hardened, his long mouth firming into a straight, angry line, causing Dene's heart to adopt an irregularly, uncomfortable rhythm. How could she be so afraid, know what she knew, and yet still feel this violent pull of the senses, this physical attraction?

'So! You have the effrontery to return, José Mañara, bringing your . . . your *amante* with you? How dare you do this to your family . . . to Lucia . . . yet again? And as for you, Señorita Mason . . .' he turned upon Dene and she shrank away.

'Luq!' José protested. 'You have it all wrong. We . . .' His voice broke off in a shout of pain, as Luq's iron hard hand caught him by his injured shoulder.

'Let go of him!' Personal fear, her tremulous reaction to his presence, forgotten, Dene leapt up as José first blanched, then slid to the tiled floor in a dead faint. 'You brute! He's been badly injured!'

There was pandemonium in the kitchen. As Dene cried out her protest, Lucia screamed and Asunción broke into loud lamentations. Incredibly, order was restored by Elena Pareja.

'Lucia!' she ordered crisply. 'Stop that noise immediately. Help me to carry Señor Manara to his room. 'You . . .' looking at Dene, 'come with us. Obviously, you are informed as to the nature of his injury.'

Luq protested, his deep voice vibrating with the violence of his anger.

'*I* wish to speak to Señorita Mason . . . at once, in my study.'

'*Más tarde*, Luq!' Elena said impatiently. 'José's need is greater than yours at this moment . . . and it will give *you* time to cool off.'

Dene had never thought to see Luq bested by a woman. Elena Pareja's influence must be great indeed, she thought, as, thankful for the respite, she followed the Doctor and Lucia, as they supported José's limp form between them.

'Dene!' Luq's voice was still angry and she cast a nervous glance over her shoulder, to meet the stare of dark, unfathomable eyes before, unable to repress a shudder, she hurried after the others.

It soon appeared that, while José was in considerable pain, where Luq had gripped still sensitive tissue, no irreparable harm had been done. However, Elena insisted that the two girls should undress him and put him to bed.

'Meanwhile, Nurse,' she told Dene, 'you may explain why you disobeyed a direct order from your employer, causing much concern and inconvenience to both myself and Señor de Léon.'

'I should have thought you'd be only too glad to have me out of the way, both of you,' Dene retorted. 'Besides, I don't have to explain my actions to *you*.'

'Believe me,' Elena said grimly, 'you would be well advised to set things straight with me, before you face Luq de Léon. In his present mood, he is quite likely to strangle you without waiting for explanations.' Dene shuddered, quite ready to believe it. 'I warned him how it would be,' Elena continued, 'if he allowed himself to soften towards another Englishwoman, and . . . further idiocy . . . a woman, who, in appearance, might almost be the sister of the one who . . .'

'Soften towards me?' Dene's voice rose hysterically, 'when he was trying to get rid of me?'

'If you had waited, instead of jumping to conclusions, you would have discovered that he merely wished you to undertake an errand on his behalf . . . an errand which would also serve the purpose of removing *you* from a dangerous situation. Instead of which, you ran away, with his cousin . . . and, poor man, Luq is disillusioned once more.'

But Luq had *always* imagined her to be in love with José. This was no sudden misapprehension, so that excuse wouldn't wear, Dene thought scornfully. Luq had wanted to get rid of her all right, so that he could carry out his purpose, whatever it was, against Isobel. Oh, if only she *had* gone back to England! Perhaps he hadn't meant her any actual harm . . . then, but now . . . now that she knew . . .

José intervened.

'Dene did *not* run away with me in the sense you imply. You insult me, Elena Pareja . . . and my *novia*. Lucia and I are to be married.' He gave the girl at his side a smile of ineffable sweetness and she nodded vehemently.

'*Si, si*, is true, Dr Pareja. My José has explained all, and I am most grateful that Dene is with him at the time of his accident, that she has made him see reason . . . has persuaded him that life still holds much for him . . . for us,' she added, her lovely face colouring.

Oh, if only Lucia weren't involved in this terrible knowledge! She and José were, outwardly at least, the nicest people at the Villa Venganza. But Elena was looking quizzically at Dene.

'It seems I misjudge you, *señorita*. Perhaps it is you who should talk and I listen?'

Dene shook her head. There was no way she was going to reveal her innermost thoughts, her emotions, and now her unwanted knowledge, to Luq's mistress. She bit her lip to still its trembling. Somehow she must maintain an appearance of ignorance. But she reckoned without Lucia.

'Dene would not hurt the Señor, Dr Pareja. She loves him. Forgive me, Dene,' she added apologetically, 'but *you* have helped *me* . . . now it is my turn, *si?* I think there are many

misunderstandings between you and the Señor. But the time of
secrecy is over. It is safe now to speak as the heart finds; and
Dene will not confide in you, Doctor, because she believes *you* to
be Luq's *amante*.'

'No, no!' Dene protested. She did not want them to tell her
anything . . . to confirm her dreadful suspicions, to involve her in
their conspiracy, make her an accessory to something . . . un-
speakable.

Elena spoke calmly.

'Lucia is right. It *is* time the truth was spoken.'

'The truth!' Dene could not restrain herself, in spite of her
fears. 'How am I to know the truth when it *is* spoken? In the few
weeks since I came here, I've been more confused than at any
other time in my life. Half-truths, lies, evasions, everyone
slandering everyone else . . . hating everyone else. This villa is
aptly named. It's a horrible place, and I wish I'd never come
here . . . never met any of you!'

'Control yourself, Nurse!' Elena spoke sharply. 'I think you
had better come with me. A sickroom is no place for scenes.'

'I am not sick,' José protested.

'Nevertheless,' Elena insisted, 'Señorita Mason will come
with me . . . to the study.'

The study! Luq would be there, and once Elena and Luq got
her alone . . .

'No . . . no!' she sobbed. 'I won't go there . . . with you . . .
with *him*!'

'You are not afraid of Luq?' José said incredulously. 'He has
the temper of the devil, it is true, but he would never harm a
woman.'

'What?' Dene began to laugh hysterically. What use to hide
her knowledge? They would never let her go. 'He's already
harmed two to my knowledge, and possibly more.' She fumbled
in the pocket of her dress and threw Isobel's letter on to the bed.
'There, read that, then you'll see *why* I don't want to go near your
cousin! I know all your secrets now . . . and, oh, God, I *wish* I
didn't!' She sank to her knees, hysteria, defiance, giving way to
abandoned grief, in terrible, wrenching sobs.

There was utter silence in the room, broken only by the sound
of Dene's misery; and she could picture them, all three, gathered
around the letter, realising that she knew everything, looking at

each other. Strangely enough, she was no longer afraid of what they might do to her. She didn't think she *wanted* to go on living with such disillusionment. The only man she had ever met, with whom she had longed to spend the rest of her life . . . and he was not what she had thought of him. She would never, ever, be able to trust her own judgment again, would never feel that way about anyone again. She might as well be dead.

Someone was lifting her to her feet . . . José.

'Wh-what are you doing out of bed?' she muttered inarticulately.

'*Someone* has to talk to you, and it is going to be me,' he said. 'We are *amigos, si?* Elena . . . Lucia . . . leave us, *por favor*.' José had suddenly acquired a new dignity. 'Elena . . . ten minutes, *si?*' There was a question in his voice, which Dene did not understand, but Elena seemed to and with a brusque nod she withdrew, Lucia in her wake.

José seated Dene on the side of his bed.

'Now, *amiga*. All this nonsense,' he rapped the letter with his free hand, 'Is the ravings of a disturbed mind. No . . .' as Dene opened her mouth to protest, 'you will listen to me. You have lectured me upon *my* duty. Now it is I who lecture you.'

Exhausted by the force of her own grief and despair, Dene listened, apathetically, disbelievingly at first, then with growing interest . . . and hope . . . as José related the events, not just of the past two weeks, but of the past two years.

Isobel Travers, he stated, had herself fallen in love with Luq de Léon, during her first visit to Spain. Returning the following year with her young stepdaughter, she had been incensed when Luq showed an interest in the girl and finally asked her to marry him. Despite the engagement, she had actively encouraged Belinda's intimacy with José, had been triumphant when the girl discovered she was pregnant.

'But her little plan did not work,' José said soberly. 'Far from casting her aside, my chivalrous cousin married Belinda. From then on, it seems, as far as we can interpret the evidence, Isobel engaged upon a vendetta against her stepdaughter. At first, apparently, she only intended to frighten the girl, drive her away though that is a charitable interpretation . . . but if so, the final incident certainly misfired. Belinda was frightened into premature childbirth, and the rest you know.'

'But Luq's revenge on Belinda, the slashed portrait, my . . . my resemblance to her?'

'Luq's revenge!' Jose laughed softly, his grip on Dene's shoulders tightening. 'You have been allowing that old story about our ancestor to colour your imagination. Luq may have a quick temper, but he would never cause deliberate harm to anyone. As a doctor, he is dedicated to *saving* lives.'

José described for Dene the events immediately following Belinda's death, including the onset of Isobel's rheumatism.

'Luq thinks, and Elena has confirmed his theory, that deep traumatic shock, the realisation that she had in effect committed murder, brought on the malady and pushed a mind already disturbed further over the edge.'

'I can't believe that Isobel was . . . was mad!' Dene protested. 'She seemed as sane as you or I.'

José shrugged.

'You will have to question Elena as to that. But it seems that insanity brings with it its own cunning, the ability to hide itself.'

'Why should I ask Elena, for goodness' sake?'

'She is a psychiatrist,' José said simply. 'and, Dene, she is *not* Luq's mistress . . . never has been. I said that deliberately, for *la Inglesa*'s benefit.'

'Why?' Dene was shocked. 'When you knew what effect it might have on Isobel? Why, she might have . . .'

'That is what we wanted,' José said soberly. 'You see, until recently, we had no proof, no witnesses outside the family to any of these incidents . . . and two doctors must sign a declaration of insanity. Elena agreed to be both our witness, and our decoy.' He shuddered slightly. 'If I had known that you were not really engaged to be married, that Isobel knew this, I should never have joked, as I did, about Luq's apparent predeliction for your company.'

'And the portrait?' Dene asked. 'Did Isobel . . . ?'

José nodded.

'Both times. The second occasion was after we left for Madrid. She seemed, in her deteriorating condition, to associate the portrait with you. There *is* a resemblance.'

They sat in silence for a few moments, then José asked anxiously:

'You do believe me, Dene? I have convinced you that Isobel lied, that Luq is not . . .'

'Where *is* Isobel?'

'By now she is in a private sanatorium . . . in England.'

'England!'

'*Si*. Apparently Luq wanted you to take a letter to the Señora's only remaining relative . . . a sister, living in England . . . explaining the position.' He grinned sheepishly. 'When we disappeared, he flew to England himself, met the sister, who requested that the Señora be treated in an English hospital, where she could visit her, rather than in a foreign country. One of Elena's assistants has escorted her, accompanied by *mia madre*.'

'*Your mother*? Has flown to England?' Dene was amazed. She could not picture Teresa Mañara out of this, her normal environment.

'*Si*.' José laughed. 'She has not always lived at Pajaro, you understand. She travelled the bullfighting circuits with *mi papa* . . . and they often made the holiday abroad.'

Dene assimilated this information.

'It's very hard to take in,' she said at last, 'hard to believe that I could have been so easily deceived by Isobel . . . and all those . . . those incidents . . . the dead pigeon, the fire . . . ?'

'All *la Inglesa*,' José confirmed. 'She was also responsible for the mysterious guitar music. Somehow she had obtained a duplicate key to Belinda's room.'

'Why *did* Luq keep Belinda's room just as she left it?'

'Because,' José said grimly, 'he hoped it would infuriate Isobel, draw her activities out into the open . . . and finally it did. Elena was here to witness the attacks on you, and . . . after our departure . . . the damage she caused in Belinda's room. Now,' he sighed and it was a sigh of relief, 'that room can be cleared, the villa purged of their presence, and we can all begin to live again. All of us . . .' he hesitated, 'except Luq . . . unless you . . ?'

'How can I face him?' Dene said miserably, 'after all these misunderstandings, the things he believes of me . . . the *awful* things *I* thought about *him*?'

José gave her an encouraging hug.

'I do not think my cousin will find it hard to forgive . . . after all, the situation in this house was not *your* fault, and he has much reason to desire an understanding with you . . .'

Dene flushed.

'I wish I could believe you.'

'It is so! *I* tell you so . . . I tell you what Asunción and Lucia have told me. Why do you not go to him, Dene?' he said persuasively. 'For a few moments there may be awkwardness, embarrassment . . . my cousin is a proud man . . . but you do not lack courage.'

Thus adjured, Dene began to feel that it *might* be possible to face Luq, if only she could be certain . . . But in the event, no action was required on her part. The door of José's bedroom was flung wide and she started up in consternation, as Luq himself entered the room. He totally ignored her, addressing himself to José.

'Elena told me that I . . . How is your shoulder?' His voice was gruff, as close to apology as Luq de Leon would ever go. 'I had no idea . . .'

'I shall live,' José said blithely. 'I have much to live for.'

'I envy you,' Luq returned simply, and now his eyes did turn towards Dene, dark, unfathomable, burning, in his lean, chiselled features.

'In fact,' José announced casually, rising, 'I think I shall go to the kitchen in search of food.'

'Oh, but . . .' Dene protested, suddenly panic-stricken, 'Elena said you should . . .'

'That to Elena!' José snapped his fingers. He paused in the doorway, a strange smile on his face. 'I do not think I shall be back for some considerable time!' The door closed behind him.

'I . . . I'd better go too,' Dene said feebly.

But there was no way she could make an exit without passing Luq, and he did not seem inclined to step aside for her.

'Why?' he said wryly, 'when Elena and my cousin have gone to such pains to leave us alone together?'

'I . . . I'm sure you have important things to do, and I . . . I have some packing to do.'

'Packing?' The word was said sharply, interrogatively.

'Well, yes . . . I . . . I expect you'll want me to leave now. I . . . I mean . . .' she struggled on, 'my job here is at an end. I'm not . . . not needed any more . . .'

'Oh, but you are!' he said softly.

Dene stared at her feet and shook her head. She could not meet those probing, questioning eyes. José had praised her courage, but it seemed to have drained away, leaving her more afraid than she had ever been in her life.

'It seems you are *not* in love with my cousin after all,' Luq said conversationally.

Dene shook her head once more, aware that as he spoke he had moved a little closer and that, with her legs already pressed against the side of the bed, there was no retreat.

'Elena has explained much that puzzled me,' he continued, his voice still quiet, carefully controlled. 'She has shown me Isobel Travers' letter.'

'Oh!' Now Dene did look up, anguished, sapphire-blue eyes meeting his in painful appeal. '*What* must you think of me, that . . . that I could believe such things of . . . of you . . . but . . .'

'Do you wish me to *tell* you what I think of you?' he enquired huskily.

Immediately, her gaze fell again. There was a look in his eyes that she feared to analyse . . . in case she was mistaken.

'If . . . if only you'd told me the truth when I first came here.' She could not help the reproachful note in her voice. 'I *would* have understood, and I wouldn't have been so . . . so gullible, or so frightened.' She shuddered, as she remembered the fears that had beset her, superstitious fears of hauntings, of unseen, unknown enemies.

'I too wish that I had confided in you.' He hesitated, then: 'But I did not want to frighten you away before I had a chance to know you better . . . there was something about you, that first day . . .'

'Yes,' she said bitterly. 'I reminded you of Belinda.'

'*Si*, at first, but only superficially . . . and there is nothing in you of her nature. In you, I found what I once believed Belinda to possess. But it was too late. You were already affianced, so I thought, to another.'

'Then . . . then why didn't you send me away?' she asked softly. A small spark of joy was beginning to burn, deep inside her, but she was afraid to fan it into flame . . . yet.

'I hoped,' he said simply, and he had moved yet again, so close that the slightest movement of her hand would bring them into contact. 'I hoped that you might come to care for me. It was despicable, dishonourable, believing, as I did then, that you were not free. But . . .' his voice became agonised, 'by the time I found out that there was no *novio* in England, I thought that it was José that you . . . and I *knew* there was no happiness for you there. Despite his amorous wanderings, José always returns to Lucia; and then I found that Isobel knew that you were free to marry and I was greatly afraid for you. It was always intended that Elena should be the decoy, never *you*.'

'And now . . . now that you know it's *not* José?' she ventured, looking up at him. She held her breath. Was she assuming too much, had she accepted José's assurance too easily.

'Now that I know . . .' he said slowly, 'I am afraid to ask if you . . . if you . . .'

Luq de Léon, afraid? Dene could not believe it, and yet it seemed it must be so, for his eyes held a depth of pleading that she could not mistake.

'If I love you?'

It was put as a question, but there was so much depth of meaning in the simple words, so much honest fervour in the lovely blue eyes looking up into his, that there could be no possibility of further doubt.

'Dene!' His deep resonant voice seemed to draw her heart from her pulsating body, as he captured her face between his hands. 'Can this be true? I am not imagining this . . . this feeling between us?'

There was no real need to repeat it, but she did.

'I love you, Luq. I think I've loved you almost from the first time we met.'

He gathered her up to him, moulding her to the taut thrust of his thighs, and she felt the vibrant heat of him through the thin cotton of her summer dress. Shockwaves of ecstasy possessed her, as she clung, responding hungrily to the pressure of his mouth on hers, as desire accelerated between them. Sweet pain welled in her as, revealingly, his chest rose and fell unsteadily to his disturbed breathing, vibrated to the powerful thud of his heart, his hands caressing, coaxing, demanding.

Her breathing was as hectic as his and she felt her longing building into a strange, agonised wanting that defied all interpretation. The closeness, the warmth of him was an intoxicant to her senses, and when his hands clamped possessively over her hips as though he would melt her body into his, she murmured incoherently against the intimate taste of his mouth.

His touch was becoming more urgent, more determined, and every nerve in her body cried out for her submission to his possession, that she should abandon herself to the infinite pleasure of more and more intimate caresses, that there should be no part of her that he should not know and cherish.

Dene could not but be aware of the expertise in his handling of her, the skilful pressures of his muscular body, his sure knowledge of how to arouse her and she was learning too how to respond, to urge her own body against the hardness of his, to explore with her hands the muscled contours of him, to wind her fingers into the thick, blue-black hair, sensuously massaging the nape of his neck, the sensitive hollows behind his well shaped ears.

She did not resist when his fingers dealt expertly with the simple fastening of her dress, the hand moving inside to cup the straining curve of her breast, a shiveringly exciting touch. She was painfully, achingly alive to her growing need of him, conscious too of the tell-tale throbbing that racked him, the involuntary tensions beyond his control. But before she gave into this tide of sensuality . . . and her heart leapt in frightened realisation of the truth . . . she must be sure of his love. She had confessed her feelings to him. With an agonised gasp she succeeded in pulling away from him, the conflict between her urgent body and her mental restraint causing a pang so real that she cried out.

'What is it, *querida*?' His voice was scarcely recognisable, rough, thickened by desire. 'Do I go too fast for you?'

Determinedly, she held him off.

'Luq, I have to know . . . you . . . you made me tell you that I . . . that I . . .'

'That you love me?' He sounded puzzled. '*Sí!*' Slowly, comprehension dawned in the dark eyes, the chiselled lineaments of his face softening, responsive to her need. 'Fool that I am, to take it for granted that you know how *I* feel about *you*!'

He took her in his arms again, but this time it was with gentleness, the urgency of his desire no less, but carefully controlled.

'*Te quiero mucho* . . . I love you very much, my Dene,' he

murmured against her ear. '*Te adoro, mi tesoro*. You are the other half of myself, as day is to night. But it is right, *si* . . . loving you, adoring you that also I should want you, need you? This does not disturb you?'

It disturbed her all right, but not in the way he meant.

'Oh yes!' she breathed, her eyes glowing up at him. 'It *is* right.' She had only needed his reassurance, that his physical desire was sanctified by spiritual emotion.

But now, strangely, it was Luq who seemed uncertain, moving a little apart from her, the strain of holding himself in check apparent in the swarthy features.

'You know that it *is* marriage I offer you, *chica*? Nothing less?'

'Oh yes, Luq, yes, I know!' She attempted to move back into the circle of his arms, but still he held aloof.

'You have wondered at my relationship with Elena. Yes . . .' as she would have spoken, 'I know this is so . . . and I will tell you so. About fifteen years ago, I wished to marry Elena . . . but then I was not qualified and I wished to offer myself as a successful man. I waited too long, and Elena married my friend Alfonso Pareja. Since that time,' he added steadily, 'they have *both* been my good friends.'

'You don't need to tell me all this,' Dene said softly, her eyes upon his lips, willing them to repossess her own, instead of wasting time in talk. Now that he had told her what she wanted to hear . . .

'*Sí*, it *is* necessary. I am no angel, Dene, I am a man. There have been women . . . but casual affairs. After Elena, I thought never to marry, until I met Belinda.' His face hardened. 'Again I waited too long. I married her, but she was never mine. But,' he added softly, 'now I am glad of it . . . glad that you will be the first woman I have taken in love as well as in desire.'

Now he allowed Dene to move closer to him, holding her, gentling her, his fingers tracing the outline of her lips that throbbed with their need for his kiss.

'I laughed at your little lucky charm, *chica*,' he said ruefully, 'but now it is I who am superstitious, afraid that history will repeat itself, if I wait too long to make you mine.'

He pulled her hard against him and her body softened to mould with his, as he shaped her, the movements of his hands intensifying in speed and urgency, re-igniting passion that had never really become dormant.

'You know what I am asking, *querida*?'

She knew and quivered at the knowledge, shifting against him in a restless, obsessive need.

Luq sat on the edge of the bed, drawing her down to sit beside him.

'It will take three weeks to arrange a marriage,' he stated.

'Yes . . .' Dene was oddly breathless, then, at the look in his eyes, an expression which told her that, although his need was almost unbearable, he would not coerce or plead with her, a sweet glow flowed through her, engulfing her from head to foot, as every instinct urged her to offer him all that she possessed . . . herself. It would not be a one-way giving. She knew that she would receive again, in full measure, the ecstasy she bestowed.

'Luq' she whispered, as she pulled him down beside her, the whole sweetly responsive length of her pressed to him, 'I'm so glad you're superstitious too . . .', and before his lips silenced her, 'third time lucky!'

Harlequin® Plus

A WORD ABOUT THE AUTHOR

Annabel Murray was born in Hertfordshire, England, and now lives in Liverpool with her two teenage daughters and her husband, who is a college teacher. He has always actively encouraged her in pursuing her hobbies, which have been legion, with writing foremost among them. Annabel had ambitions to be an author from the time she was in school.

In the interim, other hobbies captured her attention and energy. Involvement in arts and crafts led to her participation in the foundation of a local arts group. Drama, too, intrigues her, and she has appeared in many plays, produced others and even won an award for a historical play she wrote. Hiking and gardening allow her to enjoy outdoor beauty and healthful air.

None of her interests, though, is truly separate from her writing activity, for she uses all her experiences to flesh out her heroines' backgrounds. Not even her holidays are exempt. Like every serious writer, she keeps her eyes open for the unusual detail that can be transplanted into fiction from the life around her. Annabel's several novels attest to the acuteness of her observation.

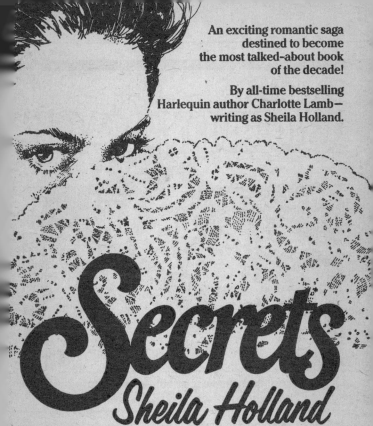